Fighter Fury

Also by Russell Sullman

To So Few
Beaufighter Blitz
Typhoon Ace

100% of the royalties from these books are donated to the
Royal British Legion

FIGHTER FURY

RUSSELL SULLMAN

LUME BOOKS

LUME BOOKS

For all those who serve in NHS Dental Services,
including a true frontline star:
Heather Barr

Chapter One

January 1944, the east coast of Scotland

The night sky was oppressive, the empty expanse crowding in on him, enveloping him within its heavy embrace.

Except, it was not quite as empty as it might first seem.

Somewhere out there, an enemy aircraft was lurking, and he was playing a deadly game of hide-and-seek with it.

He hunched forward to peer at the six-inch screen, glowing implacably from its mount on the control panel, just above the altimeter. The heat it was generating was warming the cockpit to almost unbearable levels.

The display remained doggedly empty. *Where are you, you sodding thing?*

His face was slick with perspiration beneath the constricting tightness of the oxygen mask, his backside soaking wet in a warm puddle of sweat.

Blinking gritty, aching eyes, Squadron Leader Harry Rose muttered an oath anxiously under his breath, searching the darkness as he had done so many times before.

Oh Chalky, I could really do with you here with me right now!

But Flight-Lieutenant 'Chalky' White DFC, DFM, RAFVR, dear friend and his one-time AI operator extraordinaire, was hundreds of miles away safe on the ground, and likely asleep beside his wife and baby daughter in that little cottage on the Cornish coast, *the lucky blighter!*

The hothouse Rose was huddled within was his Hawker Typhoon's cockpit, lit a brooding green by the stubbornly empty cathode screen. His eyes stole down to the photograph of his wife tucked carefully to one side, but there was no assistance there.

What idiot thought up this stupid idea?

The whisper in his mind was plaintive—*Why Harry! What a question to ask! That idiot would be you, wouldn't it?*

Don't remind me, he told it firmly.

But it was true, he *had* suggested this idea to Charlie the previous year. Despite himself, a small smile formed on his lips at the thought of the person in charge of these trials of radar-equipped Air Interception Hawker Typhoons.

The suggestions for night-fighter trials which Flight Officer Charlotte Flynn had submitted to the Air Ministry had been well received. Despite being involved in her injured husband's convalescence, Charlie had been promoted early to the rank of Squadron Officer, and tasked to supervise the trials as a reward, even though she had only been up to Ayrshire to observe the progress of her project once.

Her trip to Dundee to review the Trials when he arrived as senior pilot had been the first time he had seen her since the Red Cross had arranged for John to be repatriated from Germany, and she had broken off their relationship.

The less said about *that* visit, the better...

Eyes out again, casting around vainly for the ghostly smears of light which might reveal the glowing exhausts of his hidden foe, thanking the Almighty that the cockpit was so warm that the Perspex of his canopy was not icing over, the added vents making condensation negligible, and that exhaust flame dampers were fitted, helping protect his night vision.

The exhaust stacks had initially been painted with red lead paint, but it had not reduced the glare enough for hunting by night, hence the far more efficient dampers.

Thank goodness for small mercies!

Poor Charlie, despite six weeks of hunting, her Special Typhoon Experimental Night Unit, known as STENU had yet to achieve any success.

"Claymore Red One to Control, I have nothing, repeat, I have nothing."

Where are you, you Nazi bastard?

The voice of the controller at RAF Tealing was plaintive, "Control to Claymore Red One, he's a third of a mile ahead, angels three, are you sure you can't see anything?"

Rose could almost feel the WAAF's frustration.

Annoyed, he shook his head, as if she might see it. *Well then, you try it up here, love.*

But he bit his tongue and said nothing.

Flight Officer Elizabeth Bates was a grimly efficient young officer, tasked with guiding the project to success and fruition. Rose had never seen her smile, and she seemed to spend all her time in the AI control 'caravan', but he respected her single-minded purpose in trying to make it work.

Rumour had it that she had lost a younger brother over Duisburg in 1942 and was keen to even up the score.

However, whilst the essential initial guidance for an interception

3

was the responsibility of the controller, the final successful contact and shoot down lay with the two pilots of the Flight—Rose and a suave and manicured Free French Air Force pilot, Guy Duclos.

The moon condescended to make one of its sudden appearances, and the River Eden shone sullenly in the inclement light, below and to starboard.

The mask was tight, pushing against his nose, and he adjusted it. *Bloody hell. Am I even heading the right way?*

And then he saw something, a dull twinkle set in the darkness at the corner of his eye, just for a second. Was that the faintly smudged glow of exhaust flame?

Look aside, don't look at it directly…yes…just there…the faintest glimmer of pale blue. Enemy exhausts…?

As if in confirmation, his Typhoon juddered and wobbled as it passed through the slipstream of another, larger, aircraft.

"Claymore Red One to Control, any change in the bandit's vector and angels?"

"No change, Claymore Red One, you're closing the range, down to a quarter of a mile. Correction, bandit is vector trajectory to port. Vector trajectory to port."

"Received, Control." *Vector trajectory to port? Oh Liz, why don't you just say bandit turning, you silly old thing?* And then, as if by magic, a dark silhouette appeared slightly above and to starboard, and, as it turned, flying surfaces shone dully in the miserly light of the apathetic moon.

His heart leapt with a twist of fear and elation. *Cripes! How did I miss that?*

Certain that he would lose sight of the other aircraft if he were to check if it was displayed on his screen (the bloody thing hadn't helped so far!) Rose kept his eyes on it, opening the throttle slightly to close the distance. Looking to one side of the vague shape to maximise what he could see with his peripheral vision, Rose easily made out a pencil-thin fuselage, twinned rudders and broad wings, each bearing the bulge of an engine.

No time to waste, easy, follow her turn, but stay below......

"I have it in sight, Control...it's a Dornier 17, repeat, a Dornier 17...I am attacking."

"Oh, good luck...!" Her sudden excitement burst out into his earphones.

Slipping easily into the automatic routine, pushing down the anxiety. *Come on, Harry, get this one for her...*

Adjust for deflection, reduce the throttles by just a smidgen to hold a good firing position behind the enemy bomber, approaching just below the enemy's line of flight, the vibration of H-Hamish's airframe making the shape of the Dornier dance before him, minimal deflection with this three-quarter stern attack, and push down on the gun-button as he wobbled the control stick slightly to spray with deflection the airspace through which the Dornier would pass.

The bright flash from his cannon robbed him of his night vision immediately, their recoil slowing his fighter, white flashes sparkling where the bomber had been in his gunsight.

One

A curl of flame licking back, instantly extinguished, flaring brightly into life once more. *Aim for the flame...*

Two

And then a sudden pulse of harsh light, coldly illuminating the cockpit, and a sullen *WHUM!* felt and heard despite the strident howl of Hamish's Sabre engine.

'Ware of collision! Break away! Arms and legs working desperately,

5

the Typhoon sliding and mushing for a heart-rending instant in the rippling pressure waves of the explosion, and then she was turning, and he pulled her away to starboard to minimise the risk of flying into the debris, or worse still, into the enemy bomber itself.

Rose blinked rapidly, trying to swallow away the panic, the after-image of the cannon-flash jagged and unforgiving, grateful that he must have avoided the fragments, the cockpit filled with the sickly odour of burning metal, and he levelled off after what he judged was a ninety-degree turn.

At first all he could see was just a confused and overlapping set of light-seared patches, and he called Bates. "Control, I've lost sight of the bandit, vector, please." The controls were just a blur, and he tried to focus on them as his heart thrashed and hammered.

Come on, Liz, help me out, please.

She almost deafened him as she shrieked over the R/T, "Bandit is losing height! Bandit is going straight down! You got him! Claymore Red One, you got him!"

Ears ringing and chest filled with excitement, he found he was grinning, "Confirm your last, Control?" Already his eyes, recovering rapidly, were searching through the dark firmament.

Her voice was lower this time, the triumph edged with embarrassment, "Control to Claymore Red One, confirm bandit is rapidly losing height, zero forward vector."

He caught sight of the enemy bomber, or at least what was left of it, a writhing and twisting intense ball of yellow white, flaming shreds of its airframe detaching as the torn fuselage and broken wings gyrated wildly within the halo of streaming flames, trailing behind it a thick black column of oily smoke, an expanding fan of incandescent fragments spiralling and streaming out and down to the black waters below.

6

A sight both beautiful and terrible, but a glorious vindication for Charlie.

His two second bursts had connected, and the blazing wreckage twisting straight down was all that was left of an enemy bomber and its crew of four highly trained and experienced aviators.

Still the bubbling cry of victory and calm your voice, "Confirmed. Scratch one Dornier, Control."

Below his orbiting fighter, the remnants of the Luftwaffe bomber smashed into the sea, shattering into a thousand whirling sparks, short-lived as icy waves quickly quenching the flames.

At exactly that moment, the cathode tube brightened and died, a sickly smell of hot, burning metal and plastics vying with the stench of cordite and sweat, and he switched it off, hastily covering it with the 'tea-cosy', a special asbestos pouch provided should the bloody thing malfunction and pose a fire hazard.

Wouldn't be much of a laugh to go down after doing it to poor Jerry. With a sigh of relief, he pulled the drawstring to enclose the screen safely within it.

Much use you were, you piece of junk. Good riddance to bad rubbish. This night fighting caper needs a crew of two. At least the cockpit will cool now the bloody thing's off…

With a tour on night fighters, Rose knew that hunting the enemy by night was best done as part of a two-man crew. This single seater night fighting was for mugs.

Really? Taunted his mind's whisper.

"Claymore Red One, my, uh, thing is broken, please advise?"

Her voice was composed again, "Return to base immediately, please Claymore Red One," then, shyly, "Thank you, Harry."

*

7

Typically, when flying in daylight, Rose would have returned to RAF Tealing by sweeping back over Leuchars, before dipping down from the high green hills to skim low over the silvery River Tay, the Bridge and the stumps of its predecessor a brooding and haunting presence to starboard, before pulling up to sweep over Dundee, low enough to rattle the Nethergate Hotel's windows, if the regular complaints from her owner to him were anything to go by, then back up and over the tenements of Hilltown, before setting up his final approach to Tealing, taking care to avoid the Sidlaw Hills to the immediate north.

However, with his victory over the Dornier, achieved mostly by luck, experience and good direction, Rose chose to circle widely around to pass low over Arbroath and the Kirkton POW camp, making his approach from the west.

But not *too* low, for the Pongoes guarding the POWs, bored with the ghastly monotony of their work, may try a pot-shot or two at *him*.

If Jerry POWs had been watching the aerial hunt from within their huts, they would have seen the distant flash, and the falling, guttering cinder which told them of the death of their countrymen. Let them see the victor's roundels and know despair, quenching the hopes of the most ardent Nazis, just as his cannon had quenched the life spark of those in the bomber.

But it could have been so different, and he offered up a silent prayer, fingertips reaching out to the creased photograph to trace the outline of her face in the darkness.

My Lord, thank you, for allowing me to endure once more.
Not least for those I love.

Chapter Two

Sitting in rapidly cooling sopping wet clothes, Rose delivered his after-action report to Bates and Flight-Lieutenant 'Rags' Ball, RAF Tealing's Assistant Intelligence Officer, very aware of her delight at their success.

For a WAAF he had never seen smile, she had the biggest grin he had seen for a long time plastered across her face, and both arms were wrapped around herself as if to hold in her excitement. Her eyes shone and she seemed unable to sit still as he sipped from a mug of hot sweet tea, recounting the interception blow-by-blow.

Afterwards, she bounced to her feet, "Squadron Leader Rose."

"Please, Liz, I keep telling you, call me Harry." Despite the exhilaration of his kill, the adrenaline was draining from him and he felt exhausted. *I need a long bath, a sandwich, and a damn good kip.*

She looked as if she wanted to jump up and dance a little jig and he tried to hide his amusement.

"Harry, thank you! You've broken our duck. That's the first kill I've been involved in while in charge of the intercept station, even though you actually guided yourself in with the set."

"To be honest, Liz, it was your direction and a decent amount of luck that brought us the success. The thing is, my set was blank throughout the intercept, and as soon as I fired the cannon, I think some of the aerials broke off. That might have been the reason the set shorted out."

Her face fell, "Bugger. I need to get the boffin to repair it and recalibrate the blessed things again. I'll talk to Chiefy."

Rose smiled sympathetically. "I'm sorry, Liz. But you know the Sabre sets up those powerful high frequency vibrations in the airframe, and I reckon it interferes with the calibration."

She thought for a moment. "Hm, maybe. Last time you suggested it I thought you might be pulling my leg. It doesn't happen on the twin-engine jobs as a rule."

"True," he nodded. "Perhaps the vibration from one engine cancels out that from the second engine?" he wiped sweat from his neck. "Shock-absorbers in the mount might help, foam, or a pulse device to cancel out the vibrations?"

"I'll have a word with the Boffins." She looked down, embarrassed, fingers pulling at one lapel. "Um, Harry… can I ask you a favour?"

He looked at her quizzically, *OK, here we go…*

"Of course, Liz, ask away."

"Could you keep it under your hat that the AI went unserviceable? This *can* work, we just need time to get the set-up right, and to keep it calibrated when airborne. I'll talk to the Engineering Officer, discuss your suggestions in counteracting the tremor."

He sighed, "It's not working, Lizzy. Your directions put me in the right place, and I was lucky that the bugger began to turn just as the moon appeared and lit him up for a second. It was enough to nail him. But it was you, not that blinking set."

"Please, Harry? I know we can do it. Squadron Officer Flynn has high hopes for the trials, and she'll be devastated if we fail." She smiled anxiously. "Give us a little more time? Another month, perhaps? We're so close I can feel it. Keep quiet about the break down?" she was pleading now, "for Charlie?"

Flipping heck. If I highlight the failure the trial will likely be cancelled, and I can go back to operations. But Moll likes me up here, nice and safe!

The reduced tempo of sorties and unsuccessful flights over the wild beauty of Scotland's landscapes had been as good as a rest, far better than a tour of Training Command, and Rose felt guilty that he was safe while Excalibur was still at Little Silllo, even if the 'Tip-and-Run' raids were far less frequent. He was ready to return to the Channel Front, but another month wouldn't hurt…

That little voice again, *and if you stay, there's always the chance of another night with Charlie like the one a month ago…*

Self-consciously one hand stole up to the pocket containing Molly's picture. *Shut up, you daft sod. It's all about what's right. Nothing to do with Charlie at all…*

Hmm, OK. If you say so.

"Harry?" He realised that Liz was still watching, her face still anxious but also a little concerned by his silence.

He nodded begrudgingly, "Alright, Lizzy, another month, but no longer."

Rose thought for a moment, "And ask for something to cool the AI set, an air inlet tube, or a small fan, even? The high temperatures in the cockpit may be overheating the system."

Might help cool me down a bit, too…

To his surprise, Bates leaned forward to brush her lips against his sweaty cheek, "Thanks, Harry, you won't regret it, I promise!"

*

The following day the weather was dreadful, with stinging, driving rain and a soul-freezing gusty squall battering impatiently at the taped windows overlooking the dully glittering River Tay.

The German battleship *Scharnhorst* had been cornered and sunk a fortnight earlier on Boxing Day, a mere 36 of her almost two thousand crew surviving, the rest dying in the freezing watery wastes and howling gales at the Battle of the North Cape. The thought of their awful fate made Rose shiver and huddle closer to the comforting warmth of the grate.

He spent the day in his room relaxing, dozing over Koestler's 'Arrival and Departure', and writing a long heart-felt letter to Molly, before sauntering down to the dining room for an early tea.

Sitting at his table, idly pondering the porcelain tray of margarine and preserves, including marmalade – *yuck!*

Thank God for strawberry jam.

In this capital of marmalade making (who on earth had even invented the evil-stuff, for goodness' sake?), Molly would have been in seventh heaven. But in this world where margarine was separate from the slices of bread, and not spread on it like the heathen English would have done, the waitress reminded him tartly every afternoon, jam was his darling.

He sipped the cooling tea and wondered if the others were still at Tealing in these awful conditions.

There could be no flying in weather like this, the roads were treacherous, and Rose feared for his fellow pilot on the trials.

Duclos favoured racing home on his motorbike, but whilst he and the other officers of the AI Typhoon trial, including Rose and Bates, were roomed in the Queen's Hotel, once graced by Winston Churchill, the Frenchman preferred to stay at Kinblethmont House in Arbroath, the family there having given free house to Free French sailors, especially those of the submarine FNFL Rubis.

It was the closest to being at home for a man from an occupied homeland missing the familiar accents and vernacular on a cold and lonely evening.

When his first week as the Trial's senior pilot, Rose visited Kinblethmont House with Duclos, marvelling at the beauty and sense of peace in the surroundings of the large Victorian mansion, and been charmed by the hospitable family still there. It was a place of safety and serenity for all, and an adopted piece of France, even De Gaulle having dined there.

December had painted the trees and the glens to the house's north white with ice and frost, making an awed Rose shiver at the sharp freshness and the raw, cold beauty.

"Gosh! What a glorious sight, Guy, eh?" *I wish Molly were here to see this...*

Duclos had surveyed the scene with disinterest, a *Gauloise Caporal* cigarette drooping from his lips. "I cannot tell what you see, Flash. Is cold and empty. You like beautiful, no? Beautiful, she is my city, belle chienne ma ville, c'est Marseille. To see the Marseille docks, merde! She is beauty!"

The Frenchman swept an arm indifferently across the gleaming white landscape before them, laughed disparagingly and blew a jet of the malodorous smoke over a gasping Rose. "This? Bah! This is nothing!"

Eyes watering, Rose had shaken his head in amazement. Marseille's smelly docks over this cooly fragrant Scottish loveliness? Duclos must be absolutely raving bloody bananas!

The memory made him smile.

Sitting before the warm glow of the fireplace and listening to the rhythmic drubbing of rain and the mournful cry of the wind against the glass was soporific, and he was drowsing when the door to the dining room was thrown open and a group from RAF Tealing entered busily, a gusty draught of cold sweeping through to herald their entry.

Sod it! I was just about to snooze off then…

Grumpy but trying not to show it, he straightened from his slouch and patted his lips with the napkin, smoothing his silk scarf and checking that his tunic's top button was undone. Fighter boys have an image to uphold, after all…

Bates waved to him from the group, and he forced a smile onto his face. *Blast, they're heading this way…*

His eyes wandered to Bates' companion and stopped.

Rose and Charlie Flynn were first introduced to one another the previous year, both of them in the midst of enforced solitude from their partners, with Molly and Danny faraway but safe in the Lake District, and Charlie's husband John, a Pathfinder pilot, having been shot down over Germany, injured and taken POW. In the middle of an enemy raid, their burgeoning friendship had somehow turned into something more, deepening into a relationship in which each provided the mental support, reassurance and physical release that the other needed. Whilst wrong, it had brought them solace at a difficult time when the loneliness and pressure had been almost too much to bear.

With a lurch of his insides, startled out of a sense of lethargy by the sight of Charlie, Rose stood awkwardly, his cup tinkling onto its side and tea splashing the tablecloth, as she removed her sodden coat and cap.

Bates was drenched white and shivering. "Oh my God, it's absolutely freezing out there!" she shuffled stiff-legged closer to the fire, water dripping onto the thick rug, "I should've stayed in my van!" she half-wailed.

"Oh goodness, Lizzy, it's just a few drops of water, don't fuss, let the fire warm you." Charlie shook her head.

14

The girl's eyes were on him, bright and shining in a cold-pinched face framed by windswept fair hair soaked dark, her fringe in disarray, droplets of water shivering like jewels in her hair and a slight smile on her lips. "Squadron Leader Rose."

He had not expected to see her, this WAAF who had comforted him when he had been so alone despite the company of his friends and tried to keep his surprise and delight from showing, "Squadron Officer Flynn. How lovely to see you again! Are you well?"

"Very, thank you." She moved sideways to get closer to the fire, the flaring light soft on her skin and hair, her gaze warm and searching, "And you?"

He could sense Bates' interest and kept his voice neutral. "Can't complain." He thought guiltily of Molly and was ashamed of the excitement he felt in Charlie's presence, memories of her skin glistening by candlelight surfacing unbidden.

"Congratulations! I've just had a chat with Lizzie. Sounds like you had a good night?" she said, holding out her hand.

It was cold in his, and he clasped it, remembering the gentleness of it on his body, and he yearned to embrace and warm her, but knowing that he couldn't, *mustn't.*

"Lizzy was amazing, directed me straight onto the bandit." He smiled slightly, voice dropping, "Reminds me of an interception off the south coast last year when another rather talented WAAF did a quite exceptional job of guiding me onto a Heinkel!"

Charlie smiled at his compliment, and his lips tingled with the memory of hers, "I only got the bandits each time because I'd been directed perfectly by experts. I reckon that both of those WAAFs deserve a DFC, at the very least!"

He saw Bates' surprise and pleasure at his words, and he thought that Charlie was going to pull him into her arms and kiss him despite

15

the presence of the others, but then the moment passed. Instead, she called the waitress to them, before turning back to him.

"Sit with us and have another cuppa, Flash. I want to hear more about the Dornier my team bagged last night!"

She winked at Bates, but her smile was for Rose alone.

And then it was gone, unhappiness dulling the brightness of the girl's eyes and drawing down the corners of her mouth, "And Flash? Dear Flash, I have new orders for you."

Chapter Three

The rain had stopped but still the wind spawned angrily, sliding hungrily along the panes behind the drawn curtains as Rose sprawled comfortably on the couch beside the burbling radiator, writing pad and pen on the floor beside him, half-asleep in the warmth, feeling both glad and strangely also sad by Charlie's news.

The Air Ministry had directed that Squadron Leader Harry Rose, DSO, DFC and two bars, AFC, RAFVR, was to resume his duties as the CO of Excalibur squadron after a weeks' leave. With the knowledge came the first burn of acid in the pit of his stomach.

His replacement, another Squadron Leader with extensive Typhoon experience, would arrive the following morning, and after familiarising the new man with his duties and offering choice advice, Rose would have a week's leave owed. The prospect of time with Molly and Danny filled him with joy.

There was a light rap on the door, and he sat up in a rush, confused and bleary in his sudden transition back to full consciousness, heart pounding. What had stirred him?

The writing pad and the finished letter to Molly had fallen from his fingers as he dozed, and now he picked them up, glancing at the clock. Half past nine.

There was a second, sharper knock, and he got up to answer, but before he could reach it, the door swung open and Charlie stepped in quickly, slinging her gasmask case carelessly into one corner.

"Flash!" she rushed to embrace him, her lips finding his.

They stood together for a moment, arms tight around one another before she stepped back to close the door and turn the key.

"You should keep your door locked, you know," she scolded, waggling a finger in admonition.

The radiator creaked, bubbled and popped, as if in agreement with the girl's words.

He smiled, "Oh, Charlie, you silly thing, who else is going to come into my room?"

"You never know. What if there was a top Nazi agent staying at this hotel? Hoping to glean some secrets from personnel serving at the airfield? Or, God forbid, planning to murder one of our top air aces while he slept in his bed? The great Typhoon Rose! You really ought to keep it locked!"

"Alright then, Charlie, I will, but all this 'Typhoon Rose' twaddle is a load of old bunkum. Molly loves it of course, keeps a book of the newspaper clippings, but the lads must think me the biggest line shooter there is!" he laughed.

She took hold of his shoulders, eyes alight, "The people need heroes, Flash, and Molly adores you," her voice dropping to a whisper and embraced him again, "As do I."

Aware that he was pressing himself against her, Rose pulled back a little self-consciously, thoughts turning guiltily once more to Molly, but his words were heartfelt. "Oh, Charlie, it's wonderful to see you."

"Mm, I can tell!" she giggled, pulling the straps of his braces from his shoulders and reaching down to unbutton his trousers, "Come on, Mr Rose, no need to be bashful, I'm here to celebrate our first kill with my senior pilot!"

"Can't say I've ever celebrated a kill with my commanding officer like this before." He stepped out of his trousers as she hurriedly began to undress, "And technically, if you include our Heinkel last year, it's actually our second kill together." He had a thought, "I'd best get-"

"Don't worry, I've put my cap in." She smiled and put a finger to his lips, "Shh, now. No more jaw-jaw, it's time for action…"

Charlie had grown her hair longer, and now she shook it out of its bun, the golden wave cascading and curling against the creamy skin of her shoulders.

The wind howled outside as if in anguish, but no one was listening.

*

Later, their needs quenched, she stretched contentedly beside him and asked, "How are they, Flash?"

"They're well, thanks, Charlie. Danny's growing into a big boy, and Molly's been appointed treasurer of the local WVS. I don't know how she does it."

She kissed his shoulder and snuggled close, "We girls are strong, and can do an awful lot, you know!"

"I know, Charlie." And because she had asked about Molly, "And John? Is he OK? How are you managing? How do you manage this night fighter trial and look after him? You're incredible!"

"The same way as Molly copes, Flash. We do what we have to."

"And John?" he asked again, wrapping an arm around her.

"It's lovely, but quite hard, too. It was like our honeymoon all over again."

Rose suppressed an irrational feeling of jealousy.

"John's still the sweet, gentle man I love, and it's wonderful being with him again, but he's really suffered." She sniffed, and he felt a tear on his skin.

He folded her into an embrace. "Shh. Tell me about it, if you like?"

She took a breath, and then another. "I worry about him; he needs more surgery, and I need to keep encouraging and reassuring him. He's in an orthopaedic hospital near Oswestry for a week for a corrective operation with a brilliant surgeon, Henry Osmond-Clarke, and hopefully it'll make a big difference. We're praying for a good result. I'm going back there in a couple of days, just have to get your replacement settled in first, and then I'll take John back home after."

She wiped her eyes, "John's so brave, so strong and patient, but he's only human. We all need someone to hold us in the darkest hours of the night, don't we?"

"We do." He agreed, "And who holds you?"

She half-laughed, half-sobbed, "John does, of course. He tries so hard to keep me happy and not to burden me, bless him. He does everything by himself. Insists on it, even when it hurts him." Another sob, "He's incredible."

Again, the unreasonable stab of jealousy, "And our families do their best to help, of course, but it is wartime, after all, everyone's suffering, what makes me special? And they can only do so much, anyway."

Charlie pressed closer, "But it's enough, honestly."

She got onto one elbow and leaned forward to kiss him, her voice soft, "I've been so lucky, you kept my hopes from fading last year. When I'm with you I can be free, share my worries with someone special who truly cares. It helps so much to have you there, to have you hold me and help me to forget my everything, even if it's for an hour or two."

20

She pursed her lips, remembering. "I owe you so much, darling Flash. You kept my spirits up and distracted me from the loneliness of the worst time of my life."

She looked away shyly, "I can't tell you how much of a difference it makes to know that I can call you when I want. I know that if it all gets a bit much, I can just pick up the phone and give you a tinkle. I can't burden John; he's been through too much already."

He turned to look into her eyes, "You'd been awfully quiet, I thought I'd might've somehow upset you."

"You could never upset me, Flash." Charlie pushed her fingers through the hair on his chest. "I don't think you'd ever hurt me, Flash. You're kind and thoughtful and never ask for anything. There aren't many like that." She smiled, "You always ask and you never push. It's lovely being with you."

She sat up and rubbed her lips, "I could do with a cigarette."

She slid off the bed and picked up her gas mask container, rummaging around before pulling out a ragged packet of Senior Service cigarettes and a silver lighter. "D'you fancy one, Flash?"

Her pale skin shone in the lamplight, and he shook his head.

Harry Rose, intrepid flyer and ace, eyeing a girl who loved him, but thinking of his wife.

Both girls deserved better, but in a world of danger and uncertainty, one took every opportunity one had, lest it be for the last time.

Might I never have the chance to hold and love Molly again? The possibility was too awful to think about.

She waggled her cigarette, and he shook his head. "No, Charlie, thanks."

She noticed the picture frame and carefully laid it flat, the smiles of his family turned away, though the photograph had already witnessed their intimacy.

Rose was glad that Molly had never visited him here, how could he love her in a place in which infidelity had restored his fading spirits?

"I've brought all my toiletries down here with me, Flash. My room's up on the third floor like last time and it's like a frozen arctic waste, don't think the blessed radiator even works."

Only the ground floor had effective radiators, as he had discovered on first arriving, and Rose had used his old leg injury shamelessly to wangle himself one of the highly sought-after ground floor rooms, the staff falling over themselves to oblige the man the papers had named 'Typhoon Rose'.

"It's lovely and cosy down here, and best of all, you're here! I know some of the others are down the hall, but can I stay with you tonight?"

If Molly surprised him with an unannounced visit, it would break her beautiful heart and all would be lost, but Charlie's imploring eyes persuaded him against better judgement, and he nodded, "Of course, Charlie", praying that Moly never discovered this relationship founded on loneliness, need and sweet distraction in a terrifying world at war, where danger and fear were never far.

Outside the wind continued to moan, and he wondered if it had begun to rain again. *What could be nicer on a wet and windy night than sharing a warm room with a lovely, capable and intelligent woman?*

Charlie ground out her cigarette and eyed him speculatively, "There, you've had a nice rest. Ready for more?"

"Cripes, Charlie, you've had a long day, you should rest!"

"I'll rest when you head back south, not before. You're all mine tonight, Squadron Leader. Don't know when our next time together will be." Her voice trembled, "I didn't manage to say goodbye properly when John got back…"

He knew as well as she that this might be the last time, that neither of them might even survive the next few days. There were

22

no guarantees of a future beyond the next few minutes or so, and that tonight might truly be goodbye. He felt her hopelessness as she murmured, "So, in the meantime…"

He sighed, "I know."

The radiator burbled busily, and Charlie eyed him thoughtfully, "Do you know why you were selected to be my Senior Pilot, Flash?"

He shook his head, wondering where the conversation was going.

"I asked for you specifically because I wanted you to be safe. I wanted you as far from the French coast as I could get you. I thought you'd be safe up here. Didn't expect so many raids up here, and to be honest, I wasn't expecting that much success, the bloody sets are so temperamental. But I knew that if anyone could pull it off, it would be you."

Charlie stretched and stood, her eyes sad, "But most of all, I just wanted you safe. For Molly of course, but for me, too. My own man is safe now he's back, but I wanted Molly to enjoy the same peace of mind."

She walked across and sat down beside him. Taking his hand and folding her fingers into his, "My love was safe, but I couldn't rest, because my other one wasn't. I would wake and worry about you, every night."

A tear glistened, wobbled then slipped down one cheek, and her voice was fierce now, "I wanted you safe, Flash, you've done enough, for goodness' sake! But now the Air Ministry want you back again! How much more must you do? It's not fair! Surely you've done enough?"

"I can't hide from my duty, Charlie, John didn't. I must go to where I'm needed. The invasion is coming, and soon. We need to win. We must. For you and me and everyone else. It's never going to be enough until we've beaten them. You're doing your bit; and I must do mine."

23

How could he tell her of his weariness? How could he tell her that despite it he could not let his friends face danger when he was safe, even though trepidation and disquiet invaded the very fibre of his being at the thought of flying into combat once more?

Her face was dimmed by shadow, the bitter anger gone, "I know, Flash, I'm being selfish!"

He kissed her hand, cloying guilt as her wedding band touched his lips. "It's not selfish wanting what we all want. A normal life, a chance to enjoy a peaceful journey into later years with the ones we love. But the Nazis won't give it to us, we have to fight for it. You know that as well as I." He placed her hand against his cheek and closed his eyes for a moment, "We're lucky, Charlie, we've had much more than most. And we have tonight…"

He felt the flutter of remorse and betrayal but knew he would not stop himself when she lay against him again.

"Yes, Flash, we have, don't we? I'm glad." Charlie smiled sadly, her hand straying, and Rose opened his eyes again as he felt the flame flare bright again.

Charlie smiled, but it did not reach the sadness in her eyes, and then that soft mouth met his once again as she straddled him.

*

At last, he was asleep. She snuggled closer to him, and he sighed and muttered something incomprehensible in his sleep.

"I love you, Flash." She whispered it, her eyes on his sleeping profile, and breathing him in.

I know I ought not to be here, but, just as I love my John, so too do I love you. God, forgive the weakness of my soul and my naughtiness, but I am only human after all.

24

This love-stricken and errant heart is the only one I have, and even though it's a wayward one, it is the one you gave me.

I pray that after tonight I will have something of this gentle and thoughtful man for myself, a reminder of the special time only we knew, to treasure, love and nurture for the future, and to fill Flash's absence from my life to come.

She closed her eyes but could not hold in the tears which trickled out, falling unnoticed onto his skin.

My dearest Flash, our time is done. It's unfair to draw out this agony. The ones we love deserve better.

I must give you up, my darling, though I cannot bear to, in thanks for the good fortune of my husband's return. But a gift can so easily be taken back, and so I must sacrifice what I have with you to keep what I had before you. Our time is done, dearest Flash. Tomorrow will be our farewell.

She kissed his shoulder, the saltiness of her fallen tears sharp on her tongue.

This heart will love you for as long as it may beat, but my soul will love you for as long as I exist.

Chapter Four

Appointed acting squadron commander in his absence, Sid was ebullient with Rose's return to the squadron, even though there had been no operational flying until very recently, following a period when the Wing was being rested.

"Flash! Thank Gawd you're back!" He bounced to his feet from behind Rose's desk, "I missed a show in Exeter with a Brazilian crumpet 'coz I was acting CO! She had a rubber johnny attached to a two-stroke engine by a telescopic arm! Jacko had to go on his own."

Sid rolled his eyes, "Dunno how the silly sod managed to get there without me holding his hand, but he did." Behind him, Jacko frowned in outrage.

"It must have been properly special 'coz he was white as a sheet when they brought him back, couldn't speak 'til the morning! Got something in his eye, but he reckons it wasn't oil. Said he never seen nothing like it!"

Jacko just nodded mutely.

"Now you're back, I can go and see her." He winked, "And if you're very, very good, we may take you with us!"

In the headquarters building, his CO and dearest friend, Wing

Commander 'Granny' Smith was ecstatic, "Flash! Thank Gawd you're back! Sid and Jacko are always trying to get me to go to some sordid show or other, and there's some new Froggy act in town at the minute. They've been to see it twice already, sounds bloody awful. I've managed to avoid going, even Belle had a go at them for trying to lead me into temptation", a leer, "As if! But they keep coming back. Now you're back maybe the silly sods'll leave me alone! Do me a favour and watch some of those bloody shows with them, will you?"

Belle came in as Granny danced a jig, and was more pensive, "Flash! Oh, thank God! I'm glad you're back! I think that awful husband of mine loves you more than he does me! He's been clumping around like a bear with a sore head whilst you were gone!"

And then a tentative smile and a whispered, "Though I'll bet Charlie's cursing!" Capering around with glee, Granny picked her up and she screamed with laughter as he spun her around.

Leaving them to it, he headed to dispersals, where it was a similar story. His groundcrews, the ones who were responsible for keeping his squadron flying in reliable and well-serviced machines were ecstatic, his fitter Jimmy summing it all up for him saying, "Thank the Good Lord you're back, sir, we've had a right heavy-handed lad flying S-Sugar, very nice young gentleman, of course, but he treated her like a dray horse! We was worried he was going to bend her. She needs to be treated right, gentle like, the way you do!"

Big Dave the armourer just grinned shyly at him and nodded.

Rose's old Typhoon, the original S-Sugar, had been withdrawn from service in the late Autumn, like a lot of the older machines. Most were to be taken apart for the component stores of the maintenance and repair sections being formed to supply the need for necessary repairs during an invasion campaign. He had grown extremely attached to her, and hoped the trusty old warhorse was one of the few to be refitted and sent back to the frontline squadrons. She had been a faithful mount, and they had achieved much together.

Will Scarlet, CO of 44 Wing's other squadron, Orna, named after the sword of Irish mythology's Fomorian King, Tethra, was less welcoming. "Rose. You're back, then?" he'd grunted ungraciously before turning back to his newspaper.

Delighted, I'm sure… mentally, Rose had flipped two fingers in Scarlet's direction. Sod you, too, you arrogant tosser.

Granny beamed, "I reckon he really likes you, Flash."

Rose's new wingman was an RAFVR Pilot Officer named Jack Byron, a fresh-faced boy of nineteen who looked about eight. He was shy, quietly reserved but painfully keen, a promising and skilful pilot who had no difficulty staying in position on Rose's wing whatever the manoeuvre.

And young Jack was a fast mover when it came to the opposite sex (something Rose was not, as Molly would often remind him, remembering his shyness), already getting rather friendly with one of the Assistant Section Officers from Ops, a slight flaxen-haired girl who, from a distance, reminded Rose achingly of Charlie.

The fair girl from Ops, awed by Rose's line of ribbons and the rings on his sleeves, had timidly asked, "Jack says he's mad, bad and dangerous to know, sir. Is it true?"

Rose grinned at the blushing boy, "Mad, bad and dangerous to know, eh? Hm, Well I can confirm that he's as daft as a brush, and a touch naughty, so you'd best watch out for wandering hands! And dangerous? Well, I've yet to find out. I rather hope he is, but only to Jerry, of course!"

*

The Inn's door opened behind Rose, admitting a blast of cold air and the bristling ginger beard of Flying Officer Alan Winters. Winters raised his arms in the air like a boxer and inexplicably bellowed, "Drop your bloomers, the Navy's here!" the ladies present ignored him whilst Mavis the barmaid just rolled her eyes, and he winked evilly at Rose, "Welcome back, skipper!"

Unsure how to respond, Rose nodded agreeably, "Alan. Have you seen Sid and Jacko? They promised me a pint."

"Sid said they had to see a woman about a dog," Winters shouted, "but they'd be along prompt, like."

He leaned closer to make himself heard beneath the hubbub of the thronged bar, "Took me with 'em last time, lummee! Never again! Got crabs in me beard. The Doc made me cut it short and paint it with gentian violet. I looked a right tit." He waved at Rose's glamour boys, the elegant Thomas, Andrews, Montalmond and Trent. "Aye-aye, lads!"

With a last wink, he ambled off into the throng.

Rose rather liked to think he looked the part, but in comparison to Excalibur's gorgeous 'pilot chorus line' quartet, he looked positively dowdy. The most glamourous of them, handsome Gerry Andrews, usually sat a little separate amidst his 'harem' of adoring WAAFs. Unlike his CO, he was regularly invited to all the USO shows.

Nodding at Andrews, Rose caught the appraising looks of a couple of Andrews' flock, and he looked away, trying not to blush. The affair with Charlie had brought him through the desperate strain and loneliness of last year's tour, but to start something with one of Little Sillo's WAAFs would be madness. Molly must never discover the lovely distraction of Charlie when he needed it most, and which had kept him sane.

He could not afford to risk it all for another.

Thomas raised his pint glass to Rose, that ridiculous monocle of his catching the firelight, "Join us, sir?"

Rose smiled but had noticed the forlorn group of youngsters which were his new boys, Crandall, Gillespie and Beckwith, standing self-consciously in the far corner beside the uniform display cabinets. "Be with you lads in a moment, Peter." He called out in the din, "I'll have a half, please."

At the piano, Granny and the Wing's MO, 'Snotty' Ragg, were wrestling one another for the right to pluck at the keys and deafen them all with their wailing. Belle looked on grimly, and Rose chuckled to himself, poor thing. The loving wife, always by Granny's side. It was a wonder she wasn't completely deaf.

At the window, Percy Foster, moaning and half-cut as usual, was sitting with Quiet Willie Wight. Poor Willie, smiling gently as he listened patiently to his drunken friend.

With a cry of victory Ragg managed to upend Granny, and he leapt atop the stool to proclaim, only to have it kicked away by the prone Granny, onto whom he fell in a tangle of limbs and yelps.

Rose grinned wolfishly, the pair of daft buggers will be bruised black and blue in the morning! Pouring a pint, the red-faced Landlord, Dennis roared, "Oi! Break my piano and I'll break yer bloody heads!" Mavis gave Belle a look of sympathy. *Men! Can't live with them…*

The new boys looked apprehensive as he approached, the great Typhoon Rose, *Dear God, they look so young!*

He noticed now that standing with them were Alexander Leslie DFM, the gentle Trinidadian, and fatherly 'Pops' Graham, DFM and bar, AFM, the oldest of his pilots, and he felt warm gratitude for his kindly veterans in making the youngsters feel included and accepted. The talented Leslie would have been a delight playing the piano but had chosen to be with Graham and Excalibur's new boys.

30

My boys, he thought with pleasure, glad to be back.

These are my boys.

*

Excalibur squadron returned to operational status on New Year's Eve and was still tasked with Anti-Rhubarb and Rhubarb patrols, whilst on notice to move from Little Sillo as part of the continuing evolution and development of the 2nd TAF, and in preparation for the impending invasion of Europe.

Despite returning to the drudge of monotonous patrols after the more relaxed operational duties of Scotland, Rose was glad to be amongst his friends again, although 'Hairy' Cox's departure as a flight commander to a Spitfire squadron, whilst well earned, had saddened him. Cox was an excellent pilot and dear friend, so losing him to the Spitfire bods had been a bitter-sweet experience.

With the ominous intelligence coming in that the first of Hitler's 'terror' weapons was close to raining destruction on Britain, and the appearance of outlandish military sites in northern France which were to be the launching platforms of unmanned flying bombs, new targets to be attacked were urgently assigned.

The V1 flying bomb, designated as the Fiesler Fi 103 by the RLM (the Reich Aviation Ministry) but more familiarly known to its intended victims in Britain as the buzzbomb or doodlebug, was Hitler's new great hope, a weapon designed to be part of a new bombing campaign, an overwhelming assault by pulsejet-powered exploding robots.

The Nazis preferred to camouflage their V1 launching stations, often by hiding them in small areas of woodland, close to a road from which the supply of robot bombs and materials could be regularly replenished. The sites were built from concrete and local brick, with at least one ramp, control post, storage, servicing and non-magnetic prepping structures, and buildings for personnel.

Intelligence received from the courageous French resistance, not least of whom was the particularly daring Michel Hollard, and from photographs taken by equally brave Allied photoreconnaissance pilots quickly revealed the positions of the launch sites.

Whilst the Nazis may have been using woods as camouflage, the reality was that a small wood containing a variety of suspicious structures in an unwooded area screamed out 'look at me!'. In larger areas of woodland, they were much less obvious.

Dreadfully aware of the impending threat of heavy and imprecise bombardment of England, the Allies made an all-out maximum effort from late 1943 onwards in 'Noballs' attacks to destroy the launch sites before they became active by heavy, medium and light bombers.

The latter included 2ndTAF's Hawker Typhoon, used both as fighter-bombers and bomber escorts.

In the last week of January, Rose's Excalibur and Will Scarlet's Orna squadron acting together were tasked to pulverise the launch site newly discovered and already heavily bombed near the French town of Yvrench, ten miles northeast of Abbeville. The Allies had to keep hitting it until they were sure the site was destroyed and no longer a threat.

As a 'taster' to prepare Excalibur for their mobile role in the 2ndTAF, A and C Flights were sent to operate from a 'forward' strip, RAF Hawkinge, with a core group of groundcrew and personnel following behind in a pair of venerable Harrows, a trip which one wag later described tongue in cheek, as 'harrowing!'

The fact that their target was rather close to the home airfield of Jagdgeschwader 26, the famed 'Abbeville Boys' did not worry them in the slightest.

With Nazi Germany fighting on many fronts, the French-based units of JG26 were being siphoned off, particularly to bolster the Eastern Front and the defences of the Reich. What was left was a mere shadow of the formation which had battled the RAF in earlier years.

Knowing this, the pilots of 44 Wing RAF welcomed any interference by JG26's Bf109s, with their FW190 staffels currently defending Germany.

It was a cold, clear but gusty day when Rose led A and C-Flight in a dive-bombing attack on Yvrenche's V1 'ski site'.

He now flew a new S for Sugar, this Hawker Typhoon IB a much-refined creature over his earlier Tiffie, incorporating the new sliding 'bubble canopy' with a hugely improved view, added armour to protect the exposed radiator, engine and cockpit, and the uncomfortable vibration in the airframe reduced by modifications such as rubber engine supports and an improvised and better sprung pilot's seat which was kinder to his bottom.

Sugar Mark 2 also sported a large, four bladed propeller and Rose was both surprised and gratified by the enhanced performance when he first flew her. The Mark II 20mm Hispano was also an improvement over the Mark I, and he now had 140 rounds per cannon, almost twice that of his original Sugar.

They took off from Hawkinge, keeping low, following the land as it dipped, cheekily buzzing the houses of Foord before sweeping out across the Channel, still at zero feet to evade the questing fingers of German radar.

The plan had been to make landfall over Crotay, and they began their climb to a safe height just off the coast, but the drift caused by wind pushed them over the expanse of dunes and marshes at Marquenterre which, being on an estuary, should have been a strong part of the coastal flak belt but luckily was as poorly served as Crotay by AA defences.

The formation of twelve Typhoons approached the coast at an altitude of just over 8,000 feet, too low for the heavy AA, and just out of range of the lighter 20mm and 37mm flak guns, and in radio silence, so the defences would be left guessing about their target.

The target-site was a small rhomboidal wood surrounded by fields, pocked and cratered by the earlier bombing of the 'heavies' which had dropped heavy explosives on it at least twice.

No response from the defences as the target disappeared beneath his starboard wing's leading edge, hoping that they might not be the target and unwilling to call attention to themselves.

When he judged he was in position, Rose fused his bombs and ordered the attack, leaving Sid's flight as top cover should the Abbeville boys appear on the scene.

He pulled up Sugar's nose abruptly, feeling her slow before pushing her over onto one side until her nose was pointing downwards, setting the horizon parallel to the lines marked onto the sides of the canopy for a sixty-degree dive, and he felt that odd sensation of weightlessness, the pressure of his body against his seat diminishing, and he believed he would have floated off the seat entirely had his straps not been holding him firmly in place.

His eyeballs and ears ached, and he gasped and swallowed at the oxygen, fighting the brutal pressure that crushed against him.

Sudden sharp explosions of flak shaking her airframe and his nerves, the rattle of shrapnel sharp and harsh against her fuselage, and his fingers tightened on the stick.

A quick peek at the altimeter, the needle spinning down madly, peer out over the nose to centre it with the pocked green rhomboid, the patchwork of fields somehow faint and blurry as he focussed on the launch site.

The launch ramp itself and two of the storage buildings inexplicably were outside of the green rhomboid, and he focused on the non-magnetic building, looking rather sorry for itself with one wall caved in, *let's see if we can knock the whole bloody thing down…*

The thin barrier of sparse white flashes from exploding flak (20mm only, and not as much as he had expected) as the fused shells reaching their maximum effective altitude were above and behind him now, and he was aware of a sparkling to starboard as a flak gun pumped out a stream of the glowing dashes of tracer at him, *zip-zip-zip-zip-zip!*

There might be infantry down there too, unseen enemy taking pot-shots, careful…

Just one flak gun…? There must be others I can't see, or perhaps the heavies might have already done a better job than the Brass think…

Over the shriek of Sugar's Sabre, the muted explosions of flak were like the crackle of kindling. He could not see all the shells, but the tracer was mixed with half-seen javelins of grey and silver, and he knew that they were being slung up towards him at a terrifyingly rapid rate, the uneasy air he dived through shredded by the passage of shells from that 20mm gun below and goodness knows what small-arms fire, buffeting Sugar and Rose roughly, his testes shrinking painfully tight into his crotch and his muscles rigid with fear and strain, but there was no time to think about it as the target expanded dizzyingly in his sights.

Shrapnel sparked into oblivion against Sugar's blades, scratching futilely at her wings and sides, whispering piecemeal through the stained air she dived through.

No time to waste in thinking what to do if a 20mm shell *did* hit him, for he would know only an instants bright flash, and then nothingness.

And if he was unluckier still, then he would just feel the explosion, a violent and complete loss of control, sudden and shocking, perhaps fire and pain, and his last few seconds would be ones of intense terror and confusion and despair, before that final instant when what little was left of Sugar and himself impacted against the target and into oblivion.

Keep the gunsight pinpointed on the target, ignore the flailing shrapnel, concentrate on the long storage building already dented and pitted at one end but seemingly whole at the other, smoke and dust partially obscuring his view, making it harder for the gunners below to track them.

The vibration of Sugar's diving airframe was violent, jarring and juddering, and it worsened momentarily as he pressed out a burst of cannon fire.

It made him feel better and might even have scared those below, but now he was close enough, just over fifteen hundred feet, and he pushed the button on the throttle lever, feeling the sudden jerk and the almost uncontrollable swelling lift beneath him as the bombs fell from his racks, and he was pulling back, body pushing heavy into the seat, his head almost too weighty to keep upright, Sugar creaking and quivering resentfully, her Sabre screaming as if in sympathy with his nerves as he struggled to inflate his lungs against the crushing forces.

Impetus and the force of the dive pressed him to his seat, his vision greying and still waiting for the sudden crash of an exploding shell and oblivion, trimming the flaps in case he was to lose consciousness during the pull-out, pressure threatening to crush his eyeballs, still fighting to suck oxygen into his lungs, grunting and blinking to keep himself conscious, gasping when the concussion from a close shell-burst washed over him.

Sugar seemed to slip and yaw, the ground rushing close, ever closer, even as she bottomed out of the dive, sluggish and mushy in his hands as she fought to climb and he grabbed at her, the control column skittish in his trembling hands, his vision mercifully clearing as he pushed her nose down, down again, to skim across the field, ground-effect fighting him, knowing that Whip must be close behind, perhaps releasing his bomb as he turned Sugar into a low, wide turn to starboard.

Shrapnel pinged and clicked at Sugar, making his heart flinch and he jinked her away at full boost.

Where are you...? Smoke was rising from the wood, a dirty blot in the clear sky, the explosion flashing for a split-second and his eyes searched frantically for the enemy gun. *And how many MG posts?*

As if in answer to his question, an arc of glowing tracer wavered sloppily over Sugar's canopy, and his head swivelled to port, a second necklace of fire-bright rounds snaking out, too far behind, emerging from a meager line of hedgerow bordering a stubbled field to his left, and he headed away, already out of range of it, turning back tightly after a mile or so, the bright flash of explosions over the target beneath the drifting pall of smoke.

Watch out for the power lines to the south...

There, just yards from that lone tree with the broken bough where the hedgerow was a little thicker, the stubble a little flatter, and he squeezed the gun button, cannons spraying a swathe of metal that splattered and shredded a length of the shrubs, earth spurting and kindling flying beneath the ruinous fury of his Hispano's, a single tiny figure in field-grey flung backwards, *did I imagine that?*, the machine gun nest destroyed before Sugar was back within its effective range of 2,300 feet.

One less for the boys to worry about...

A shadow flitted across his fighter, and he thought for a gut-wrenching moment he had been caught with his pants down by the yellow-nosed Abbeville boys, but luck was still with him, for it was just the last of C-Flight, what was the boy's name? Crandall, nice lad, keen as mustard.

Crandall's Tiffie mushed out of its dive, nose up but flying level, before heading upwards and out again, jinking hard as he fled, geysers of heat and light and debris like a punch against her fuselage as his bombs exploded behind.

A quick look around, no bandits, and no columns of oily smoke coming from the pyres of crashed aircraft. Far above, faint through the smoke and oil-greased canopy, shapes flitting and light glinting on Perspex.

Please God, keep all my boys safe.

Rose pulled Sugar into a wide sweeping turn, her Sabre thundering at full throttle, taking them out of range of the 20mm cannon, wondering where the enemy fighters were and hoping that there weren't any other flak guns nearby.

Climbing steeper now, the seat unyielding against his back, with fresh columns of smoke rising from the battered V1 launch site, he felt suddenly very tired.

It's time to take the lads' home...

Chapter Five

Quarter the sky and sea, aileron to clear behind, check mirror, glance at the control panel and check the gunsight.

Rose spared a wistful glance to port, the grey jumble of buildings lined along the West Cliff Promenade in the early light of the day seeming like half-forgotten friends, once looming dark over them on the evenings they had shared a walk, before returning to her parents' flat.

Ten miles ahead of them lay Colwell Bay and the entrance to The Solent, smudged dull by the morning mist. Mindful of the AA battery based near the Needles Lighthouse, he guided Sugar a safe distance from the Isle of Wight and the sullen chalk monoliths.

It was the eastwards leg of the patrol, the sun low and painfully bright in his mirror…

The fighter-pilot's mantra interminably repeated for the umpteenth time.

Quarter the sky and sea, aileron to clear behind, check mirror, glance at the control panel and check the gunsight.

And back westwards… Stick over into a wide turn to starboard, sunlight glistening sharply on the surface of the water terrifyingly close below.

Quarter the sky and sea, aileron to clear behind, check mirror, glance at the control panel and check the gunsight.

Zzzzz…

A fleeting break in the pattern of his search to check on the boy, diminutive inside the cockpit of his Tiffie, head revolving as his had been, his kite fishtailing gently, occasionally wing dipping to starboard then port, then level again, *good lad.*

The sun seemed higher, the approaching dusk dull in his rear-view mirror, and he would have been paranoid, apprehensive, but the knowledge that there was a highly sophisticated T16 radar set monitoring the airspace had given him a false sense of safety.

Now he cursed that complacency.

Never relax, for that will be the instant of your ruination.

The sun low and in front, painful in his eyes…

Quarter the sky and sea, aileron to clear behind, check mirror, glance at the control panel and check the gunsight.

There. That patch of green in the heathland, the little park at Meyrick, where they had enjoyed a summer picnic and Charlie had -

"Blackgang to Toffee Red One, vector 130, angels zero, ten miles."

Heart thumping blood hard through him, "Received, Blackgang. Vector 130, angels zero. Wilco."

Turning, turning, knowing the youngster was with him, sea so very close beneath one wingtip, ease out of the turn to head outwards and away from the Isle behind them, the sun shining bright behind as he indicated to Byron to get into battle spread formation.

Two Typhoons drawing apart, line abreast a hundred yards, and giving them thirty seconds before turning to approach the unknown contact from its port quarter.

For some time there was nothing, just the sea and sky merged into the haze.

And suddenly, a pair of Bf109s, gleaming like shards of coloured glass against the glimmer of the darkening water below and behind them, throat tight as the distance closed dizzyingly fast…

Abruptly, the silhouettes changed as they began to climb, up and into a wide turn towards them, a flash of intense light as it caught against enemy canopies, his hope to 'cross their t' and blast them from behind unsuccessful as the enemy turned into the onrushing Typhoons, spreading apart to mirror the British formation.

At least we have the sun behind us…

And then, *but might there be more of them concealed in the shining light behind?*

No time to wonder. "Break port after we cross, Red Two, mine's the leader," he breathed, chest tight and blinking away the sweat.

"Wilco, leader." Calm despite the obvious youth of the voice, even over the crackle of the R/T.

Good lad, keep it brief, no unnecessary chatter.

Rose lined up on one of the tiny, rapidly foreshortening shapes, its guns sparkle firing at the Typhoons, huddling behind the protective block of his Sabre without realising he was doing so as fiery rounds flashed past startlingly close, precision and experience correcting the stick, and he pressed down firmly on the firing button, the airframe quivering in sympathy with the thumping cannonade of his Hispanos.

Shells pumped out of his cannon in a tight swathe into the path of the leading 109, but somehow it braved the storm and flashed past and over, Sugar buffeted roughly in a blasting rush of sound and air, apparently as undamaged as the bandit in the fleeting face to face firing pass.

Damn it!

No time to think, already harshly breaking to starboard as reflexes took control of him, knowing young Byron would be turning to port.

Stick back hard into the stomach, harder, grimace as the forces pummel at him and grey his vision.

Where is he?

Greyer still, black spots dancing before his eyes, lips dragging into a snarl of anger and frustration, filling his lungs with oxygen, head turning to scan the murk, Byron's B-Bertie small with distance, pulling hard into the sun after the glittering cruciform of the little German fighter.

And what of the other?

Eyes desperately searching, *where are you?*

There. Sharp lines, a glint on canopy betraying the enemy even as he fled, the Isle of Wight faint with haze and laying open before him.

The bastard wasn't turning into him, no sharp knife-fight here, the German pilot's attention focussed on the Isle, his target unknown, the Bf109 tiny and distant against the darker smudge of land.

Involuntarily Rose's right hand reached out and his fingers touched Molly's photograph, just for a moment.

I have to get him...

Oh God. Might Jerry be after Blackgang itself? The mobile radar station with its T16 radar to the west of Ventnor, foiling again and again the best laid plans of Goering's finest. God knows that it alone was a high value target, and it would not be the first time RAF Blackgang had been attacked. The previous summer it had been targeted by a tip-and-run raid, nearby Niton receiving the enemy bombs instead. During the raid, one bomb actually bowled over a WAAF, Sheila Barnard, as it skipped past, breaking her arm in the process but miraculously continuing on its way before exploding a safe distance beyond. Despite the experience, she had been remarkably cheerful when the boys of Excalibur visited her in hospital.

But if not the mobile GCI station, then perhaps the aerials of RAF Ventnor or even RAF St Lawrence, Ventnor's reserve?

Dear Heaven, don't lose it! As if it had heard him, a blob of oil flew back from the propeller to splash across his vision, and he cursed, as if visibility weren't bad enough already with the gathering haze.

Throttle pushed through the gate and the Sabre growling fit to deafen him, he pushed her hard after the enemy.

Rear-view mirror, all clear, a hurried glance around, nothing. For an awful instant he lost sight of the enemy fighter as his attention swayed between it and Jack's lonely fight over the sea, heading out towards the Old Harry Rocks to the west.

But this old Harry was needed elsewhere and could not help young Byron.

Dear God, keep the boy safe, please…

As he raced after his own bandit, Rose fancied that even through the light haze he could see the collage of the fields and the south-easterly slant of St Boniface Down, the station itself towards the highest part of the Down.

Quick, quickly, girl! Push forward on the stick to slide her downwards, Sugar's speed building, gradually easing her back into level flight, Sugar shivering as if in anticipation as the distance between them diminished, his muscles aching from holding her steady.

Rose fancied now that he could see the indistinct smudges that were the two separate clusters of towers of RAF Ventnor, and alarm flared at how close they were.

Rear-view mirror? Nothing, mercifully clear. Rocking in his seat with anxiety, willing her onwards…

He sighted on the blur of the Bf109, gauging the moment as the sleek little Luftwaffe machine lithered and bobbed, and pushed down again on the trigger for a second's worth of 20mm fire, twirling smoke trailing his torrent of shells, the harsh vibration of his cannon conspiring with the quiver of her airframe to shake his thumb from the button, feeling it in his crotch and spine.

And it worked, for there was a sudden flash on the enemy fighter, and it yawed to one side before sliding back to settle back onto the distant towers, but he had lost more of his lead over Rose by flinching away from the 20mm fusillade.

Yet the recoil of his Hispanos had slowed Rose, too, and the chase continued.

Come on, girl! Mirror, clear. *Oh Jack, be safe!*

As if the boy had heard, the R/T crackled, "Toffee Red Two to Blackgang, scratch one bandit, any other customers?"

Good boy! Relief surged through him, oh good boy, Jack!

But there was no time for celebration, for the threat before him remained. He could see the bulge of the bomb hanging below it, and he wondered that the German before him was continuing despite the RAF fighter rapidly closing behind him. Some sprog with dreams of glory? Dangerous and fearless in his keen innocence.

Certainly, the German lad couldn't out-run, out-turn or even out-climb Sugar, but he could have jettisoned his bomb and stall-turned in an attempt to escape in the haze and mist but had foolishly chosen to risk it all in order to deliver a blow that would surely cost him his life, the bomb slowing him by too much.

The Bf109 was dropping, low enough now to disturb the surface of the water, the furrow rippling outwards behind it, its slipstream making Sugar's airframe judder and bounce and complain.

They were so close! And now the memory rose unbidden again of the ranks of dead girls in torn RAF blue, covered from the world beneath a creased and soiled tarpaulin, their memorial a red-brown cloud of smoke and brick dust, hanging low over a ruined and burning airfield.

Blood, tears and bitter despair.

The memory of the dead girls made Rose feel ill, and anxiety curled through him. *I'll not let it happen again…*

Mirror, clear…

A fine spray of water spattered against the oil-stained windscreen, the running water making the image of the enemy fighter ripple before him, and he knew that he must fire soon, before they reached the resort at Ventnor, for otherwise his shells might scatter destruction and death for those who lived there.

And then apprehension. Have I enough left in my ammunition trays?

The boy was too far to help, but he might be able to intercept the raider if Rose failed, "Toffee Red Leader to Two, re-join at Point BG."

"Received, leader."

Carefully…

Once more he pushed down the gun button, and the stench of his fear and hot cordite was the finest counterbalance for the sight of the ruinous hits flash bright across the little grey-blue fighter in his sights. Drifts and puffs of smoke and paint and shreds of metal, a thin stream of white sliding back across the 109's fuselage.

And again, Sugar slowed from the recoil of his cannon.

A glance into the mirror, thankfully empty.

Yet still it continued onwards to the little patch of green with its magical stick-towers.

Damn you! Why don't you die?

He licked tight lips, cordite bitter on his tongue, seething with frustration, stiff muscles willing the bloody thing to come apart beneath his cannon.

And then it happened. One moment it was dancing jerkily in his gunsight, haphazard flashes strobing along its fuselage and smoke

45

erupting from his impacts, a trail of twisted fragments with the thin tendril of flame and white smoke, a fragment of debris flashing like a comet for a split second as Sugar's propeller scythed it away at a tangent.

And then there was just the boiling explosion, the 109 ballooning into a red and yellow fireball of stabbing light, searing painfully into his eyeballs as Sugar's shells set off the enemy bomb. The explosion expanded alarmingly before him, the sullen *BOOM!* muted under the scream of Sugar's Sabre.

Crying out in fear and braced against his seat he hauled back as hard as he could, and he felt Sugar's slackness as she fought to gain altitude, rearing and wavering, through the edge of that growing hell-bright miasma of fire and severed wreckage, a surge of heat washing over them, dulling the Perspex, but Rose and his trusty Sugar enjoyed continued good fortune as nothing in that hail of shredded fragments of man and machine through which she passed was big enough to do her damage.

Only the expanding pressure wave of the raging tumult flicked at Sugar, and she jigged precariously to starboard, but he caught and held her with shaking hands and staring eyes, the sickly odour of burnt metal making his nose crinkle with distaste.

At last she was safe, and he swallowed the tacky lump stuck in his throat, heart throbbing painfully as the seaside town of Ventnor appeared through the gloaming, pale buildings speckled with sunlight and slightly blurred through the streaks on the Perspex, but still beautiful.

Jack. Got to find Jack.

Quarter the sky and sea, aileron to clear behind, check mirror, glance at the control panel, all well. No other threats visible. No sign of any other raiders, *watch out for them, eyes open.*

Fingertips for a moment gentle against her picture.

Thank you, my Lord, for keeping me safe.

Little puffs of dirty brown smoke suddenly erupt around him, *crump-crump-crump* and a patter of shell fragments and disturbed air, stopping as he waggled his wings irritably, the recognition stripes on the underside of his wings and fuselage obvious to the gunners on the ground. *Trigger-happy pongoes…*

"Toffee Red Leader, scratch one bandit, do you have any other trade?" he grimaced at the stridency in his voice.

The girl's voice was shaking with excitement, shrilly gulping out, "We saw it all, Toffee Red Leader! Congratulations! And thank you! Next time you're passing, come and see us, we'd love to thank you in person…"

He grinned with stiff lips but could imagine the chief controller's scowl at her familiarity with Rose, the cordite still harsh on his tongue and reeking through his nostrils.

Rose indulged himself by flying over the RDF site, gawking at the two groups of skeletal aerials clustered close to one another, gaunt fingers pointing up at the sky, the pair of much smaller wooden towers at the reserve station, RAF Lawrence, faintly visible some distance to the west.

Rose waved dutifully at a mixed group of WAAFs and airmen leaning against their bicycles, waggling his wings one last time before turning westwards again to re-join his patrol line, to wait for the readiness boys to take over from them even though it was almost dusk, so that Jack and he could refuel and rearm and prepare their combat reports, glad in their success and survival.

Why had his enemy not jettisoned his bomb and turned to fight when he could have after that first pass? He had no chance once he had decided to just bore on and try to bomb. The bombing run had been a Forlorn Hope, yet he had taken the gamble, and lost.

47

Courageous or thoughtless? Inexperienced or hopeful? No one would ever know.

There would be no rows of dead girls today as there had been in 1940 when RAF Foxton was bombed, just small groups of disconsolate Luftwaffe groundcrews gazing vainly into the empty sky, waiting fruitlessly for those who would never return.

Quarter the sky and sea, aileron to clear behind, check mirror, glance at the control panel, feel the bulge of the little pink teddy bear and the lucky pebble in his pocket, touch her photograph and imagine the sweetness of her voice and the softness of her skin.

We saved them, Moll.

Oh, merciful God, you saved us, thank you.

Chapter Six

Attacks on NoBall targets kept 44 Wing and a large part of the 2ndTAF busy in the early months of 1944, occasionally escorting fast medium bombers or the slower four-engine 'Heavies'.

But there were also plenty of other targets to provide bomber escort for, with squadron-strength 'Rangers' later in the day, reaching further inland to attack targets of opportunity and with the hope of catching (or drawing) bandits into the air.

The trips were often unproductive, and they would return tired and frustrated with cannons unfired.

With the prohibition of attacks on rail transport since December 1943, watching a troop train or one laden with trucks or tanks puffing peacefully away unscathed was equally maddening.

But more often than not Excalibur engaged in bombing targets of their own.

With their Typhoons restyled (to their chagrin and Scarlet's undisguised disgust, *we're fighter pilots, for goodness' sake!*) as 'Bombphoons', 44 Wing became intimately familiar with both the infrastructure and sights of Northern France.

In most of their attacks on the launch sites, they found little opposition, with the Luftwaffe jealously hoarding its shrinking group of veteran pilots, and the flak units being wisely allocated to defend operational sites, rather than incomplete construction sites.

After weeks of continuous bombing, many of the northern French launch sites were severely damaged, with programmes of repairs constantly set back by each next raid. Consequently, the V1 sites were pulled back.

By the time Rose re-joined Excalibur, the enemy defences they faced were not what they had once been.

Nonetheless, a single 20mm gun could catch and kill a raider just as well as a massed battery of 37mm or 88mm guns, as could a solitary bullet from a Mauser. And they did. Light defences were no excuse for complacency.

This was true for the one of the last NoBall raids involving Excalibur in February of 1944. Thus far, the squadron had managed to avoid anything worse than slight battle damage to their Typhoons.

*

The coast, faint in the light haze, passed beneath Sugar's nose as she passed through seven thousand feet, just below scattered cloud, heavy flak already bursting above them, and Rose pushed forward back into level flight, Dieppe a dark grey smudge around three miles to the north-east of them; Pointe d'Ailly below and to port.

Far above light glinted on the wings of the twenty or so Spitfire Mark IX's which were their escort, but they did not expect any Luftwaffe intervention today, as usual.

From this height he could survey the irregular green expanse of bocage, wide pastures and forests of the Pays de Bray, the sticky clay soil for dairy pasture in an area known for its sumptuous butters and cheeses.

But there was no time for sightseeing, for their objective was situated within that expanse, a large V1 complex fifteen miles from the coast, veiled in the midst of thick forest close to Ardouval.

They had all seen the most recent reconnaissance photographs and knew where to look, in the patchwork centre of the central wedge of forest, around fifteen miles south-east of Dieppe. But searching was unnecessary, for the target was well defined by the jumbled and irregular collage of deep craters, banks of floating smoke and explosions marking the end of Orna squadron's attack, easily visible from a mile above and some miles afar.

The squadron was in formation behind him, and Rose took them past the target so that they might recover from their dives facing towards the coast for egress, but the defences were under no illusions that this second squadron formation of Typhoons would pass them by, and the lighter flak guns opened up immediately, creating a daunting carpet of explosions for them to enter, the black puffs of 37mm interspersed with the white of the more common 20mm, and the heavy flak speculatively continuing ineffectually.

He pressed erratically on the rudder pedals to manoeuvre against the onrushing gale of explosive metal (but not too much, for Byron was close by), knowing that all the aircraft behind would be doing the same, the enemy gunners here tracking them disturbingly close.

Rose saw the last of Scarlet's Tiffiebombers fleeing, the pulse of light beneath where its bomb had fallen, tracing a thin white line of smoke behind it against the rich living greens of the forest below.

There was no need for radio silence, no one was fooled about why they were here.

"Toffee Leader, fuse bombs." Rose reached up his right hand, sweat pooling beneath his buttocks and stomach, scrotum tight and tingling with apprehension, first flicking the paired bomb selector switches, and then the nose and tail fusing pair, *ready.*

It had been agreed early on during this dive-bombing lark that whilst individual bombing may suit a small formation against a poorly defended target, larger formation attacks against heavy defences would be better suited in pairs, and now young Jack Byron sat to starboard in spread line abreast.

Lord God, protect us…

Almost in position… and… *now!*

"Toffee Leader attacking."

Stick hard back, nose rising, and almost immediately over to the right, Sugar rearing up to slip over to one side and nose over downwards, aileroning her into position and trying to ignore the twinkling of the massed guns below, like a forest of flashbulbs, flinging ruin at Jack and himself.

Focus on the target and overlook the reality that he seemed to be flying through a funnel filled with broken, swerving lines of tracer, the blossoming smoke of flak bursts, the air so thick with flak that it seemed impossible not to be hit, and he felt the tight throb of pain in his muscles, jaw working as the altimeter spun down impossibly fast and the target shivered large in the gunsight and Sugar pitched and staggered in the tumultuous air, the crack of shells and the clatter and jangle of shrapnel distant.

The blood was thrusting through him and his heart thumped a staccato rhythm in harmony with the raucous banging of his cannon, down on the bomb release button, Sugar lurching sideways hideously as a shell burst close by, *'bang!'* and the clatter of more fragments against Sugar's skin as the bombs fell away, knowing the shell had ruined the trajectory of his bombs into a miss, and he was hauling back, viciously into his belly, Sugar working hard against the stubborn embrace of the dive, momentum pulling at her and at the blood in in his skull even as the horizon appeared once more in the windscreen and into in his fading vision.

The stick trembled and his ears felt as if they would burst as Sugar's Sabre shrieked and she slithered through the rough air, and as she did so he saw beneath the trees, thinly veiled by smoke and poorly-concealed beneath artificial netting and branches, the rectangular shapes of a pair of huts and beside it a 20mm gun, the quad mounting clearly swinging after him, and even as his instincts bawled at him to get out of it, he was dragging Sugar a couple of degrees to starboard, feeling her nose slide, and crushed down the button, his involuntary cry of fear resounding strangely in the cockpit, a murmur in the midst of the clamouring madness.

The tracer was reaching out for him, as bright as the sun, the figures of the crew imprinted on his mind even as his shells clawed and ripped them into bloodied rags.

No time to enjoy his success, for already a line of tracer was swinging his way, and he felt Sugar buck as flak burst close around, the flecks of shrapnel picking and punching her, feeling the explosion as it tore at the air.

Got to get out of it, quick!

He flapped the stick and struck the rudder pedals, throwing her into a jinking climb at full boost of +9lb/sq.in., pulled into the seat as she fled to safety from the intense fire below and behind.

His eyes were stinging as rivulets of sweat ran down his face and slipped beneath his goggles, and he wiped them quickly, eyes dropping first to her picture, *made it, Moll, somehow, we made it…*

Even as he instinctively felt for Molly's little teddy bear and Charlie's glass-smooth pebble, his eyes sought out his wingman, and saw that

Byron was rapidly closing on his wing, smoke stained and battered— *thank God! The boy made it through that maelstrom!*

The air was dirty with flak, and they circled the site at eight and a half thousand feet, staying clear of the lighter flak and moving around to confound the 88s, watching as the others made their attacks before pulling out.

One of Scarlet's boys had crashed, the column of smoke thick and accusatory in the dense woods near Torcy-le-Petit commune, but there was no parachute draped across surrounding trees to give them hope.

His men attacked, twinned pairs dancing, darting shapes diving in turn to race through the curtains of tracer and flak bursts, emerging miraculously each time from the drifting veils of smoke, though smeared and bearing battle-damage.

And then it happened.

The penultimate pair of Typhoons were falling through the thickening obscurity of the smouldering and burning buildings of the launch site, and Rose was anxiously searching the firmament for signs of enemy fighters when there was a pulse of light, pricking through the drifting banks of brown-black staining the air, and he groaned as one of the pair twisted apart, a second explosion marking its end, the wings folding backwards.

He couldn't look away as the flaming comet smashed into the target in a flaring bloom of fire. Unnerved by the loss of his partner, the other Tiffie dropped early and swung away from the flak. He was too high, an easier target as he pulled out prematurely, and Rose cringed inwardly as explosions erupted all around it, but miraculously the lone Typhoon made it through, climbing past them a quarter of a mile away. He could see the hole in one wing, testament to a truly tough fighter and a very fortunate escape.

Who was it? He wondered bitterly, *who have I just lost?* He felt the heaviness of despair clench like a cold fist around his heart, the taste of loss harsher than cordite in his sour mouth.

He reached out to touch her picture, but he felt no better.

His final pair were passing them now, low down and manoeuvring hard, only beginning to climb at full throttle and full boost as they cleared the light flak perimeter.

He cleared his throat, but said nothing, desperate to go, but knowing that he was leaving one of his own behind in this place of pain and death.

They had come here to attack the enemy and confound his hateful projects, and in so doing had likely killed tens if not hundreds of them, and throughout the Wing's attack there had not been an appearance by the Luftwaffe, so what right had he to begrudge the payment due?

Excalibur had lost one, and they had been lucky if the intensity of the anti-aircraft fire was anything to go by, but it was hard to describe this as an incidence of luck when they had lost someone who had only just begun to live.

They left behind themselves a battered V1 launch site, its operational readiness pushed further back and more Allied lives saved from the robot bombs, but amongst the soot and ashes lay the remnants of one of their own.

*

"Who was it, Whip?" Rose marched up to Whipple on stiff legs, the C-Flight commander's face was pale and strained, that bloody great scary dog of his nowhere to be seen.

"Young Beckwith, poor little blighter," Whipple pulled out his pipe, stared at it as if he didn't know what it was. "It was just his third sortie. He was a good lad, careful and conscientious, would have done well, given half a chance."

Beckwith! The poor sod. Eager eyes, a serious mouth and hair slightly longer than regulation length. It wasn't the first time Rose lost a young fighter pilot, but it still hurt. Goodness knows, it didn't get any easier.

Whip wiped the sweat from his face and sighed, "Hardly got to know the lad. Dead keen, thought he'd have done well. Bloody shame."

"He was from Leeds," Rose murmured, half to himself.

"Leeds, eh? Fancy." Whipple clenched the pipe angrily between his teeth. "Well, Leeds lost another of its sons today. Poor little blighter," he repeated.

"Yes." The muscles on Whipple's face were tight with anger, and Rose patted his shoulder. "I'm sorry, Whip. I'll write to his parents." He couldn't think of anything else to say.

Whipple looked down and sighed, "No, Flash. I'll write. He was one of mine."

No, Whip. He was one of ours. The hurt in his chest proclaimed it.

But he didn't say it.

The lad had trained for war, flown Typhoons into combat, and died attacking the enemy. A boy dying a man's death, daring and dreams unfulfilled.

And all his idiot of a CO could say was, 'He was from Leeds'. That was just a part of who he had been.

Rose wanted to kick himself.

Whip must have seen his expression. "Those of us who make it will have to make sure that everybody remembers the ones who don't, eh, Flash?"

Rose turned away, thinking, *that's what I should have said,* not a feeble, *oh, he was from Leeds,* like some brainless prune, and now the memories of his meeting with Beckwith the previous month in the Ramrod Inn returned.

As was his usual practice with new pilots after becoming Excalibur's CO, Rose had invited Beckwith for a pint and a chat in the Ramrod Inn usually called the 'Twitchy Stick' by the men, and now Rose recalled the little newspaper cutting the boy had shown him when he had asked if Beckwith had a wife or girlfriend.

"No, sir, at least not yet. There's a girl, but she doesn't know how I feel. Doesn't even know who I am, really." Almost diffidently the lad had removed the piece of newspaper lovingly from his wallet, "I don't know if you remember her, sir, but she was in all the papers at the time because she met with Stalin in 1936."

Rose took the cutting and unfolded it carefully, it was a page from the Blackpool Gazette and Herald, "Railway Queen Crowned," he read it out aloud, looking at the faded picture of a pretty young girl with a dark bob clutching a huge bouquet and wearing a crown, a bashful teenage sovereign smiling self-consciously at the camera.

The boy's eyes had glowed with pleasure, "Elsie Audrey Mossom," he breathed the name with reverence, "Tenth Railway Queen of Great Britain, 1935. I fell in love with her when I saw her dance in the Blackpool Tower Children's Ballet. She's an absolute smasher!" He gave a slight smile, "Audrey's a few years older than me of course, but that doesn't matter, does it, sir?"

Rose had assured him it didn't. After all, wasn't Rose five years younger than his Molly?

"What's a Railway Queen?" he had asked; feeling daft in his ignorance.

Surprise showed on young Beckwith's face. "Oh! Why, um, girls whose families work in an industry can enter competitions to be crowned the queen of their particular industry. Audrey was the queen in 1935, sir. Imagine! The Railway Queen for the whole country!"

He carefully took back the cutting from Rose, looking at it for a long moment before tucking it back into his wallet. "She's a professional dancer now, and was wed in 1940, but it doesn't matter. I love her and I'm going to marry her, but I want to complete a tour of operations before I write to her. Girl like that, I'll have to fight for her. Need to be someone if I expect her to leave her husband."

Rose, with his own experiences of a lovely married woman, remained silent.

Leaning back, eyes on the redcoat and RAF uniforms in the display case, Beckwith doodled distractedly with spilled beer on the tabletop, "She doesn't know me yet, but one day she'll be Mrs Audrey Beckwith."

He had nodded firmly to himself, "Mrs Audrey Beckwith. Doesn't that sound grand?"

Despair washed coarsely through Rose at the memory. The boy's plans and dreams had ended brutally in an instant, a 20mm cannon shell grinding the daydreams of years into oblivion, and Audrey Mossom, the Tenth Railway Queen of Great Britain, would never know the boy who had joined the air force so that he could be worthy of her.

Lost in his dreams of his queen, he may never even have known a woman in the short thread of his life, dying as a warrior whilst not having had the chance to become a man.

And now he was gone. Rose felt his eyes sting and blinked the moisture away.

Granny tramped past, face like thunder, "Cheer up, you tart! We kicked Jerry's arse! They won't be launching at our civvies with their bloody chuff bombs from there for a while yet. We put a lot of holes in their base." He sniffed, "C'mon, let's get the debrief done, and get ourselves around a sandwich and some tea. Got a fag?"

Irrationally, Rose felt a spark of anger with his dearest friend., "I lost one of my lads, Granny."

"I know, Flash. It's a fucking awful war." Granny grabbed his arm and shook him, his words deliberate, "And he won't be the last, my old son, believe me. The invasion is coming and it's going to get a lot bloodier. A whole lot bloodier. Our lives for those we hold most dear, eh? The lad you've just lost helped to keep those fucking bombs from being launched. People who would have died now won't. But they still might, so we need to finish this bloody thing, and there'll be a lot more lads like him lost on the way. I may be one, too, but if that's the price, then that's alright by me." Rose saw the rage in Granny's face, and knew his OC felt the pain of loss, too.

"Me too, Granny?"

"Little Danny needs a daddy, even if it's a dopey pisspot like you, Flash, you soft pickled sod, so don't you dare go for a burton! If you do, I'll kick your scraggy backside right over the watch tower so hard they'll have to pull my sock out of your silly arse, d'you understand?"

Rose forced a smile onto his lips and straightened his shoulders. "Hm. Not a very pretty picture, that. Don't think I'd like it much. Alright, come on then, Granny, let's get that cuppa, shall we?"

Granny nodded, "Lets." He looked across the airfield, into the distance, "He was a hero, Flash, like all these lads that we lose. They always are. They're only kids but they fight as men."

Granny remembered an eager but anxious young Pilot-Officer named Rose at RAF Foxton in 1940, and felt as if he might weep, *kids who fight as men.*

"They're heroes, every one of them. Only we know it, but the Almighty willing, when we win this blasted war, it'll be the boys like Beckwith who will have bought it with their precious futures, for the ones they leave behind, and the ones yet to come."

Let that be the boy's epitaph.

He was a hero.

Chapter Seven

The table rocked dangerously, and Rose's tea slopped onto the tabletop as Granny threw himself onto the seat opposite.

"Wot you doing, tatty drawers?" Slouched on the seat, his OC dragged greedily on a creased cigarette before skilfully tossing the butt into Rose's cup, a spark of embers glowing for an instant on the walls within. Pulling another from his pocket, he lit it with a flourish.

Rose's Wing Commander leaned forward and eyed him critically, "Crikey! The chops on you! Fuck me! Like a battered haddock! What's wrong, chum? Got trapped wind?"

Grumpily, Rose pulled out his handkerchief and wiped the splatter from his uniform tunic and face, noting the tiny droplets dotting his tie and shirt, "Just enjoying a quiet cup of tea," he looked pointedly at the sodden butt floating in his tea, "or at least, I was trying to."

Granny scratched his neck, and blew out a stream of smoke, the fumes rolling over Rose. "Blimey! Ain't you the grouch? I've got so many delicate dollies in my Wing now! You can still drink it, just take out my fag end! What's wrong with you? Don't you know there's a war on? You going to sit there howling into your brew, or you want to hear about the Heinkel mine-laying bombers setting up shop in Jersey?"

Rose coughed, eyes slitted and watering, pausing in his scrubbing, "Mine-laying bombers?"

"Hah! Thought that would get your attention, you bolshy bugger." Granny nodded with satisfaction, "Apparently Jerry's got a brand-new aerial mine that they're going to seed the Solent with, which would be rather bad news for the ships gathering there for the invasion."

"Oh, yes?"

"Oh, yes. Auntie Hermann's deployed a flight of He-115's in the Channel Islands. A mate at the Admiralty tells me that they've developed a new magnetic mine, super-sensitive, can destroy a ship even if it's been degaussed, and let's be honest, you've seen how many ships there were in The Solent and Southampton Water, haven't you?"

"Could have got out and walked across, there were that many of them!!

"Well then, thought it would be nice to nip over to wish 'em *gute nacht*, eh? Might nip over to Jersey tonight, old randy plum, want in?"

"Rather! Squadron attack?"

"Nope. I thought two sections, a couple of pairs making a single pass a minute apart. You and your lad Jack'll attack first, one pass, then Brat and I'll follow up as you two clear off."

"Bombs?"

"Couple of 500lb bombs for each of us, I thought, strafe the floatplanes and drop bombs on the facilities set up for them. But remember the mines are the main target, not the Heinkels. OK, potato? Now give me a fag, and stop flapping your chops at me, will you? Can't hear myself think!"

*

62

The rays of daylight were seeping away, just a glowing thread now highlighting the distant horizon as the night hunted the sun.

He checked that the boy was close, but not too close, lest a tyre burst on take-off. Byron was looking at him, awaiting the signal, the dark shape of his Typhoon B-Bertie huge and imposing, the spinning disc a veil of diffuse light at its nose.

A quick check of her trim, the instrument console showing all was well, and a deep gulp of blessed oxygen, one finger lightly brushing against her picture for a moment.

At his request, the lights lit up the runway and he pushed the throttle fully forward, holding the torque with the rudder hard over as Sugar began to roll, the weight of the bombs helping to steady her, gradually building speed and then they were airborne, soaring upwards. It was a perfect night for a Rhubarb, the moon low to the east in a sky thinly strewn with low cloud.

Above them Granny and Brat were circling with their navigation lights on, helping Rose and young Byron to form up on them.

The formation dropped down low over the channel, no more than a hundred feet above the choppy, oily-black surface of the water. The moon a glow climbing above the horizon, and they flew southwest to loop around the westernmost of the Channel Islands; the powerful Sabres of their Typhoons swallowing the distance in just a few minutes.

Soon the dark mass of Guernsey rose out of the water to port, a long, low, brooding shape, its profile outlined in the moonlight, and the formation separated, Granny and Brat climbing and turning to starboard in a large clockwise circle.

Rose and Byron, however, dropped lower, to seventy feet above the black sliding surface, and Rose shivered involuntarily as they turned forty-five degrees to port, the twenty miles between the islands flashing past in just three minutes, and shortly the dim bulk of Jersey appeared to port as well.

Rose keyed the R/T, "Safeties off, fuse bombs," he half whispered, the words thick in a throat dry as dust, fear a rushing current through his heart. Byron clicked a response.

And then time seemed to speed up, the moonlight revealing the pale upright finger of Corbiere lighthouse, and he felt a flutter of satisfaction that they were on track.

The second headland of St Brelaide's Bay passed, and St Aubin's Bay suddenly lay open before them even as a lick of tracer from one of the blockhouses wheeled aimlessly into the sky behind them.

Pictures of the Nazi blockhouses had shown disturbing and very alien, smooth-sided angular constructions so very out of place on those peaceful, grassy slopes and beaches, like some ominous futuristic prop from Lang's 'Metropolis'.

The blood was pounding through his temples, punching at his thoughts as his eyes sought out Hermitage Rock at the south-eastern end of the island, the site on which Elizabeth Castle and the Priory Church were built.

He turned away to starboard, knowing that young Byron was close by, skimming low over the water, circling to allow them a long approach to the waters of the sheltered eastern side of the islet.

Mati told them of how the Germans nightly moored the Heinkel floatplanes close to the causeway, allowing fuel trucks and ordnance lorries to be carefully driven out to arm and fuel the aircraft at low tide.

The floatplanes would take off and land under the cover of darkness, when the tide had risen, and Granny expected that with a spot of luck they would be fully armed and fuelled at dusk.

Just in case, their bombs had been given a short delay fuse, so that

Rose's section were able to escape the explosions whilst not endangering Granny's subsequent attack.

When he was satisfied that they had created enough distance for the approach, Rose guided them back onto track.

A small warship, long and lean, was moored close to the eastern side of La Collette, and Rose offered a silent prayer that its crew (and gunners) would be doing what most sailors did when in port.

He pushed Sugar onwards, edging her nose down, thumb automatically checking that the safety was off, and three or four searchlights flicked on hesitantly from the islet and St Helier harbour mouth, a single line of glowing coals lacing out from the castle into the black sky, but too high.

A line of pontoons extended from the islet to the headland and beyond it, in the moonlight, he caught sight of the spiky jumble of aircraft on the flat gleam of the bay.

And...*now!* He pressed down hard on the gun button, and his thumping cannon ripped out a rush of shells which flung up a line of advancing waterspouts, clawing across the water to pluck at the pontoon, a small boat was pulling it to one side, perhaps to release the first of tonight's raiders, and a glimpse of figures throwing themselves from it into the water, a point of light, a blinking light green lamp, thrown into the air by one of the figures, even as tiny droplets of seawater from the waterspouts freckled and ran across his windscreen.

He focussed on the winged shapes beyond as they passed close beside Hermitage Rock, tracer flickering out from the small blockhouse there, and the second blockhouse on La Collette opened up as if in sympathy, the gunfire still too high and nowhere close enough to worry about, but still Rose hunched down, his mouth metallic and bitter with fear.

The lofty battlements of Elizabeth Castle flickered past in an instant, above and to port, and although the castle was only being used as a cement store, it was well defended, and now the fortifications erupted ferociously with the boiling flare and flash of guns, but the Typhoons were too low and too fast for the enemy gunners to adjust their sights, almost too fast to hear the awakened defence's cacophony.

And then his avenue of advancing waterspouts met with the first row of three Heinkel floatplanes, lined up very nicely, taking the full force of the broadside of shells, hits sparkling behind the climbing curtain of water as his cannon shells splashed across the central flying boat, but no fire or explosions, whilst the one on the end blew up spectacularly and he sensed the force of the explosion and felt the tiny fragments carried by the expanding shock wave which scrabbled powerfully at Sugar, even as he released the lever and felt her rear up as the bombs fell away, and then Sugar was sliding to the left and he pulled her straight, and knew that his bombs had fallen too late to land amidst the first three Heinkels—*sod it!*

But more floatplanes were lined up beyond the first row, on the far side to where the causeway should be, and there was a better than even chance that his bombs would land close to or amongst them.

Swiftly they shot past the Outer Ward and Charles fort, the islet falling behind as flak cascaded up, and he checked on the boy, seeing that in the attack young Byron had lost ground and was now catching up with him from starboard, a searchlight swinging wildly from Raleigh's Yard, even as their bombs pulsed out furious light, like short-lived suns.

An exploding fuel truck seared the bunched aircraft with blazing sun-bright annihilation, setting off more explosions in sympathy, lighting up the windows and fronts of the buildings lining St Aubin's Bay before them and fire-tinged columns of curling smoke and twisted, burning shapes behind them.

Now that they were clear, he worried about Granny and Brat,

tensed muscles aching as light flickered dully from the flak and fire receding behind.

His friends would now have to brave the stirred and unforgiving defences.

Lord, protect them in that turmoil…

Granny picked him to attack first with the advantage of surprise, but now guilty anxiety for his friends plucked at his nerves, we should been second, not first.

He keyed his microphone, "Toffee Done."

There. Now Granny would know they had bombed and were on their way out.

At full throttle and at two hundred feet, Rose's S-Sugar and Byron's B-Bertie thundered northwards across the island, climbing as the ground elevation beneath increased gradually, the ear-splitting roar of the Sabres and the subdued crack of explosions from the Bay awakening its residents with the promise of liberation.

Once past the coastline they dropped back down low again for the leg home, and he rewarded himself with a glimpse of her photograph, *thank God, we did it, Moll,* but within minutes Rose's earphones crackled urgently.

"Toffee Red Leader from Two, aircraft two o'clock high, heading northeast, about two miles, angels zero." The boy's voice was calm, but Rose sensed the excitement in it.

Heart banging, Rose anxiously peered into the moonlit night but couldn't see a thing, although the blob of black oil which had flown back from his propeller boss didn't help. *Cripes, Jack's eyes are sharp!*

"I can't see it, Two, take the lead."

Might it be a night fighter? And if so, one of ours, or…?

"Received." B-Bertie eagerly forged ahead, and Rose pulled back about a hundred yards and to one side.

Within a minute or so he could make out the faint grey shadow floating above the water, flying at an altitude of no more than a few hundred feet and seemingly unaware of their approach, but Byron saw much more.

"Two to Leader, it's a floatplane, twin engine job. I think it's another Heinkel 115."

Rose half-squinted, and nodded to himself, Jack was right, one must have taken off before they had carried out their attack! This was the one that got away.

Or almost had if they had anything to do with it...

"I concur. Red Two, you are formation leader, want to show him that he's going the wrong way?"

"Sir!" the boy's voice was keen.

He watched approvingly as Byron manoeuvred quickly into position, keeping well out of range of the MG15 7.92mm machine gun which the dorsal gunner would be equipped with.

Again, he marvelled that the enemy minelayer seemed blissfully unaware of the Typhoon approaching from behind, the slim bomber continuing as if without a care in the world.

It was something Rose had discovered during his tour on Beaufighters. Even when the moon was bright, enemy bomber crews did not often notice his presence behind them until it was too late, something he found quite inexplicable.

With that thought in his mind, Rose quartered the sky to ensure that no one was going to creep up on them while they crept up on the He115, although it was rather dark despite the moonlight, and he hadn't seen the floatplane until it was quite close...

Suddenly the Heinkel lumbered to port, aware at last of its pursuers, and a stitch of glowing tracer spurted out, falling uselessly away from the Typhoons, out of range.

Loaded with a heavy sea mine, it was a little less manoeuvrable than a tin bathtub, and no match for the powerful fighters following it.

Byron on the R/T, "Attacking…"

At just under maximum range of his 20mm Hispanos, and still well out of range of the enemy guns, Byron opened fire, and in the darkness a constellation of white flashes flickered and sparkled, mirrored in the water below, the enemy bomber jerking and shaking helplessly beneath the impacts.

The floatplane was losing height, a trailing cloud of smoke, dust and debris slumping onto the surface of the water, and then Byron's shells found the almost full fuel tanks and for a moment the dark shape of the floatplane seemed to be riding on an exploding comet's tail.

It was only for a moment, and then the sea mine itself detonated in a glaring pulse that seemed to light up the sky, and they broke away, Rose to port and Byron to starboard, as the wreck of the minelayer, wreathed in flame, tumbled silently into the sea.

Rose blinked his eyes rapidly as he tried to dissipate the afterimage of the flash on his retinas. "Leader to Two, that's another confirmed. Well done, Jack!"

"Hello, Leader, thanks! Will re-join on your starboard wing."

"You greedy tarts! Could've left us one!" Another familiar voice crackled in his earphones.

Rose looked over his shoulder, and sure enough, two fleeting shapes appeared from out of the darkness, closing with Byron and himself. But he waited with one hand ready to throw Sugar into evasion, wary of being fooled, *just in case*, until the ghostly shapes resolved into two pugnacious-looking Typhoons.

Granny and Brat. He felt relief course through him at the knowledge his friends were safe as well.

Thank God.

Coming in over the perimeter fence he glimpsed the slim figure of a WAAF standing alone beside her Hillman staff car, and he knew that now that she had seen her husband return safely, Belle could rest easy, at least until tomorrow.

What we put the ones we love through he mused as Sugar's propeller finally creaked to a stop and her airframe stilled, knowing that unlike Granny and Belle, he could not be with Molly this evening, keenly feeling her absence, but knowing that in many ways it was worse for her, each minute alone and not knowing. Every waking second eclipsed with the fear that a telegram might be on its way bringing the news she most dreaded, terrified each time the phone rang.

At least Charlie has her husband, glad for her happiness, but envious that she was no longer there to provide him sanctuary from the stress, responsibility, and loneliness of his wartime command.

He had no cause for jealousy. Hadn't he enjoyed the same good fortune of seeing Molly every day back during the battle, and then throughout 1941? And how fortunate he had been to have Charlie when he most needed the support of another? How lucky that she had willingly shared herself completely with him?

Rose knew he was luckier than most. No postings to some fly-ridden North African desert or mosquito-infested far eastern jungles for him, his entire war served in the defence of home, near enough to the ones he loved.

There were many who would envy him.

Oh, but how he missed Molly's warm embrace, breathing in the fragrance of her skin and hair, softness beneath his lips and fingers, the only place where he was free of the anxiety and foreboding lurking in the recesses of his mind, endlessly gnawed away at the edges of his spirit.

Byron joined him, grinning ear-to-ear, and Rose roused himself from his melancholic thoughts and slapped his young wingman on the back, "That makes two! Well done, Jack!"

The boy blushed with pleasure and embarrassment, "He wasn't able to do much about it, sir!"

Rose shook his head, "You won't believe how many blokes I've flown with who would have made a meal of shooting down that Heinkel!"

Granny strode up, parachute casually over one shoulder and the ubiquitous cigarette hanging disconsolately from his mouth; a weary but grinning Brat Morton, now a Flight-lieutenant with the DFC and DFM, straggling along behind.

He stuck out his hand, "The drinks're on you, Maddie!" even though Byron was neither mad nor bad, he had proven himself dangerous to the enemy, and been christened 'Maddie'.

Granny nodded lugubriously at Rose, "And Mr Rose here is right, it took me years to train him to shoot straight! Couldn't hit a moving barrage balloon from ten paces!"

Granny blew a stream of noxious smoke into Rose's face.

"You lads blew buggery out of the floatplanes, wasn't much left for us. It was lit up like a tart's boudoir, and the flak was hairier than my arse, so we dropped our bombs on that Jerry destroyer instead. Last I saw, she was smoking like a good 'un and settling in the water. We'll see what the PRU wallahs find, but I reckon she's a goner!"

Granny grinned evilly at him as Rose coughed and wiped his streaming eyes, "No good sobbing, Flash you soppy tart, Jerry didn't think your aim was going to be any good, either!" he sniffed, "Leave the bawling to their frauleins, eh?"

Chapter Eight

The war in the Western desert had been one of endless movement for the Allies, advances and retreats, in which (as Granny discovered in 1942 when a member of the Desert Air Force) not only the ground elements of the British Army but their air support swept backwards and forwards with the rapidly changing tides of war.

During the hard-fought and equally hard-won campaign, the RAF aircrews, more used to operating pre-war from fixed bases were forced to learn a new and mobile way of conducting aerial war.

These roving airborne elements went on to form the First Tactical Air Force.

The desert campaign was a salutary lesson for those charged with planning the future invasion of occupied Europe.

To keep a battlefront from becoming a static line of defence and offence like the Western Front of the First World War, it was vital for fast moving ground forces to be backed up by air support based nearby, minimising the time between the request for help and the arrival of aerial support.

To adapt this approach for the European theatre, wargames were fought in 1943, the lessons learned leading to reorganisation of established units and formation of new ones, the evolution and development including a whole new RAF element, the Second Tactical Air Force. In effect, the Allied invasion would be Blitzkrieg in reverse. Yet while the disparate allied formations in France in 1940 had been arranged and organised to work together in mere months, the enemy had been preparing for almost four years. Indeed, *Der Fuhrer* had appointed the great Desert Fox, Rommel, to reinforce and oversee the defences of the Atlantic Wall.

It was decided that the ground formations involved in the invasion of Europe would be allocated their own separate aerial support.

The 2nd TAF as it came be known included 83 and 84 Groups, each highly versatile including fighter, fighter-bomber, medium-bomber and reconnaissance units.

Two or three squadrons would be allocated to an airfield, and two airfields form a fighter wing.

One unfortunate consequence of this reorganisation of Fighter Command's squadrons was the separation of the flyers and their aircraft from their beloved and trusted groundcrews and most of the ground-based elements of the squadron.

The mobile ground component would be allocated to a particular airfield behind the front, able to relocate to other airfields as the front advanced, and be responsible for servicing whichever squadron landed at the airfield.

The pilots and a core nucleus of ground personnel of each Wing would move between airfields as necessary to remain close to the frontline and provide prompt assistance as necessary.

Breaking up units in this way created a great deal of ill-feeling, but in the end, most squadrons adopted particular airfields and ground personnel.

Whilst this reorganisation of RAF squadrons was being

implemented, a few quiet words in the ears of old friends at the Air Ministry meant that Granny's 44 Wing RAF remained essentially untouched.

Whilst there was a trickle of postings away, most of Granny's people would not accept transfer to other units, despite enticement followed by menaces and intimidation.

Granny's Wing was now a part of 83 Group, 2nd TAF, but would continue Anti-Rhubarb channel patrols and Rhubarbs into Europe for another month before re-mustering to full strength and beginning the intensive training required for the Invasion which was surely coming.

Furthermore, it would give them time for the transformation to mobility. Their first move from RAF Little Sillo in Dorset was overseen by a tough little NCO from the 2nd Battalion, The Parachute Regiment, lent to them by the legendary paratrooper 'Johnny' Frost.

Corporal Romanescu was a sinewy, leather skinned man in his mid-thirties with the ribbon of a Distinguished Conduct Medal on his chest and had been a circus trapeze artist before the war.

Knowing how much of a nightmare mobilising an RAF Wing would be, Granny made full use of the grizzled soldier's pre-war knowledge and experience of moving a large circus establishment by road from place to place.

Whilst not free of drama, they had avoided some of the difficulties, identifying rest areas and potential sites for a night stop in case of mishap on the convoy clogged roads.

The move provided an opportunity for training some of the Wing's newest pilots in low-level attacks as they made dummy-attacks on their mobile elements during their trek, the meandering line of vehicles with their excellent and dedicated ground personnel visible from miles away.

Meant to remain 50 yards apart, the vehicles bunched up to stay together—trucks, transporters, tenders and ambulances jumbled along by despatch riders and jeeps in front and behind.

Despite Rose's qualms of a Luftwaffe attack, the move was undisturbed by Goering's Finest (Ta very much, Hermann), and with the minimum of problems (Ta very much, Corporal Romanescu) the Wing reached their destination safely (Ta very much, Traffic Control Wing, Corps of Military Police).

The convoy was first sent to RAF Warmwell, but on arrival was directed to Tangmere. They remained in West Sussex for four days before they were once more on the road heading for their last destination before France.

44 Wing RAF's new base was a military airfield initially intended for the US Eighth Air Force.

What should have been USAAF Airbase 270 became No. 120 Airfield of No. 83 Group, 2nd TAF, otherwise known as RAF Havelock Barr.

However, very soon after it was completed by a battalion of US Aviation Engineers at a cost of almost one million dollars, some bright spark in General Eaker's staff discovered that the runways were sufficient for routine take-off and landing but rather shorter than required by a bomber in distress.

RAF Havelock Barr was situated a couple of miles from the tiny hamlet of the same name and close to the Norfolk coast. Whilst not a tented delight (the fast-moving elements of 2ndTAF were to live under canvas, the expected continental field conditions) 44 Wing were allocated Nissen huts, icy in the winters, and baking in the summer.

Granny managed to requisition a rather delightful little cottage nearby, and his senior WAAF, Squadron Officer Belinda 'Belle' Bolt (unbeknownst to the Air Ministry, also his wife) set up home there with him, although officially billeted in the nearby 'Waffery'.

Rose enjoyed a similar arrangement when on night fighters in 1941 and being able to see his bride every day had been pure heaven. It was serenity and comfort after the boredom of patrol or the stress of combat.

It was different for Rose when he rejoined Excalibur squadron.

Molly and little Danny were far away and safe in the Lake District during his tour as a flight commander with Excalibur squadron at Little Sillo in '42-'43, the grinding stress of operations made bearable by the delightful distraction and support of Charlie nearby, an injured soul who shared his feelings of helpless isolation.

In 1944, with the war now entering a critical phase, he would have neither mental solace nor physical release.

And as a leader, he was no longer one of the gang, but separate and responsible for all of them, an invisible barrier separating almost two hundred members of Excalibur squadron from their lonely CO.

As Rose discovered when he put up his half-stripe the previous autumn, command is a solitary and demanding place to be.

Chapter Nine

The sun had not yet burned off all the dew, and the expletive was torn from him as he slipped and fell onto his hands and knees, "Damn it!"

He grabbed at his stick impatiently and got back to his feet, wiping the dirt from his hands, and stopped to draw breath.

"Crikey, Moll," he wheezed, "what are we doing up here anyway?"

Molly stopped to turn and smirk smugly down at him, barefoot in the grass, shoes in hand, "I told you to save your energy this morning, didn't I? But, oh no, you had to have your wicked way with me, didn't you?"

"What's a chap to do?" he replied defensively, trying to get his breath back, noting grumpily that she wasn't even out of breath.

"When one wakes up with a gorgeous popsie clad only her birthday suit, well then, it's only to be expected that he might indulge in, er, intimacies." He haughtily retorted, rather liking the way the dew glistened on her toenails, the red contrasting with the lushness of the grass.

"Oh, Harry! What a terribly nice way to say you fancied a fuck!" she smiled prettily.

His breath caught in his throat, "Oh, I say!" Despite his

complaining, aching muscles, he felt his groin warm at her words and the morning's memories.

"Well, come on then," she inclined her head, "Time and tide and all that…"

"Little walk before heading for home, she says…" he grumbled under his breath, and then, watching her bottom sway before him as she thrust her feet through the rough grass. "Cor! Who needs a carrot…?"

"Did you say something, Harry?" she called back over her shoulder.

"Er, I was just wondering what we were doing here, my little spiky hedgehog." He eyed the grassy slope ahead doubtfully.

Molly turned to face him, but continued upwards, walking backwards, her movements light and easy, and he admired the sight of her midnight tresses tangling and blowing across her face in the cool breeze as she replied, "I wanted to see the giant. I came here when I was at school, but the teachers wouldn't let us look because of the obvious. Don't know why they bothered bringing us in the first place."

They were making their way up Trendle Hill in Dorset, the site of the famous Giant of Cerne Abbas.

The Giant was a mysterious 180 feet high figure carved into the rock and filled in with chalk, wielding a knobbly club and sporting a huge erection. It was a sight which would normally have been clearly visible when airborne in Little Sillo's circuit but was not because of the Home Guard's camouflage of bundled brushwood covering it.

"Well, being here makes a fellow feel a bit average," he said plaintively, raising his walking stick for a moment, glad he had brought it and knowing he would never have got this far without it. "I've not got a lumpy club, but I do have a walking stick."

He shook his head sadly, "But I can't compare otherwise."

"Harry! You are silly! What would I do with something like that?

I'm quite content, thank you very much. Satisfied, you might say. Of course, you do prattle a lot of nonsense and you've never read Virgil's Aeneid, but one can't have everything, can one?" She winked cheekily at him, "I'm not sure you can even read, but not to worry. You'll do, at least for now!"

"Ta very much, I'm sure. Care to explain why on earth we're here?" he replied grumpily.

Molly nodded, head down and her buttocks rolling nicely beneath the dew-darkened corduroys, "I read somewhere that if one sits on the Giant's private parts for fifteen minutes, it aids in one's fertility."

He stopped, aghast. "I'm not sitting on his blasted balls for fifteen minutes. What if someone should see me? What if some of the lads fly over and see me there?" then, with slight outrage, "How dare you, madam? I'm as fertile as the next man!"

She tittered and rolled her eyes, "Well I'm not interested in the next man, foolish boy, only in you. And it won't just be you, silly boy, it'll be both of us. I'm going to sit there with you for fifteen minutes. You can sit on his knobbly club later if it makes you feel better."

"I will, you sassy creature, but it won't. But why must I?"

"Well, you know what they say about a Tiffie's vibration?" There was a rumour that the high frequency vibration in a Typhoon's airframe had an adverse effect on the fertility of its pilot. "I've been thinking that it would be very nice for Danny to have a little brother or sister."

"Won't the Home Guard be a bit peeved if we move their camouflage? I don't fancy being poked in the bum by a rusty bayonet."

She sat down, took his hanky to dry her feet and pulled on her walking shoes, "Don't worry, we'll leave it as it is, that's why I brought this thick blanket. Your poor bum won't be poked by bayonets or brush wood, or even soaked by dew."

"Oh, alright then, if we must." Rose looked back down the hill longingly to the village, the staff car from Little Sillo's Motor Pool hidden amongst the buildings.

All this nonsense about visiting the sights when I could have flown up to her! What a waste of time.

"I'm not sure about this," he said, eyeing the thickets uncertainly, then, anxiously, "D'you think there might be spiders in there?"

She felt the laughter bubbling in her throat at the look of trepidation on his face, *of course there will be, silly boy, hundreds of them.*

The dew-encrusted cobwebs were clearly visible in the branches, glittering in the light like beaded crystal embroidery. "Oh, I shouldn't think so, darling," she lied airily.

Hopefully, "Can we head for home after?"

Molly led him through the brushwood to the Giant's chalked genitalia, vigilantly avoiding the webs, and carefully cleared a small space just big enough for them both. She set the blanket down, opening it up, and sat on it, patting the space beside her.

"No, dear. After this we're going to the earthworks further up to do the same thing, and if the maypole is still up there, we'll have a little dance around it, and *then* we'll head north."

Dear God. Have a jolly little dance around a maypole set on top of a hill with a naked man etched on it? And not just any old naked man, but an exceptionally large naked man with an eye-wateringly massive protuberance?

Cripes! What would the lads think? He could already imagine Sid and Jacko's comments...

But he knew that he would do anything she asked.

Rose made a surly face but crawled obediently into the space, and she hugged him tightly. Instantly, he felt better. *Gosh, that feels rather nice...*

Something was mercilessly poking his backside and he asked," Shift over a bit, Moll, I think I'm sitting on a pebble."

"You poor boy," she grinned, "to have such a sensitive bottom. I feel a little like the prince who married the girl in that fairy-tale, y'know, in 'The Princess and the Pea?'"

He smouldered at her, "I'll bet it wasn't just the pea she felt against her arse that night!"

She giggled, "She must have driven him spare on their wedding night!"

Maybe it was her closeness, or the mention of wedding nights, or perhaps even some primal magic associated with the ancient location at which they sat, but Rose felt a tingling in his loins, and he leaned into her, "Fancy a smooch, glamour pants?" he whispered hopefully, curling one arm lasciviously around her waist.

Molly slapped his hand lightly but embraced him back, her arms tightening protectively around him, feeling a frame thinner than she remembered, and she felt like crying. "If you're lucky!"

The breeze whispered through the brush wood, making it creak fitfully as he kissed the top of her head lightly, one hand sliding down to her hip. "Well, that's alright then, because I'm always lucky with the really beautiful ones!"

She reached down to unbuckle her belt ruefully, laughter in her voice. "Hm. Is that so? OK. Come on, then, you bad boy, but you'd best be quick, before the Home Guard turn up!"

The swish of the grass and the gentle sighing of the wind faded as he shifted closer to her, her breathing loud in his ears and the fabric of her trousers coarse against his fingers as he tugged at them.

Rose traced her ear and neck with his lips, his hands sliding from the rough cloth to the silken curve of her buttocks even as Molly reached around to undo his trouser buttons, fingers gently releasing and then guiding him, rounded buttocks pushing down and opening against his zeal.

He pulled a fold of the blanket over them both before wrapping his arms around her again, pulling her into his close embrace, hands cupping her breasts, and her fingers intertwined with his as Molly rocked gently, smoothly, accepting and deliciously moving against him, the sinuous, fluid scent of her readiness and the perfume rush-dabbed on earlier blending sublimely with the rich fragrance of wet grass, brushwood and earth.

Beneath the cover of the blanket their breath mingled like a desert wind, her cheek hot against his and the sounds from her throat like the soft murmurings of a sun-dappled brook as he met her movements with his own, a matched urgency quickening them until he could hold back no longer, and he jerked, arms tightening and gasping involuntarily against her shoulder, overflowing into the yielding warmth, pushing, pushing far into the delicious pliancy, and Molly relaxed back against him, sighing in both contentment and release.

They lay still a moment, bodies united, and senses dimmed, joined as if by the heat and intensity of their passion.

Holding her in his arms, Rose felt an overwhelming sense of well-being and peace.

Oh Moll, I wish we could stay like this forever...

Rose shifted against her side, the breeze cool against his exposed behind, slanting his body over to kiss her, tasting the softness of her warm reciprocation. Luckily, there was no trace left of the marmalade she had had for breakfast (*yeuch!*) and he breathed in deep, inhaling her fragrance.

Molly returned his kiss fiercely, the bristles left behind by his hurried shave rough against her skin, and she felt tears prick warm behind her eyelids as she remembered the shy but kind, honourable and attentive boy she first met four years earlier.

His eyes were still eager and needful, but weariness had replaced the freshness.

Dear God, keep my darling Harry lucky, and keep him safe. For me. For our child. Give us the years ahead, many years together, and the life I dream of with each breath, years fulfilled with joy and contentment until the distant twilight of our lives.

Please.

*

A policeman greeted Molly as she strolled back down the hill, and she noted how the anxious expression on his kindly face eased into one of relief when he saw the mirth on her face.

He came to an easy semblance of attention and touched his helmet respectfully, "Are you alright, ma'am?" he glanced at the folded blanket and walking stick she carried.

She caught sight of Rose peering balefully at her from the back of the Police Wolseley.

"Why, yes, thank you." She looked over his shoulder. "My husband seems to be in the back of your car, Sergeant, has he done something wrong?"

The policeman glanced back at his car, "Begging your pardon, ma'am, but I saw the young gentleman running down the hill holding up his trousers in a very excited state as I happened to be driving past, and he seemed to be acting in what I can only call a very unsavoury manner. Suspecting that there might be questions to answer, I apprehended him." He glared at Rose, who seemed to wilt behind the glass.

Molly covered her mouth for a moment to hide her smile. "Oh dear. I must apologise for his behaviour, Sergeant…?"

He smiled at her, touching the peak of his helmet again. "Baxter, ma'am."

She took the daisy circlet from her head. "We were up on the hill, and I foolishly promised him a kiss, and, unfortunately, he got a little carried away. The problem is, he's not very keen on spiders, and I think one startled him while he was in an unfortunate state of undress."

Sergeant Baxter looked at his glum prisoner doubtfully, whilst Rose adopted a look of injured innocence behind the glass.

"Good Lord! A spider, you say?"

She nodded.

Baxter shook his head in disbelief and sighed, "A spider. Blimey." Grasping the car door handle, he asked, "Will you vouch for him, ma'am?"

Molly nodded again, "I can."

"In which case…" he pulled the door open and gestured for Rose to exit. "Out you come, sir." As Rose got out, the policeman eyed his ribbons, "A spider?"

"It was really, really big," Rose countered sheepishly, stretching his arms out wide apart to demonstrate.

The bloody things made his skin crawl and he had instructed Jimmy to always ensure there were no bugs in the cockpit before he got in telling him, *"I might mistake a spider on the inside of the canopy for an enemy fighter and break off an attack unnecessarily…"*

Now he blushed beneath the policeman's gaze, and felt he needed to say more, and added weakly, "Honest."

Baxter puffed out his cheeks, looking unconvinced.

"He's normally terribly brave…" Molly began defensively.

"Yes, Ma'am. So I see." The policeman responded heavily.

He turned back to Rose. "I don't approve of your behaviour, sir, but we'll say no more about it for now, let's just say we take a rather dim view of gentlemen running down Treadle Hill clutching their trousers at half-mast."

Baxter sniffed disparagingly. "We might have a large etching of a naked man on our hillside, but the gentlefolk of this parish really don't need rank vulgarity cavorting itself shamelessly in their streets. It really isn't done." His tone was stern, "I'll thank you to kindly refrain from doing so in future."

"I shan't, Sergeant, scout's honour, I'm really very sorry," Rose said, feeling the flush prickle its way up his neck and onto his ears.

Baxter scrutinised him for a moment, and then his face lit up. "Oh, I say! Aren't you Typhoon Rose?"

Molly glowed with pride, but Rose's blushes deepened, wondering that if he wished it hard enough, a hole might appear into which he could disappear. "Um, yes, Harry Rose, hello, how do you do? Pleased to meet you."

"Why, you're quite the hero at our station, Mr Rose. It's a pleasure! Wait 'til I tell them I met you! Typhoon Rose!" the policeman beamed.

Oh God, I'd much rather you didn't...

Baxter chuckled and shook his head. "A spider! Well, I never!"

Aargh!

*

They watched as the police car disappeared into the distance. "What a nice man," she said.

"It really was huge, Moll," he said tentatively.

He felt her hand slide into his and she laughed. "I know, my darling. I saw it fall off your bottom as you ran down the hill screaming like a banshee. I think it must have been almost an inch long."

The male ego is a sizeable but fragile thing, and now Rose could feel his deflate a little. Sensing that his dignity and manhood was in question, and feeling slightly shabby by his unmanly behaviour, he made to withdraw his hand from hers, but her fingers tightened around his and squeezed as if to reassure him.

"It felt as big as a damned tractor, Moll." He shuddered at the memory, the blessed thing had felt huge, skittering about on his exposed skin, "Felt as if the bloody thing was trying to crawl up my backside, and I think it's claws scratched my bum something rotten; I think I can feel the blood pouring down the back of my legs."

"Oh dear. Well, the thing is, if you drop your trousers for me to check, we'll probably be arrested for lewd behaviour and a gross lack of moral turpitude, so I'm afraid you'll have to be very brave. We can bandage your poor injured bottom when we get home," she tittered.

"The blood will have dried, and I might be stuck to the seat. What then? Hm?" He squeezed her fingers

She huddled up against him, "We'll cross that bridge when we get to it, shall we? I think there might be a crowbar in the boot."

He huffed but pulled Molly closer, remembering the feel of her beneath the blanket. *God, but she felt good…*

Rose hitched up his trousers, "A kiss may help soothe the pain?"

She placed a hand on his cheek, "Oh Harry, you are such a daft old thing," but she kissed him anyway, and he tried to pull to her into his arms, but an elbow gently nudged him away, "You've just been arrested for running around half-dressed, so behave yourself. Come on then, Mr Typhoon Rose, let's get back to the car. We've a long journey ahead of us, and it would be nice to get back home before nightfall."

She grabbed his hand and pulled him along after her, "And, my darling, do stop being a pain in the bum, there's a good boy."

*

86

She felt his absence in her bed even before she had fully awakened.

Molly was accustomed to sleeping alone, only occasionally sharing when little Danny managed to evade Noreen and wriggle his way under the covers into his mother's warm hug. During Rose's time at the Air Ministry before Little Sillo, and then afterwards with Excalibur, save for episodes of leave, their marriage bed had been a place of solitude.

Yet despite the normal loneliness of her bed, Molly sensed his absence, and she awoke and sat up, alert and aware, her bare shoulders catching the chill of the room as the covers slipped.

Rose was sitting in her favourite place, the old armchair before the picture window in which she had nursed infant Danny, nursing their child and praying for Rose's safety.

He was staring out into the night, eyes faraway, and the moonlight caught his profile, edging it with cold light, the shadows of the room behind him.

"Harry?" she ran her tongue around a sticky mouth. "Harry?"

He blinked and guiltily got to his feet. "Moll, I'm sorry, love, did I wake you?"

She saw with surprise that he was trembling. "Harry! Goodness me! You're freezing!" she jumped out of bed and wrapped herself around him, "Come back to bed, darling."

He looked embarrassed, "I'm not cold, Moll," he could not meet her eyes and placed his cheek against hers, her hair covering his face, "It's the damnedest thing, but I woke up shaking like this! I got out of bed in case I disturbed you."

How can I tell her I woke up terrified? how can I tell the only thought in my mind was that I might die? Molly's nearness was my only sanctuary from fear, is it now gone? Dear God leave me that at least, please! I can't let her see me like this! I couldn't bear it if she thought me a coward!

"Oh Harry! My darling! What's wrong?" she clung to him as if to let go would be to lose him.

He tried to sound blasé, "Prob'ly just coming down with something. Might have caught a chill playing with the naughty little man in the garden."

Rose could see by her expression that she did not believe him, "Harry, come to bed. Let me hold you." He saw the fear in her eyes, this exceptional woman who had won her excellent George Cross risking everything to save others and chosen him over other braver and better men. He angrily cursed himself for causing her concern.

Mortified by his shameful display of weakness in front of Molly inexplicably calmed his anger at himself, and Rose was guided back into their bed.

Soothed by her warmth as she swaddled him with herself, his painfully thin body finally stilled, the fear dwindling back into the essence of unease which was his constant companion through each waking hour.

Molly cradled him in her arms and wept silently for the shy and gentle boy she fell in love with during that Summer of 1940, his innocence lost in the cruel turmoil of war, and prayed that he survive beyond the madness.

Given time, she hoped her love would heal his hidden wounds.

Soothed in her embrace, tense muscle relaxed, thoughts settling to drift.

And finally, Rose slept.

Chapter Ten

Rose was checking and initialling the latest requests from Excalibur's engineering section, catching up on paperwork and wondering to himself why Engineering always needed so many spare oleo legs and tyres for the bomb dollies when there was a light rap on the doorframe.

Grateful for the interruption, he looked up from the barely legible requisition form with the incomprehensible scrawl and said, "Yes?"

Sid smiled ingratiatingly at him from the doorway. "Flash? We're off down the Crown and Trumpet, wanna come? I know you like sitting in the dark all on your tod with a dry twig up your arse, you bein' the noble CO and all, but you need to come for a drink and, if you're really lucky, you might even get a shag."

Jacko peered at him from over Sid's shoulder nodding doubtfully, "A shag?"

Rose smiled at his two flight commanders, Sid Brown of A' Flight and Jacko Briggs of B' Flight standing in his doorway like a mismatched Tweedle-Dum and Tweedle-Dee in RAF blue, the ribbons of the DFC, DFM and '39-'43 Star which each of them wore beneath their wings proof of their competence, experience and, not least, good fortune.

Though he still wondered how on earth the far from verbose Jacko managed to run his flight so well.

The thought of a relaxed drink and a chinwag with his friends, and the uproarious spectacle of their Wing Commander's discordant but enthusiastic destruction of songs such as 'Chevalier' and 'I don't want to join the Air Force' was immensely appealing, but the truculent piles of stacked forms on his desk silently assured him it was a bad idea.

A Squadron leader's job is never done…

Putting down his pen he rubbed his eyes and sighed, "Can't, chaps. I'd love to, but there's far too much to do."

"You have to come, Flash, we might even be able to find you a girl willing to play with your old man. Might be a bit of a job, of course, but I'm sure we'll manage. You might need to pull your cap down over your face and look away, though, 'cos girls prefer a bloke to be at least halfway decent looking. Don't want to scare 'em off, do we?"

Rose's lips twitched. "You daft buggers, I don't need a girl to play with my bits. My private parts are quite happy as they are, ta very much." He picked up his teacup, but it was empty, and he sighed and placed it back onto the saucer.

"Mais non, mon capitaine, mon cheri, mon apetit. You can't keep the poor little thing tucked away forever, it's inhuman. You need to wet the baby's head, if you'll pardon the expression."

Jacko nodded, "Wet the baby's head!"

"Yeah," Sid enthused, "The old man needs to be wetted by popsie reg'lar, see? If you don't get it wet, it can dry up and fall off! You wouldn't like that, believe me! You'd miss it even though you don't use it!"

Rose shook his head, "Crikey Ada, Sid! You spout such a load of old tosh!"

Sid stepped closer, Jacko shuffling in close behind him, and his voice dropped conspiratorially, "Not scared of Totty, are you, Flash?"

Jacko's eyes peered at him over Sid's shoulder. "Scared?" he whispered, eyes bulging.

"What d'you mean? Scared of totty?" he roared at them, deciding to bang his hand down on the desktop to emphasise his ire, *CRASH!* (*Ow! That hurt!*).

Jacko flinched, eyes sliding anxiously, but Sid was unperturbed and grinned easily at him, "Nothing to be ashamed of, Flash. Bints *are* scary."

Jacko shivered and wrapped his arms around himself, "Scary."

Sid nodded, "But not *too* scary… "

Aargh, I shouldn't have done that. His hand ached, but Rose flexed his fingers and ignored the pain, "I can choose to replace my flight commanders, y'know, lads."

Sid sniffed scornfully, "Go ahead and try it, mon apertif, you'll not find better'n me and Jacko."

Jacko hugged himself tighter and winked at him, "Me and Jacko!"

True, and I wouldn't want anyone else, either, and they know it, the conceited sods. Rose waved his hands at them in a shooing gesture, "go on, piss off you mad buggers and let me get on with my paperwork!"

Ignoring him, Sid tucked his backside comfortably on the side of Rose's desk, before looking secretively over his shoulder, and a pile of precariously perched forms toppled onto the floor. "I say, Flash, you ain't a virgin, are you?"

Jacko slapped his chest with both hands as if he were having a heart attack. "Virgin?" he looked horrified.

Sid leaned closer as Jacko picked the forms from the floor. "It's against Kings Regs. Dint'cha know? Can't have fighting men being led by virgins! It's not allowed! Not proper, see?"

"Not allowed, not proper." Jacko piped up, smoothing the creased forms before placing bundles of them onto three or four separate unrelated piles.

"God! Can't you stop blathering bollocks, Sid?" asked Rose plaintively, opening and closing his stinging hand, with one eye on Jacko as he disastrously mixed up the piles of forms. At last, he could take no more, and he slapped Jacko's hands away in exasperation, "Look, for goodness' sake, Jacko, don't touch! Leave them alone, will you?"

Jacko's lower lip wobbled, and he sulkily tucked his hands under his armpits.

Sid shrugged, "Yeah, if you can get your old man into the right hole, proves your aim's not off. Can't lead fighting men into battle if you can't aim for toffee." He looked apologetic, "I might have to phone the brass to tell 'em you're a virgin. It being in the Regs, an' all."

Jacko nodded eagerly, "Not allowed!"

Rose glowered at them both and picked up the framed photograph of Molly holding infant Danny in her arms and thrust it at his friend and A' Flight commander, "There! That good enough for you?"

Sid looked at the photograph for a long moment, Jacko peering eagerly over his shoulder.

"Give us a butcher's…" He took it from Rose. "Hmm, not a bad looking popsie. 'Course she'd look better as a blonde."

Sounds as if Sid wants me to stab him in the eyeballs with my pen…

"But there's no way popsie like this would be with someone with a face like yours, though, Flash."

Jacko nodded. "No chance." He sighed, "Gorgeous."

"You pair of gormless twits, how many times have you met with Molly?" he stared at Jacko, "And wasn't it you who was playing horsey with my little Danny just last month? Ran you bloody ragged while Sid was doing his best to chat my wife up!"

Sid looked baffled, and tapped his chin with one finger, "No… no, I think you're imagining it, old cock. I'd remember if I'd met a hotty totty like this one. She's a beauty. Just my type."

Jacko gasped and reached for the frame. "Ooh! Hotty totty!" he smiled at the picture, "Danny! Daaanny! Giddy-up!"

Sid wrinkled his nose, "You know, Flash, old lad, I reckon you pinched that picture from someone who's been luckier in the face area than you, if you'll pardon me for saying so. That little 'un in the photograph can't be your little pudding. He's too cute. With a mug like yours, your nippers won't be oil paintings," he held up his hands and shrugged apologetically. "Sorry, speak as I find, I do. Can't help it. Honest as the day is long, ain't I?"

Jacko grinned cheekily and cackled, "Ugly mug, Flash! Can't help it!"

"Not your fault, can't help how you look, eh? Born like it."

"Born like it," tittered his echo.

Sid took the picture back from Jacko and carefully put it back on Rose's desk. "Nah, a girl like that would tell a bloke like you to sling yer hook. Classy popsie like that, she'd never let a bloke like you near enough to kiss her, let alone put a bun in the oven. But don't you worry, your Uncle Sid knows a nice girl who'll relieve you of your virginity gentle as a whisper, you'll not even notice it's gone."

He slapped the side of his head and pointed a finger at Rose, "Coo, luvaduck! I've got it! I'll sort you out with Adrienne! You'll like her, Flash! Belgian totty, wears an eye patch on account of an act she used to do with a donkey in Paree, todger like an Oerlikon, almost had her eye out, less said the better, eh?"

"Less said," Jacko agreed reverently.

Sid smiled ingratiatingly, "But, most important, she'll shag you! If you turn down the light, she'll not be able to see your mug, nor notice how small your old man is! And then you'll be able to say you've been with a woman! You'll be just like a real man!" He was all grinning teeth and self-satisfaction. "Bloody hell, mate, I can make a man of you! I'm a genius!"

Jacko clapped his hands like a child and nodded enthusiastically, "Genius!"

Sid patted his chest modestly. "And I'll give you a bit of advice on what to say, too. I'm a man of the world I am. I *understand* women, see? I know 'em like the back of my hand."

Rose rolled his eyes and frowned. "You'll be getting the back of my hand across your insolent chops if you keep this up, you cheeky bastard,"

Sid looked hurt. "Just trying to be a mate, that's all. Trying to help you out. No need to be like that, Flash."

"Naughty Harry." Jacko shook his head reprovingly.

Rose didn't know whether to laugh or scream. Instead, he settled on picking up his pen and waving it at them both. "You've had your fun, you pair of thoroughly obnoxious reprobates, now get out of my office and go and annoy someone else. Why don't you two go and see The Ginger Ring again? You never get tired of it, as far as I can see."

Jacko's expression was woeful. "Gone! Gone away!"

"Yeah, she's gone! Heard tell that she's taken her show to the Yank bomber bases in Lincolnshire, right popular she is. Bloody Yanks," grumbled Sid dolefully, before adding wistfully, "Blimey, she was amazing. She had a lovely fancy article. I miss it, y'know? And the colour of her hair down there, like a fiery sunset, it was. Cor lummee, Flash, made me right happy, it did, lookin' into that sunset…" He sighed glumly and lapsed for a moment into sad reminisce.

Jacko's lower lip trembled with emotion, and he closed his eyes and bowed his head in respect, a comforting hand resting sympathetically on Sid's shoulder.

Rose bit down on the hysterical screech of laughter threatening to bubble uncontrollably from his throat. *Oh, for the love of…!*

Had 'Boom' Trenchard, the 'Father of the RAF', been unfortunate enough to be privy to this conversation between a Hawker Typhoon squadron CO and two of his flight commanders, Rose reflected, the poor old sod would probably have collapsed.

Suddenly cheerful once more, Sid clapped his hands together, making Rose jump. "Flash, old pal, come on, don't be an old stick in the mud. Come with us, there's an act on in town, it's the Jones Sisters. Apparently, it's fashioned on an old vaudeville act, 'cept when they lift their skirts, they don't have a kitten tucked into their drawers!"

Jacko gasped again, face glowing with enthusiasm and wonder, almost bouncing on his toes with excitement, all thoughts of The Ginger Ring forgotten, "Ooooh-er, cor! No drawers! Heh-heh! Come on, Flash! Heh-heh!"

For heaven's sake! Rose threw down his pen in exasperation, a blob of ink spurting onto the blotter, and he slumped, creaking backwards into his chair and grabbed his head with both hands, wailing, "I've work to do, you scatty sods, now, for the last bloody time, will you both just piss off?"

Sid heaved a deep sigh of defeat. "Can't say I didn't try, mon petit bon-bon. No skin off my nose, pal, but no totty titty or crumpet on your eyeballs, nor on your wee winkle, neither," he sniffed disapprovingly, "Come on, Jacko…"

Jacko looked disconsolate. "No totty titty," he shook his head, and tut-tutted sadly.

Despite himself, Rose found himself grinning at them, "For goodness' sake! Get out! Just clear off, will you?"

Jacko simpered at him from the doorway. "No totty titty," he pouted in a falsetto stage whisper, smiled sweetly, and switched off

Rose's office light before closing the door gently behind him, ignoring the shout of outrage from within, and leaving his CO fuming in the dark, wondering what the King's Regulations said about throttling one's (in)subordinates.

Chapter Eleven

With the sure knowledge that war was coming, and soon, the Admiralty in London realised the absolute need for coastal defence and escort vessels, and with a whale-catcher design proposal by an expert ship builder in Middlesbrough, Smith's Dock Company Limited, the Royal Navy's legendary Flower-class of corvettes was born.

Although the remit was for coastal work, these heroic and tough little warships and their equally heroic and hardy crews became stalwarts of the long-range convoy scene, playing a crucial part in the battle against the U-Boats, their crews bleeding and dying to get the convoys through to an embattled nation.

'La Royale' (the French Navy), seeing the huge potential of these fighting vessels, commissioned a number of 'Flowers' of their own, to be built in French shipyards.

None had yet been completed when the Nazi juggernaut slammed into the low countries and France capitulated in the terrible summer of 1940.

Under new masters, the yards would complete these corvettes to serve the Kriegsmarine.

One of these ASW ships was the 'Fleur de Pavot', (poppy flower), appropriately renamed by the Kriegsmarine as the 'PA-5 Alpen-Mohn'.

Like her sisters at the Ateliers et Chantiers de Saint-Nazaire Penhoët shipyard, PA-5 Alpen-Mohn was finally completed in December 1943, action by French workers successfully delaying the shipbuilding for more than three years, and immediately entering Kriegsmarine service as a PA-class patrol ship on coastal escort duties.

In early January 1944, orders were cut for PA-5 Alpen-Mohn's transfer for Scandinavian and Dutch waters.

*

They took off just as the first drab glow of dawn revealed the high ground undulating just to the south of the field, four Typhoons in loose line abreast, flying low over the darkened sea, visibility poor and cloud base at less than a thousand feet.

The meteorological officer was a solemn WAAF Flight Officer named Maitlis who seemed to live in RAF Havelock Barr's Met Office, and she earnestly assured Rose that the poor weather conditions extended all the way across Europe.

In the hour before first light as they made their final preparations, he felt the usual touch of anxiety curl through him, cloying expectancy and worry, the knowledge that whilst this sortie might be one which might be unmemorable and forgotten by next week, it could just as easily be the one that killed him.

Again, he checked that Molly's little pink teddy bear and Charlie's glass-smooth pebble were safely and securely tucked away in his battle-dress pockets, for he could not fly without them.

The harsh crack of Coffman cartridges and thunderous snarl of Sabres came from across the field, as he strode purposefully to his fighter, knowing that Scarlet's boys were setting off for their anti-rhubarb dawn patrol, not bothering to turn as he reached his kite and heard the other Typhoons roar along the runway and take off into the lightening murk.

His hands slid along Sugar's sides as he checked her surfaces, like a man caressing his lover enjoying the way she felt, even as he pulled on flaps and ailerons, picked at covers and hatches, ensured the bulbous shapes of her bombs were secure.

Like a lover, she would contain him, and after it all, when the frenzy and action was done, safely return him to a place of peace once more.

The Almighty willing.

*

As usual, Maitlis was right. The ceiling of low cloud remained beneath a thousand feet all the way across the North Sea, visibility down to a couple of miles or so, with rolling banks of mist and occasional spits of drizzle. It was perfect weather for a coastal Rhubarb, if claustrophobic, but it would also help the enemy, keeping them concealed until the very last moment.

The journey was uneventful, and just under twenty minutes later they could just barely make out the lighter patch that were the dunes of Texel and the periodic and subdued gleam of its lighthouse, just north of the pale teardrop of Noorderhaaks, guarding the southernmost entrance to the Wadden Sea and Den Helder.

The glimmer thrilled him, for the German garrison normally kept the lighthouse lantern off, in the hope of British ships running aground, and only lighting it when a friendly convoy was making passage nearby.

They had arranged beforehand that the formation split into two pairs, to patrol the waters north and south, the haze and their low altitude (with a bit of luck) offering them some protection from the flak situated in Texel and the coast between Den Helder and Rotterdam.

But with Texel's light on, they might come across the German convoy. Even a small resupply vessel would be a worthy target. Of course, if the ship or ships was already deep within the Wadden Sea, that was another matter altogether, with plenty more flak to have to deal with...

And not just the flak, there's always fighters with convoys... though with dirty weather like this...?

"Toffee Red Leader to Toffee Blue One, pull back, line astern by a mile, and follow us in."

"Understood and received, Toffee Red Leader." Jacko sounded almost normal. It was extraordinary how the man was a highly competent and capable flight commander in the air but a dollop of utter gormlessness on the ground.

Turning low over the water he took the formation north, skirting close to the coast, but not close enough to make themselves an easy target for any flak batteries that might be on the islands. They would be concealed by the gradually thickening mist and essentially invisible at zero feet, and only a single necklace of glowing shells lanced out towards them but was too far off the mark to do more than glow prettily in the haze.

The lighthouse on Vlieland was also lit, and Rose's heart leapt at the glow as his wingman, young Jack Byron called out, "Toffee Red Two to Leader, ships at two o'clock!"

There were two of them, a little warship and a slightly larger cargo vessel in line abreast, smudged faint outlines in the mist, just over a mile away, cutting white furrows through the dark sea beyond Texel and Vlieland.

And praise be, still no sign of fighters!

He stabbed 'send' urgently, no time to waste, "Fuse bombs, Toffee Blue One, take the cargo vessel, we'll take the warship."

"Received."

No fighters, by God!

No time to think or to plan, just enough time to arm his bombs, push forward the stick and *attack*.

They were skimming the sea now, as low as they dared to confound the few flak batteries there might be, a quick check and Jack's B-Bertie was a dark shape on his wing to starboard.

Slipstream raising plumes of spray and creating their own bank of haze behind, showing anyone who cared to look where they were, with the North Sea wind pushing them to one side and the treacherous lift induced by flying so close to the surface of the sea pushing them upwards, stick and rudder, curving into a three-quarter attack from the stern, the canopy running with rivulets of oil and water.

And still no fighters! Yet his neck and shoulders were stiff with tension, knowing that flak awaited in front, and enemy fighters might yet appear behind.

No response from the enemy, the ships continuing to plough their way stolidly through the stiff grey waters, the outline of the dazzle-painted warship indistinct.

Nonetheless, beneath the harshly angled painted patches of blue, grey and black, the shape of the little warship was familiar, the shape the same as those valiant little ships occasionally seen sheltering in Plymouth, Portsmouth and Southampton, but there were no rows of depth charges on its quarterdeck, and at its stern flew not the White Ensign but the scarlet of Nazi Germany.

They must think we're friendlies…

Fighting the controls to hold her steady, Rose hunched forwards and pushed down on the firing button, his cannons snarling and thumping, the airframe juddering and his vision blurring, ready to pull the bomb release as they drew closer.

This vessel was not an anti-submarine ship like her British sisters but rather a surface warfare and flak escort, and now at last she responded even as the flares of interrogation rose above her.

Bright fireflies flickering across her upperworks as tracer stabbed out viciously towards the Typhoons, faithfully followed by a vivid line of fiery red shells, light sparkling in the gloom, his own shells racing low across the water to batter destructively against her, water erupting into rising waterspouts and spray, the flashes of her AA guns merging with the explosions of his shells.

The little ship faded and disappeared behind an expanding hazy curtain of water, gushing smoke and debris, the line of tracer from her swinging wildly away before ceasing altogether, only the mainmast visible as she loomed in his streaming windscreen, a rising cacophony of flak and shrapnel rattling a tattoo across her fuselage.

And then he was pulling up and to port, his bombs released as the mainmast slid past his starboard wingtip, *oh God, so close,* the vessel a dark blur beneath him, already pushing the stick forward to lose height once more as his Typhoon zoomed further than he would have liked when released from the weight of the bombs, the spatter-clatter of debris and the crunch of *something* punching into the fuselage behind him forcing his heart into a mouth tight with dread.

Smoke and spray and waterspouts as enemy rounds, the fire thinner than before, stitched the sea to the side and ahead, ringed by dashes of glowing luminosity which would have looked lovely from a distance and would have pleased the heart had it not been trying to blow him out of the sky.

Bang! Close enough to hear above the scream of her Sabre, unlike the subdued 'crack' of the other, distant dark fiery billows of smoke and

102

expanding concentric shells of pressure and shrapnel, the concussive shock sweeping over Sugar, and he fought to hold her steady as one wing was thrust starkly upwards by the fleeting wave of compression, even as the heart-stopping crash, ping and rattle of shreds of shrapnel signalled the near-miss.

He pushed Sugar down as far as he dared, muscles aching and straining and heart thumping out a frenzied tattoo like a drum, anxiously eyeing the controls, jinking Sugar as glowing red balls flew angrily over his canopy, the sound of the AA rounds zipping and whimpering past.

Rose cowered behind the protective shield of thick armourplate at his back as he raced away from the enemy warship, low, lower, *lower still*, lest the troops on Vlieland join in the fun, hoping and praying that young Jack Byron had successfully broken away to starboard and was doing the same, running for the cover in the patchy haze of the Wadden Sea, and all the while expecting and waiting for the crash of impact from the enemy guns to tear him into twisted and bloody ruin.

The ones which flew past Sugar weren't a problem, the ones which didn't were.

Don't look back until you're clear, don't want a splinter or cannon shell in the face…

Neck twisting this way and that, easing her into a sideslip one way and then the other, jinking up and down, eyes restlessly searching for the fighters which should have been there, but miraculously were not.

Don't look a gift horse…

What would Moll think if she were to see him now, face twisted with fear beneath the mask, rocking backwards and forwards in his seat as he willed Sugar on, praying that nothing was damaged bad enough to breakoff, that her Sabre would not fail him in this Nazi-dominated Sea?

How could he share *this* with his wife? How could he describe this? Heroic Harry Rose, *Typhoon* Rose, cringing in his sweat-soaked seat in a blue funk as he expected a shell to blast him out of the air at any instant…

Once he thought he had gone far enough, once the tracer and the red glowing balls and the rearing waterspouts of near misses had ceased altogether, the light stuff from Vlieland still silent, and he sneaked a quick glance over his shoulder, saw that the haze behind him was tarnished by a mushrooming cloud of malevolent black smoke, just the hint of a bright flicker inside it, something burning. Was it the cargo ship? Had Jacko and his wingman hit it?

Had Jerry hit *them*?

And what of the Nazi Flower-class they had attacked?

And then his questions were answered, for there was a flash of light, a searing pulse ballooning for a moment to one side of the bank of black smoke, and Jacko's breathless murmur over the R/T, "Yikes!" and Jacko's wingman, Flying Officer 'Baggy' Scrutton, "Bloody hell, almost went up with it!" as a fresh black blotch grew to taint the milkiness behind.

Jacko and Baggy must have hit her hard, but how much damage had they received in turn, either from flak or from the result of their attack on the target?

The stench of cordite and sweat was thick in the cockpit, coating his tongue and throat. "Form up at point Tommy, lads." Point Tommy was twenty miles over the North Sea above cloud to the west of Den Helder. "No second runs, just get out of it, OK?"

Rose was surprised that the few words left him breathless, and he coughed and gasped and swallowed, pulling Sugar around west for home, pulling back on to climb, anxious eyes still glancing in the rear-view mirror.

No fighters, but his senses searching, seeking tell-tale indications of trouble, automatically scanning the dials for signs of danger, but she flew as smoothly as before, her Sabre thundering as powerfully as ever, no worrying vibrations or sounds.

He sighed with relief as Sugar plunged from the mist into thick cloud and turned for the rendezvous.

Time to go home.

Chapter Twelve

The others were already in the Intelligence Officer's debriefing tent at dispersals, a few words with Excalibur squadron's senior engineering NCO about the revs counter having kept Rose behind.

As he walked across the grass, enjoying the coolness of the breeze against the heat of his face, the deafening thunder of approaching Tiffies made him look up to see Granny and Brat sweep in over the airfield boundary, returning from their anti-Rhubarb patrol.

He turned back and saw his C-Flight commander, Flight Lieutenant Arthur 'Whip' Whipple DFC, and with a sinking feeling saw that his bloody awful dog was with him.

His pace quickened, and he saw that Whipple had seen him too, and turned away, knowing Rose's discomfort with large, eager dogs. Unlike little dogs which only nipped, the big ones could tear a chap to pieces.

But it was too late, for the great head on the bloody beast was turned towards him.

Oh crap…!

The monstrous creature released a joyful fusillade of barks, and came bounding for him, ignoring Whipple's frantic shouts.

Oh no! Damn it!

He began to run, chest tight with apprehension, awkward with his parachute still slung over one shoulder. Like a fool he turned to look, moaning with despair when he saw how close the hideous brute was. Behind it by some distance ran Whipple, still futilely calling it to heel.

The breath caught in his tight throat like sticky phlegm, and the sound of its paws slapping through wet grass and the eager panting of the horrid creature was like the sound of impending damnation…

As he cut across the tarmac of the boundary road, he missed seeing the approaching fuel bowser, the squeal of its brakes warning him at the last moment, and hauled along by his momentum, he almost ran into it before going around, knowing with a sinking feeling that he had lost ground to the creature.

Rose managed another ten lurching steps, lungs blown and burning, before the unspeakable horror was upon him, and it felt as if he had been tackled by a hefty Rugby prop forward, the sudden weight crashing into him and flinging him onto the tarmac face first.

He flinched beneath the onslaught, waiting for those slavering jaws to clamp down on his neck, or flip him over and tear out his throat.

Coarse asphalt, cold and wet against one cheek, a coarse lapping tongue, warm and wet against the other, and he choked as the brute slobbered at him, drool dribbling into his mouth and eyes and nose, hot sewer breath, surging in wave after stinking wave over him as it whimpered happily on top of him.

"Aaargh!" he spat out the damned thing's slaver, "Get this bastard thing off me!"

And suddenly the weight holding him down was gone, and he scrambled to his feet, wiping the odious fluids from his face with one sleeve.

The creature was struggling wildly, forepaws off the ground, but Whipple had both hands on its collar, and smacked its rump gently. "Down, Daffie, down!"

Rose glared, "Whip, can't you put that sodding thing on a bloody leash, for Christ's sake?"

Whipple's face was defiant, "She just gets excited when she sees you, I can't stop her when she goes! She really likes you! And please, Flash, don't call her a 'bastard thing'. She's really sweet if you get to know her. And her name's Daphne, Daffie to her friends," he added reproachfully.

"Well, I'm not her friend, Whip, and never likely to be, so keep her on a fucking leash, will you?"

Whip flushed at Rose's words but pulled Daffie closer.

"But… "

Rose cut him off brutally, "And for heaven's sake get her a bloody bath! She smells like a bucket of shit!"

He heard giggling from behind him, and he turned to see a couple of WAAFs had dismounted from the fuel bowser, Daisy Sugden and Audrey Wheeler, and he felt the scorching darkness of irrational rage steal over him.

"You two! What the bloody hell d'you think you're doing?"

The merriment slipped suddenly from their faces, and they came uncertainly to attention, looking less than smart in their creased and baggy overalls, greasy caps pushed back, and the rage bubbled over knowing they had witnessed his humiliation.

For over a minute he ranted and raved at them, the fiend's saliva sticky on his face, haranguing two teenage girls in stained overalls, their faces beneath the streaks of grease and oil pale and pinched in the cold and from his sharp words, mute and obedient and trembling.

And even as he shrieked like a madman, he knew how very wrong it was to do so, so terribly wrong, and his anger at himself for his behaviour made the words from his mouth even harsher, perversely punishing the girls for his own shame.

When he saw their eyes glisten, his mouth stumbled to a halt, and was silent at last, horrified by himself.

But it was too late.

Their cheeks burned under his anger, while his burned with disgust for himself. *Oh Harry, you absolute tosser. Is this hollering martinet the man who you truly are? What would Molly make of this frothing madman if she could see him now?*

Harry Rose, fighter pilot and decorated hero, publicly acclaimed and feted by the newspapers as 'Typhoon Rose' (much to Molly's secret pleasure), blaring like a maniac at a pair of quaking girls, the WAAFs obedient to service regulations and unable to utter a word in their defence.

Screamed at by their CO for the loathsome crime of laughing.

What would the newspapers say if they could see him now? Would they laud Typhoon Rose's ferocity against a pair of nineteen-year-old girls??

How could one respect the rank, if the man wearing it did not reciprocate? Granny would always remind him *be worthy of the rank and the authority you are entrusted with. Respect them, protect them, love them as your own.*

And who would not have laughed at his ludicrous predicament with that bloody animal? Inside he curled with embarrassment, but how to apologise? COs don't apologise, or do they?

He stared at them for a moment, hating himself, and then without a word of dismissal turned on his heel. Whipple and his bloody hellhound had cleared off sharpish as soon as he had begun to shriek, and around him figures went back to what they had been doing before he started his show.

Only the station warrant officer, Mr Masters, craggy, magnificent, the scary sovereign of the Orderly Room and the ever-reliable custodian of RAF protocols, returned his stare and nodded, "Sir."

Just one word, spoken in an impassive tone, yet somehow heavy with disapproval and reproach, and the added shame which he felt making him cringe.

Oh, for goodness' sake! I just want to sit down and have a cup of tea! Just one cup of tea, and maybe a sandwich? Is that too much to ask?

He stopped, sighed heavily, turned once more, and clumped back to the girls.

Still they stood at attention, but on the cheek of the taller one a single glittering line, smudging a distorted path through the streaks of grease and oil on her cheek.

He felt the creeping shame and remorse burgeon through him.

You total bastard. They're just a pair of girls, enjoy your power over them, did you? You absolute bastard. Is this the man Molly married?

Quietly he spoke to them, apologising with contrition for the injustice, soft words of regret and appreciation for their service; for the ground crews were the ones who worked faithfully and tirelessly in all weathers at all hours of the day, with precious little recognition or thanks.

He openly recognised two of them now and uttered his words of apology and gratitude with sincerity before dismissing them.

They were sobbing as they climbed back into the cab of the AEC Matador, and he detested himself.

You bastard. You selfish, unfeeling bastard.

As the WAAFs trundled away in their bowser, he could not know his stock had risen further. Oblivious of the devotion of those he served alongside, Rose did not see what they saw. They saw how much he cared, his efforts to improve their lot, yet he found himself wanting, his actions less than they deserved.

No show of affection for Excalibur's CO from the grim-faced station warrant officer, but a slight inclining of that great leonine head, and a fleeting glimmer of approval in his frosty eye as Excalibur's sweat streaked CO made his way for debriefing with the Intelligence Officer.

Aye, lad, you'll do. There's more to being a man than a pair of bollocks, thought the WO approvingly, despite being a man who would rather have all his teeth removed with a rusty pair of pliers than apologise (to which his long-suffering wife could attest).

*

Rose sat listening to the others, sipping hot tea and learning the attack had been a huge success, resulting in the likely sinking of both ships without loss. Jacko and Baggy exultantly reported their cargo vessel breaking into two and the corvette burning and listing heavily.

Their greasy faces were marked and animated by adrenaline and success, their voices loud, and Rose should have been exhilarated at their good fortune in being in the right place at the right time despite the poor weather, catching the ships by surprise and without air cover.

But he could not forget the WAAFs, and he burned with self-loathing as he remembered the tears on their cheeks.

Dear God. Who have I become?

Baggy Scrutton said something, and the others laughed. Rose joined in, even though he had no idea what had been said.

Granny pushed noisily through the tent flaps, the typically crumpled cigarette hanging dangerously from his lower lip. "Hallo, boys, bit of a sticky do, was it?"

Mati coughed pointedly at him, and Granny grinned irreverently at him, blowing a stream of smoke in his direction. "Blimey, Mati, that's a cough and a half, you sound a bit grim! Go and see the quack when we're done, right? Can't have you dropping down dead of the clap when we need you for the war effort, eh?"

The Intelligence Officer looked nonplussed, "Er…"

Rose stood to add his signature to the report as the others filed out, and Granny waved the cigarette at him, ash dusting the floor, "Flash, my old bag of knackers, wait for me outside, will you? I'll not be long; we saw bugger all on patrol. Be finished with my report in a jiffy."

Mati fixed him with a disapproving stare, "D'you know the jiffy is actually a proposed unit of time, Granny? It's equal to the time it takes light…"

Granny blew the Intelligence Officer a juicy raspberry, "Blah, blah, blah, don't give me any of your science cobblers, Mati, 'else I might propose to stick your pencil where the light don't shine. And in case you're wondering, the Granny is the time it takes for my foot to reach the crack of your arse when I stick my boot up it."

Mati shook his head in exasperation, smiling despite himself, as their Wing Commander leaned over and dropped his cigarette butt into Rose's mug, "Oops, sorry, old fart. On second thoughts, Flash, don't wait, just nip over and get me a bun and a cuppa from the NAAFI van, would you? But not the relics on the counter, OK? Them's for the likes of you. Tell Meg you're collecting it for me, she keeps mine specially. Ta."

Granny picked up a biscuit from the tin plate on the table and pointed it at Mati, "Come on, my old son, get the thing filled in quick as you like. There's an iced bun out there waiting for me to get around it." He pulled at his trousers, "Cripes, I think my drawers are caught in the crack of my arse, it's itching something chronic."

Mati shook his head, "Honestly, to think that I could have been serving on a normal Typhoon Wing. I should have stayed at the Air Ministry," he added darkly, pulling a blank form carefully from the pile.

Granny grinned toothily at him, biscuit crumbs falling down his front, "You know you'd miss me too much, old lad. You're the bloody IO here, ain't you? Don't happen to know if we've devised something clever to stop one's drawers riding up while on patrol, do you?"

As Mati rolled his eyes, Granny looked up at Rose, "Chrissake! You still here? Go get my bun, you insubordinate tart, and if you so much as lick it I'll kick you so hard you'll be unwrapping my sock from your tonsils!"

Rose caught Mati's amused eye, his earlier shame driven away by Granny's words, "I know, Mati, it's shocking, isn't it? When I see the calibre of our leaders, I sometimes wonder if we're actually going to win this bloody war…"

*

Meg was still pouring the tea when Granny reached the van, and he took his mug and 'special' bun with a wink, the girl simpering in response.

"Come on, sticky knickers, let's go and sit down over there," he said to Rose, nodding towards the HQ building.

"So, Granny, what's the gen?"

"Uh-oh…" Rose followed Granny's stare and saw that Belle was on her way to them. "Bandit, eleven o'clock…"

The young WAAF Squadron Officer nodded amiably to Rose, "Flash."

He smiled, "Belle."

113

"How was Holland?"

He wiped his lips and shrugged, "Noisy and misty. A touch dicey."

"Good to see you got your boys back safe." She put her hands on her hips. "I was going to have a chat with you about a couple of my girls."

Heart beating and feigning ignorance, feeling the flush climb up his neck and into his cheeks, *uh-oh, indeed…* "Oh?"

"Yes. I thought I saw you having a rather protracted go at Daisy and Audrey, but they tell me you had some rather generous and kind words to say to them, said you were very sweet."

Sweet? Cripes! "Ah." *Might they have forgiven my childish outburst?* "That's…um, nice."

"Hmm. Isn't it?" she raised one eyebrow, "I was going to have words, but it seems I don't need to. I'm glad."

Not half as glad as I am, Rose thought with relief, and trying not to let it show…

"Just remember, they do their best and they're hard working. Be kind, please Flash. Daffie doesn't belong to them."

Aargh! Who else had seen his humiliation at the paws of that blasted mutt? "I know, Belle, I know, I'm very sorry." He bowed his head, trying to look remorseful.

"Not sure you need to apologise for anything, Flash. I think they rather like you."

Granny was smiling evilly at him, his bun half eaten. "Don't you go taking advantage of my WAAFs, you dirty dog! Just because they like you." He looked censoriously down his nose at Rose, "I'll be keeping an eye on you, you cheeky little bugger. Keep your todger tucked away and your mitts off their tits."

Belle turned her eyes onto Granny, and they became a great deal frostier, "Talking of keeping an eye on cheeky buggers and keeping mitts off tits, *sir*, I think we'll be needing to have words later."

Granny's smirk slipped, "Eh? What?"

"I saw you leering at Meg in the NAAFI wagon just now, and I thought that smile seemed quite a bit friendlier that it really needs to be."

"Oh no, Belle dearest, no, I wasn't smiling at Meg at all." Granny's face was still greasy with sweat and it was difficult to see if he was perspiring further under Belle's critical gaze, but Rose rather thought he was, feeling his friend's discomfort.

Granny's voice was obsequious, "You misunderstood, darling toffee apple. I was looking at her, of course I was, but I was thinking only of you. I was thinking to myself just how gorgeous you are in comparison," he wheedled unctuously, "and how very lucky I am to be married to you. That's what made me smile, the wonderful thought of you, honestly."

He presented Belle with his finest *charm-your-knickers-right-off* smile. "Darling Belle. I was happy. So happy. I was so very glad that you're my missus, and the sheer joy of knowing it made me smile with pure happiness. I was only thinking of you, Belle, honestly, and I just happened to be looking at Meg while I was smiling, that's all."

He slurped from his mug, adding piously, "I was overflowing with adoration and bliss."

She snorted with derision, "A likely story. More like overflowing with bullshit. As I said, we'll be having words later, Wing Commander, *sir*. in the meantime, though, I think I'll take that." She snatched the half-eaten bun from his hand and, giving Granny a dirty look before turning smartly on her heel and resolutely marching away.

His friend watched her go, waiting until she was well out of earshot, then cleared his throat and half-whispered lest she might still hear him, "*Tsk*. Women. Easy to love 'em, nigh on impossible to understand 'em."

Rose stifled a grin, enjoying the sight of his normally very self-assured friend's rare embarrassment. "I'm sure Belle would find your insights on relationships really interesting, Granny." He sniffed expectantly, "So, you said you wanted a word?"

Granny licked the icing from sticky, grimy fingers. "I was enjoying that! Anyway, yes, the powers-to-be have decided that all Tiffie units have to go through specialised training again just to make sure we're up to speed in time for the invasion."

Rose looked at him curiously, "Will it be this year, then?"

Granny nodded firmly, "Has to be, daft fart. What with all those bloody hush-hush weapons Jerry's developing, we need to get this bloody thing over as soon as possible. Group's decided that Typhoon Wings're going to continue as fighter-bombers, but each squadron will be specialists in either bombs or rocket-projectiles."

He wiped his fingers on his trousers. "We'll be taking turns to go to Armament Practice Camps, and I thought Excalibur would stick with bombs, and Will could train up his lads with the RPs?"

"Suits me, Granny, aiming the damn RPs is quite the job. Got to have the kite flying in a line without any kind of yaw or roll, while trying to aim." Rose could feel his lids dropping, and he rubbed his eyes, but it didn't help.

"Yeah, winds can bugger up where the rockets go, and trajectory droop is the hardest bloody thing to correct for." He smirked, eyes twinkling, "Although can't say I've ever had any problems with droop, as thousands of popsies can gratefully attest!" he leered.

Rose groaned and rolled his eyes. Must be a line shoot, surely? Dear heavens! Couldn't be true, could it? That Granny had slept with hundreds he did not doubt, but *thousands?* His mind reeled, if it truly was thousands, Granny had probably worn the bloody thing down to a blunted nub.

Rose himself had known only three women intimately, and was quite content, but Granny's easy confidence was something he envied. How did he do it?

Granny picked something from his teeth with his little finger before continuing, "Anyway, me old fag packet, enough of your gum-flappin' about droop, alright? I don't care about your problems, so long as you can fly. The squadrons may have to be specific to using one or t'other, but you and Will still have to train up your lads in both systems, Flash, just so all the pilots of the Wing are adaptable and switch as the need arises."

Granny pulled a squashed piece of his bun from a hollow tooth, flicking it carelessly away.

Feeling suddenly queasy, Rose put down his half-eaten sandwich on one of the whitewashed rocks behind them. "Sounds like a sensible idea, Granny. Improves our flexibility in battle as a Wing. When and where?"

Rose stifled a yawn. *Cripes, Granny will think he's boring me! Daren't close my eyes, 'else I'll likely fall asleep.*

"Next week at some place in North Wales, No. 12 APC at Llanbedr, apparently." Granny looked amused, "Cor, you young 'uns, can't keep yer eyes open! Feeble beggars!" he poked Rose, "Got a fag, old man?"

Rose rummaged through his pockets. He usually kept one or two cigarettes about him for such requests, and finally found one which looked as if he had sat on it.

Getting tiredly to his feet, he passed the poor little tattered thing to his CO. "Much as I'm enjoying our little chinwag, Granny, I'm bushed." He yawned again, "Oh, Lor', 'scuse me! I need a long hot soak and then a crafty forty winks."

Granny smiled, "Best wash poor Daffie's slops off your chops first, though, eh?" The creased cigarette hung disconsolately from his mouth, as if ashamed to find itself there, and nodded at Rose's half-eaten sandwich, still perched on the rock, "But, before you bugger off for a dip in the tub and a kip… mind if I have that?"

Chapter Thirteen

Dearest Flash,

I have something to tell you!

Something Very Important Indeed, and how I wish I could tell you in person!

I am with child!

One which I made with you, and I'm so excited, and filled with happiness!

I am with child, our child, a glorious harvest, seeded by one I love, and there are no words that can describe my joy! You are not mine, yet a part of you is becoming a part of me and will be mine forever!

But this news I cannot share with the world, and nor can you, my love, for it will surely break the dearest hearts of those we love.

Please know that John is as kind and decent and patient as you and will raise our child with love and devotion. And with time, he and I will give our child brothers and sisters.

This is the most wonderful thing I could imagine, for now there shall always be a part of me which is also a part of you, a living memory of one so precious, someone I may love and treasure in your stead.

What a strange thing it is to have but one heart, yet to have given it completely not once, but twice.

And now I have given it a third time, to our baby.

Please know that I shall love our child with everything that is me, just as I love you. This gift will fill that place in my heart left empty by your absence, for I cannot have what belongs to Molly, nor should I yearn for it when I have a shining soul such as John's joined to mine own.

I am fulfilled by him completely, yet still I yearn for you, the sense of you, the feel of you, even as I know that our child will fill that aching hollow with light and joy.

*

Charlie put down her pen with a sigh, and picked up the letter, before laying it flat again.

How can I tell him? I can't. And I shouldn't.

She looked at the ceiling. *But then—How can I not? It would be too cruel to deny him the knowledge of his child.*

But how could I live if I knew another was raising my baby? How could I live without my child? How can I expect him to?

She placed a hand lightly on the slight swell of her abdomen, feeling the warm glow of the new life growing within her own, one soul growing within another, *my precious little one…*

Charlie *tutted* to herself and shook her head.

Flying Typhoons operationally in wartime is as hazardous an occupation as there could be, and a distraction was the last thing Flash needed now.

He must never know. She picked up the letter again, read it through once more, considered for a moment, and then regretfully tore it into small pieces and threw the shreds of paper into the grate.

I'm sorry, dearest man…

120

She sat back and watched the fragments curl and blacken in the flames with a heavy heart. *It's for the best. Poor Flash, he mustn't know...*

The paper was just a smear of glowing ash when there was a light tap on her door, and it squeaked open to reveal Belle, a wide smile on her face.

Charlie stood and they embraced, "Belle! What a lovely surprise! What are you doing in town?"

"Just needed to pick up some papers from the Ministry, and I thought I'd nip along and see you. Feel like I've walked for miles looking for your blessed office. Do you have time for lunch?" her eyes settled on Charlie's abdomen. "Oh, I say! Charlie? Have you been scoffing all the cake...," she smirked wickedly, "or...?"

Charlie blushed, adding to the healthy glow on her face, and a frisson of pleasure and pride flowed through her again. "John and I didn't mean for it to happen, but it just did!"

"John?" Belle teased.

Her cheeks blazed bright. "Yes, who else would it be?"

Belle cocked an eyebrow, and favoured Charlie with a saucy wink, "I reckon a certain Tiffie pilot I know might have had a damn' good go!"

Charlie blushed harder, her face red-hot, "Oh no, Belle! No! this is John's baby!"

Liar, liar, pants on fire...

Belle sat down, crossing her legs and primly smoothing her skirt over her knees, eyeing Charlie dubiously from beneath the peak of her cap, "If you say so."

Charlie heard the shrillness of her denial and lowered her voice, knowing her face was glowing bright in betrayal, "And John must never find out about Flash! Promise you won't say anything?"

"Don't worry, Charlie, you know I shan't say anything. Ever. Does your CO know?"

Charlie looked alarmed, eyes widening, "About Flash?"

Belle sniggered and flapped a hand, "No, you silly goose, about the baby!"

"Oh." She looked relieved, "Yes. He knows. He's asked me not to say anything yet because the Trials are going well, we got another bomber last week, that's three kills! Lizzy's ecstatic! Flash's advice about the Tiffie night fighter was actually rather helpful, and I'm involved in a number of other theoretical trials with Research Section, too. All a bit hush-hush, I'm afraid. He said he'll try and keep me for as long as possible."

She smiled at the memory of the alarm on her Department Head's face when she had shared her news. "So, I'm here for a little while longer!"

"Thank goodness! All my friends are getting pregnant and leaving the service. Won't be long before I'm on my own. How is John?"

"He's wonderful! I'm so lucky to have him back!" Was she imagining it, or did Belle sound broody…? Charlie's voice softened, and she tried to sound nonchalant, "And how is Danny?" she looked at the fire, ashes all that were left of her most recent unsent letter, "And Flash?"

Belle smiled, "Danny is Danny, I feel as if he's between my legs all damned night, the dreadful, cheeky, randy swine, and he's still eyeing up the girls as well, the rotter, but I love him, God help me. And Flash? Dear Flash. He's fine, Charlie. Flying umpteen sorties, like all of them, helping us to win this war leading from the front, like all of them. He's a bit thin and tired, and he actually ranted like a maniac at a pair of young WAAFs over something silly, something I never thought I'd see. He apologised to them straight after, of course, and I think he shocked himself. Flash is one of the lovely ones, and Danny adores him. He's worn out, bless him."

She shrugged and shook her head sadly, "Like all of them."

122

The pain on Charlie's face was clear, and Belle continued, "But don't worry, dear, they're to be rested any day now. The Typhoon boys will be an important part of the invasion force, and they need to be in tip-top condition when the time comes. So, they're going to get another period of training and retraining. But keep it under your hat."

"I love him, Belle. I love my John so very much, but I do love Flash, too." Her eyes were wet, and she looked away, "I wish I didn't, but I do."

Belle reached forwards across the desk, and gripped Charlie's hand gently, "I know, love."

"I'm scared for him. I'm lucky, much luckier than I deserve, because I have John. But poor Molly? If Flash…," her voice broke, and she swallowed the thickness in her throat, "Poor Molly. Flash is all that she has."

A tear slipped a line of silver down her cheek, her fingers tightening around Belle's, "Please God, keep him safe…"

*

"We're to cut back on Ops, Flash."

Rose sat down in front of Granny's desk, the distant sound of a Sabre being run-up in the background. "What?"

"We're the aerial artillery, my old trollop. They can't afford to throw us away piece-meal. We're losing lads we need for the invasion. Time for us to make good our losses, train and retrain, refit and reequip where we need to. A spot of leave then down to earth to gird our loins," Hhe smiled. "We'll be pretty busy, so leave will have to be short, I'm afraid."

"So long as I can get a weekend or two with Molly?"

"I should think so, old trout. Make the most of them, because a

123

little bird tells me we're going to be hitting Jerry hard, and trains are back of the target list again, too."

Belle peeped through the open doorway and stepped into Granny's office. "Good heavens! Still talking about your loins, Danny?" She smiled warmly at Rose. "Hallo, Flash, I've just been to Group. Guess who I met?"

His pulse quickening, Rose tried to hide his excitement, "Oh yes, Belle? Who?"

"I think you know!" Her eyes crinkled, sparkling with devilment.

Granny leered at him and Rose pretended not to see. "How was she?" he asked noncommittally, and knowing he was blushing, coughed to hide his embarrassment.

Belle nodded, "She was well, had a wonderful glow about her when she was talking about you. She wanted to know how you were and asked me to give a hug and a kiss."

Granny sat up straight, alarm on his face, "You touch my missus, you pustulating prune, and I'll stick my boot so far up your arse you'll be able to see the toecap with your eyes closed!"

She rolled her eyes at her husband and frowned, "For goodness' sake, Danny! It's only a blessed hug! From my best friend to yours!"

"What if he tries touching you? Eh? What then?" Granny replied petulantly.

She giggled and shook her head, "Oh, Danny! Honestly! Stop being childish! Stop it!"

Her husband glared at Rose, and waved a fist, "Touch her and I'll knock you right out, you saucy sod."

Rose grinned at him, reflecting that, for a man whose morals were looser than those of an alley-cat, Granny was overly defensive of his wife. "How can I hug Belle without touching her, mighty leader?"

Granny sat back with his arms folded, "Exactly."

Belle slapped Granny's arm lightly, "Good grief, what a silly man you are!" she turned to Rose, "I'm sorry, Flash, it looks as if you'll have to get that hug from Charlie in person!"

Rose crossed his legs and sat back, "I think it's for the best, Belle." He cast a jaundiced eye at his CO. "I don't think I'd much like being beaten by Granny."

Granny blew a juicy raspberry and stuck up two fingers at Rose. "Sod off, you dizzy fart."

Belle stared hard at Granny, "I'm blowed if I can see the reason people seem to like you, Danny. I'm going for a cup of tea, Mister Wing Commander Smith, *sir*, and in the meantime, I think you'd better apologise to poor Flash for being such a frightful bore!"

She stopped at the door and looked back, "Join me after you've said sorry?"

Granny pursed his lips disinterestedly and looked at the ceiling, crossing his feet on the desk. "We'll see. Maybe." He idly creaked back on his chair, "What will I get if I do, hm?"

She smiled coldly, eyes flashing, "A loss of privileges if you don't, sir," and she was gone.

"See, Flash, that's what you get for being married," Granny whispered, one eye on the empty doorway, "You end up being a woman's plaything, a puppet to their every whim and desire."

"Doesn't sound too bad to me," Rose grinned, "And might I just ask why you're whispering?"

Granny scowled, voice still lowered, "If you're trying to imply that I'm scared of a popsie, I'll punch your lights out!"

"Never even considered it, although said popsie happens also to be your lady wife," Rose crossed his arms comfortably, and raised his eyebrows, "So, Granny, sir, about that apology?"

Granny swept his feet off the desk and bounced to his feet, already reaching for his cap, "Don't worry about it, old man. You're uglier than a goat turd, your breath makes my eyes water, and you get on my tits something chronic, but there's no need to apologise. I'm used to you, now."

He jammed his battered cap onto his head, and added airily, "Now, if you'll excuse me, I'm off to see if *I* can get on someone's tits!"

Turning at the door, "And, if you're wondering, you silly arse, I'm going because I want to, not because she told me to, awright?"

If you say so. Rose eyed him, trying not to grin, "Forsooths! Methinks my lord doth dissenteth too mucheth!"

Granny frowned, "Are you taking the piss?"

And with that, his friend stamped off in hot pursuit of Belle, leaving a bemused Rose behind, glad for his friendship with that exceptional fighting leader and unique man.

Chapter Fourteen

The German coastal radar network was an essential part of Hitler's Atlantic Wall, the extensive defensive wall of ramparts and shoreline fortifications, stretching from the Pyrenees to the Norwegian coastal border with Soviet Russia, designed and built to resist and repel any invasion attempts on what he had named 'Festung Europa', and crucial in giving the Axis forces early warning of invasion.

Being an integral part of the Wall, the radar operators were well protected, with much of the radar systems safely tucked away in subterranean shelters, what little was visible above ground contained within thick concrete bunkers.

As a result, despite repeated attacks by 2nd TAF, the stations were hard to knock out completely, only the detection equipment on the surface vulnerable to aerial attack.

Each of the radar stations found along the Wall were a tough nut to crack but cracking enough of them along it was essential so that the defenders remained unaware of the destination of the coming invasion.

44 Wing was tasked, along with others in 83 Group, in knocking out radar stations along a stretch of the Atlantic Wall on the Belgian coast, between Middelkerke and Wenduine.

At the same time in May, the prohibition of attacks on the French railway system was finally removed.

They were six in number, pugnacious in the dull half-light, Rose flying along with Sid and one Section of A-Flight, a hundred feet above the sullen dark waters, even as the early morning sun cleared the horizon, the pilots silent to prevent the enemy any opportunity of getting a 'fix' on them, eyes directed outside, but thoughts inwards and unable to enjoy the fast-receding spectral layered shades of dawn.

It was dim in the cockpit, and Rose looked from his instruments to her photograph, the unease he always felt drawing at his innards, the sound of the enemy 'Karl' radar jamming transmitters fretting faintly in his earphones.

Cloud ceiling was three thousand feet, a broken layer climbing up to eight thousand, which promised to complicate any attempts at bombing from height, for their target today was a Large Coastwatcher unit and a twinned pair of Limber Freya radars in a 'bed spring' dipole array, a framework of two panels, one receiving and one transmitting, mounted one above the other.

Enormous when standing in its shadow, but tiny and blurred and almost invisible at low level when viewing it through one's smeared and oily windscreen at over 350 miles per hour from miles away and being shaken to bits by the howling Sabre.

PRU reconnaissance photographs had been invaluable in choosing the approach, for the array was placed directly between two groups of cottages on a distinctive concrete square, two corners of the platform occupied by 37mm flak positions.

While it was, as Sid succinctly put it, 'a bit shit', Mati smiled gently and reminded them that near misses on the target were likely to land in the German gunners' laps, hopefully lessening the risk to the next Typhoon.

However, it was a forlorn hope, because the sites were bristling with anti-aircraft weapons of multiple calibres, and there would be plenty having a go at them.

Even from this part of the coast there was the smattering of black flak bursts, mainly long-range heavy stuff which was more familiar with slower heavy bomber formations in fixed bombing runs, rather than weaving and jinking Typhoons.

Not terribly keen to be on the receiving end of that veritable forest of guns, Rose led them in line astern low over the coastline around ten miles to the southwest of the target, across the featureless concordant Flemish coastline of Belgium, *careful Harry, hold her steady, beware of windshear!*

Through the dusty haze of the dunes, over the sea dike and the grassy stretch of cliff past the main coastal road, two grey Wehrmacht trucks swinging to a halt and gone before he could give them a squirt, on towards the flat patchwork of fields and the grey horizon faint in the early morning mist ahead.

The puffs of flak ebbed behind as they raced in low, traded for chains of tracer and other small arms that tore after them, and Rose felt the punch of something against Sugar's side as they ran for the dubious cover of the mist, the thump of his heart like an echo of that single hit, yet Sugar flew on.

Ostend was a grey-brown jumble to the northeast, the thin line of the runways at the military aerodrome of Stene at Raversijde/Middelkerke indistinguishable from the city, the renowned Aachen Battery jammed in somewhere amongst the muddled sprawl.

Mati had suggested that a flyby of the Count of Flanders' estate might be a morale raiser for the Belgians, to which Rose had smiled thoughtfully and agreed, before looking across to Sid and shaking his head imperceptibly and raising his eyes to the heavens, mouthing silently, *not likely, mate!*

And now he eased back the throttle and nudged the rudder bar to drag them around to port, pointing Sugar's nose southwest of the centre of the port, to where the edifices thinned.

It was all very well seeing the PRU pictures and knowing where the damn things were on a piece of paper, but it was quite another to be at zero feet fighting ground effect buffeting and peering through a smeared and greasy windscreen, searching through a thin veil of mist at a stretch of Flemish scenery and trying to find a target that would be essentially invisible until close to.

He felt the creep of anxiety and apprehension and pushed it down, *no time for that*, looking for the aerodrome the Luftwaffe had built on what had been farmland, for their target was about a mile west of the airfield perimeter.

He could feel the sweat running down his body, adjusted Sugar's nose by a degree or so, eyes narrowed in the search, ignoring the glowing tracery of machine guns and the unseen small arms, pushing her lower, knowing Sid and his men would be circling wide at about a hundred feet, and would peel off in turn in the attack.

His jaw was aching and his neck stiff, and he tried unsuccessfully to relax his clenched muscles. His eyes just occasionally searching the sky for enemy fighters but forced himself to concentrate on the ground ahead, knowing the others would warn him if the Luftwaffe made an appearance.

Straining for the two clumps of fishermen's cottages.

Stene itself was no danger, Mati assuring them that there were only a few Junkers 52 trimotors and some Henschel army co-operation aircraft, so no danger from that quarter, hopefully.

There! There they are!

Tiny, but growing rapidly in his sights, he could see the concrete square now, the line of coastal guns along the dike beyond.

Sugar trembled and he soothed her, hands gentle on the control column even as his own nerves screamed at him when a white burst of 37mm flak erupted above and behind, metal shreds rattling and tinkling against her.

No more time, low concrete bunkers behind the oblong array, flak spotting dark all around but he was pushing down on the gun button, the clatter of his cannon jarring and cordite plugging his throat, earth spurting and the flash of hits amidst flying dust, a knot of men running to another reinforced low bunker and then he was releasing his bombs even as he saw his lines of 20mm storm past the target and slam into the roof of one of the furthest cottages as Sugar lifted at the instant of bomb release and he pushed forward on the stick into the danger and pulled his finger from the gun button, horrified that his cannon shells had ripped through the cottage. Under his breath he muttered a prayer, so familiar to him now: *Dear God, let me not have killed any civvies!* but the line of flak guns on the dike was near, and Rose pushed down on the gun-button once more.

He felt the compression chase past as his bombs exploded, feeling Sugar skittish in the torn air but he edged her nose to point at one of the approaching guns.

An engraved moment, a cumbersome artillery piece mounted in a circular concreted parapet, its crew caught in an instant of flight as his cannon shells hammered in at a sweeping tangent across it, feeling their terror mirror his own, cannon bursts enveloping them in a twisting shroud of smoke, dirt, blood and metal splinters.

Airframe jerking from the recoil of his Hispanos and the vicious kiss of shrapnel.

Push down as the cliffs drop away, lower…*get lower…*

And then it was all behind him, just the beach, a breakwater blurring past, Sugar's Sabre in full boost screaming as if in triumph or terror.

Stick side to side, backwards, kick rudder from right, left, right again, the sweat pouring off him and the forces grabbing at him as Sugar slid and slipped, jinking wildly before the flak could adjust their deflection, feeling the sea draughts plucking at her…

Flak was light, far lighter than it should have been, so Sid must be attacking now, Jerry must be lining up on his Tiffie, and his eyes anxiously scanned the controls, searching for the warning signs of disaster, but all was well.

He reached for her picture, but his head was turning already, searching in the broken cloud for the bandits that surely must be out there.

Nothing.

Oh Lord, my God, thank you!

Once out of range he heaved her around, eyes anxious as Sid swept out to sea, a web of tracer chasing after him, the flickers of his bombs exploding fiercely on a target partially hidden by smoke, the drifting banks ripped asunder by the expanding pressure waves of the bombs, and Rose feared Sid must surely be hit, but the other Typhoon safely joined on his wing as they circled offshore just out of range, stained and blemished from the cauldron of fire.

The others attacked in turn, their angles of approach and distancing unalike, Sergeants Tim Morris and James Clement, tipping and slipping through the roiling, tumultuous air, then the aptly named new boy, Pilot Officer Tony Green (who released too late, his bombs demolishing the cottage Rose's cannons had already flayed), jinking so close to the ground that Rose thought he must surely crash, and then it was Flying Officer 'Dandy' Alan Trent, the smartest man in the squadron and one of his handsome 'chorus line' quartet, skimming through the smoke, cannon winking and bombs dropping perfectly amongst the zephyrs of smoke and shrapnel.

A bright point of light glowing at the base of one wing on the tiny shape below, swiftly expanding to swathe Trent's Typhoon in a boiling globe of intense flame, the ball of fire seeming to slow down and float upwards before tumbling to bounce once, twice, a third time directly over a flak post and the dike to smash itself onto the beach, the cataclysmic explosion setting off smaller explosions as buried mines added to the cataclysm, adding sand to the smoke, dirt and concrete dust already thick in the air.

Rose cursed foully, anger and sorrow pulsing through him, even as their tail-end Charlie, Flying Officer 'Ginger' Bridge, emerged through the rolling, ragged banks of dust and smoke from the target, his wings in turn cutting through the column of oily smoke issuing from the ragged hole Trent's Typhoon had torn into the sand.

Seeing his colleague shot down had given the experienced Ginger a fright and he dropped his bombs slightly early, blowing a crater amid the first group of cottages.

As the last of the raiders, the light flak gave poor Ginger their full attention, but with the smoke and confusion and his speed, he was luckier than poor Trent, twisting away without serious damage.

"D'you want to beat up that bloody airfield, Toffee Leader? I've some ammo left." Sid's voice, heavy with despair and fury.

Rose's voice was harsh as he pushed down his anguish, "No, Sid. We've given the target a bloody good pasting, and I've had enough Jerry flak for the morning. Let's go home. we've done enough."

It was only a matter of time before enemy fighters made an appearance, and there was no point in tempting fate any more than they had.

One lost was too much, more than he could stomach.

Rose took a last look at the listless pall of smoke and dust hanging heavy and low over the shoreline, remembering the dapper Flying Officer, and felt the guilt in leaving him behind amongst the enemy dead, but war is merciless, a vicious thing of cruelty, spiteful edges and blood, and he turned for home.

I'm sorry, Dandy, to leave you.

We've paid again with our precious blood; I just hope it was enough. If we destroyed the radar, at least Dandy's death won't have been in vain.

A glance to Molly's picture, another outside, eyes sweeping across the sky but thoughts elsewhere.

Dandy had been an experienced and skilful pilot, holder of a DFC. Yet all his experience and skill had not saved him.

Luck is fickle, and flak indiscriminate.

Who's next? Me?

*

He jerked awake and sat upright in bed, lathered in a cold sweat, heart thrashing a tattoo against his breastbone.

He wondered if he had cried out and felt the burn of shame.

It felt as if he was not alone, as if he were being watched, and his staring eyes picked out the shadow standing silent in front of the door, the hairs on his neck crawling.

"Hello?" he croaked, then stupidly, "Dandy?" a thin sound, the hairs on his arms standing on end, even as he realised that the shape was only his greatcoat and cap, hanging from the hook.

Despite himself, he shivered, half-expecting a shadow to move, and switched on his bedside lamp, swamping the room with light.

What woke me up? It was unusually quiet outside, not even the muffled scrape of tools on metal.

Had Dandy returned to protest his fate to the man who had led him to his death?

In the far distance he heard the low mumble of aero engines, not the desynchronized mumble of the enemy, but rather the sound of Roll-Royce engines (a Lancaster? Going or returning?).

But it was not the distant grumble which had awoken him.

He wiped his greasy face and thought again of poor Dandy Alan, ashes on a Belgian beach, and felt that strange feeling of helplessness and despair wash over him. And fear.

Dear God, please let me live…

The lamp was still lit when he finally fell asleep, brow troubled by dreams forgotten by the morning, her framed photograph clasped to his chest.

Chapter Fifteen

Evere was established before the First War by the German Empire, and had welcomed Charles Lindbergh seventeen years later, a week after he had coaxed the *Spirit of St Louis* to land at Le Bourget.

A Belgian Air Force bomber airfield 6km northeast of Brussels, Evere was handed over to the Luftwaffe by the victorious German Army, seeing much use by its new owners.

It was currently in use by naval reconnaissance and transport commands and was also the home for Stab/KG6's Ju88s.

With a single concrete runway less than a kilometre long and connected (thanks to wartime expansion) by a taxiway to the nearby Melsbroek bomber airfield, Evere was an important Luftwaffe transport hub.

There were eight attackers, eight Typhoons in line abreast and at zero feet, B-flight led by Jacko, accompanied by his CO and young Jack Byron.

On the starboard sided of the formation, Rose and Byron scraped the treetops of the swathe of woodlands to the north of Brussels, the faded expanse of Brussel's rooftops to the west, light flak and small arms fire slanting past them too high, and he felt the excitement and fear surge into him as he caught sight of the rough diamond shape of Evere ahead, a flat green sheet punctuated by the solitary finger of its runway, raised Flak towers at the eastern dispersals and the trees beyond only just visible, like small chess pieces arrayed on the far side of a green tablecloth, barracks at their base.

Already the flak bursts from the airfield's defences ahead were bursting uselessly above and to one side, but it was light stuff, and from only a couple of guns.

Line abreast, the Typhoons braved the thready flak as they passed over the silver curve of the Charleroi Canal, nerves singing as they bobbed up and over the looming powerlines running parallel with the northern rail tracks, dropping down again, the Cologne Road close to the airfield's north-western perimeter busy with traffic.

They ripped over the barbed wire of the high wall, pushing against the upswell of air, shielded from the flak by the hangers and workshops, and Rose pushed Sugar down again to zero feet, knowing even as he did so that Jacko and his boys were dropping their bombs, twelve 250lb bombs in all, fused with three second delays, crashing through the roofs of the German occupied Renard and ERLA buildings.

A pair of parked trimotors flashed beneath them, gone even as they registered in his eyes, and he eased up Sugar's nose, ruddering slightly to align her with the easternmost of the flak towers, and noticed a line of aircraft parked before it, half hidden by the hangers midway to dispersals.

A line of tracer glittered into the flak-spotted sky, and ahead on the eastern end of the runway light shone on twinned spinning discs, an aircraft crawling slowly towards the two-mile-long communicating taxiway leading to Melsbroek.

It was already too far to port and moving away, and he would have to turn into Byron to bring his guns to bear on it, so instead he corrected minutely to pull the gunsight through the pointed tip of 'his' flak tower and down onto the parked aircraft, pressing the trigger as he did so to blast a long three second burst of 20mm shells at his target, smoke and concrete dust instantaneously billowing to envelop the tower as his shells clawed at the concrete, flashes sparkling on one or two of the aircraft.

"Candy Leader to flight, stay down boys, 20mm in front of the main airport buildings." Jacko, calm and incisive, a stranger in the air.

Rose was dimly aware but unable to look as yellow light bubbled on the runway, Byron's cannon blowing the taxiing Junkers into a boiling ball of fire collapsing onto the tarmac.

The airfield stretched open before them, and he felt horribly exposed as they raced across over the grass, the myriad flashes in the towers and on the ground revealing the depth of Evere's defences, the air before them ruptured and blotted by flak, but too high, too high, the dithering enemy gunners fearful of hitting the two hangers at the eastern boundary.

His spirit shrivelled with fear as he pulled back to leap the hangers, rising towards the flame-hearted puffs of flak, pushing the bomb release perhaps just a little earlier than he should but hoping that with a little luck they would crash through the hanger doors before the time delay on their fuses was up, feeling rather than hearing the spatter of splinters of shrapnel against Sugar's flanks, but the flak was still too high and farther to starboard than it should have been.

'Baggy' Scrutton: "*Christ! Did you see that?*" and Jacko's, "Low! Stay low!"

He skimmed the hanger as close as he dared, the sombre grey ranks of Brussel's cemetery close to starboard, dropping down towards the ground again, clearing their target in the blink of an eye as the treacherous cushion of ground effect air tried to bounce him up into the ravening storm of bullets, cannon shells and tracer.

The middle flak tower was hidden within its own miasma of dust and fragments, and he knew Byron must still be alongside, but he dare not look for they were so low that if he did so, even for an instant, Sugar would slam into the ground.

Be safe, Jack. Be careful, stay low…

No breath to call out and no need, for the boy knew what to do in this blizzard of metal and fire.

His muscles ached, breathing stertorous in his headphones, holding Sugar as steady as he could, feeling the bombs erupting behind, knowing debris from the explosion might yet strike him, the proximity of the ground and the shrieking air, rent by metal and pressure, trying to shove him up into the flak and down into the ground simultaneously.

The mask was pressing painfully into his face, tight against skin greasy with sweat and stretched into a rictus of fear and fury, eyes prickling with strain and sharp perspiration, slipping the gunsight towards the first of four parked aircraft at dispersals near the southern corner perimeter, a Heinkel 111 minus its propellers and three Junkers 52 transport aircraft, and he squeezed down again in the gun button.

The closest Junkers already bore a shattered nose and cockpit (*from my first burst?*), and his second, longer burst of shells tore through the trimotor's fuselage and demolished the tailplane of the Ju52 next in line, the aircraft disappearing beneath a mantle of fiery flashes and smoke, mechanics running like ants scurrying in all directions, his burst ripping past to churn an avenue of torn earth and grass, sweeping harmlessly past a stopped truck, the driver's staring face a blurred blob in the cab.

He was too close to the flak tower for it to depress its guns far enough even if the enemy gunners were to risk shooting so close to their own, and he jabbed the gun button again as he pulled back up to smash an obliterating fusillade of explosive shells once more into the flak tower. Clouds of dust and fragments bloomed, pull back on the stick, hard rudder and aileron, slide-climbing to one side of the tower, screaming over the southwestern boundary wall, pulling over the trees and the electricity pylons.

"Jack, mind the power lines," he huffed, inching Sugar down low towards the patchwork of fields, into the fitful cloak of smoke rising from the pointing chimneys of the grimy brickworks to starboard, low as he dared, a quick glance across the controls, another to port, and the speeding shape of Byron's B-Bertie closing rapidly, stained and holed by the flak, the smudge of another Tiffie faint in the distance.

Sky and mirror, "Two?" *Bloody hell this mask is tight.*

The boy's voice was strained, breathing hard, "I'm alright, sir."

"How's Bertie handling? She looks a bit dented."

"She's feels fine, sir, controls are good, Sabre's running smooth, revs and temps are fine."

Nothing leaking or flapping, no smoke or flames, "Give me a once over, Two." He adjusted the mask with a quivering hand, *there, that's better…*

As he watched the sky and climbed to a hundred feet now that they were out of range of Evere's flak, Byron dropped back to pass behind and beneath and then abreast of Sugar to starboard.

"Some small holes in your rudder, sir, but Sugar looks OK."

"Toffee Red Leader, I'm lost, is three a crowd?" the other Typhoon drew closer but remained slightly behind, Rose knew Flying Officer Dai Owen, one of Jacko's Section Leaders was at the controls.

"Not at all, Blue Five, tuck in, join us, do. The more the merrier."

Ask it, ask him what you don't want to, "Dai, did we lose anyone?"

"I didn't see anyone go in, sir, but there was a lot going on."

"Toffee Red Leader to Blue Leader, are you receiving?"

Jacko, breathing hard, "Received Toffee Red Leader, all heading for rendezvous."

"Understood." All! They had escaped that seething cauldron without loss! *Thank God!*

He touched her photograph, but his attention was on the controls and enemy sky. *We survived, Moll, but we're not safe yet. Still just over half an hour to home.*

With Byron and Owen tucked in close, Rose led them up to a safer altitude, turning for home and sanctuary. Distant Brussels barely visible now, Evere invisible were it not for the faded columns and pall of smoke being blown eastwards by the breeze.

Thank you, Lord, for our salvation and your mercy.

Chapter Sixteen

Granny sat back and blew a circle of smoke comfortably at Rose as he took a last sip from his cup, the clatter of tools on metal drawing the Wing Commander's eyes to the groundcrew working on his Typhoon, P-Popsie.

"I was an Abbeville boy, once," he said, and waited for a reaction.

"Err..." Rose rubbed his watering eyes, and tried not to cough, "I must be tired, Granny, I could've sworn you just said that you used to be one of the Abbeville boys?"

They were sitting at Dispersals, and Rose was on Immediate Readiness.

"Oh, you heard right, Flash, you soppy twit. I was," came the smug reply.

Rose pulled a face, "Honestly, Granny. The more you talk, the less you make sense, I swear."

Granny plopped the cigarette butt into the dregs of his tea. "Thought that would have you wondering! Well, the fact is, when Excalibur popped over to France in '40, we landed at Abbeville first. Flew from their before being sent to the Belgian border, just before the balloon went up." His eyes glazed in recollection.

"It was a right tip, just a rough grassy field, really, somewhere Sid would call a shitty dump, nothing like the dear old pre-war RAF Aerodromes we were flying from, back in Blighty. It was called Abbeville-Drucat back then, dear old Donald used to call it call Abbie-Drab." He smiled sadly for a moment, and Rose sighed at the memory of his first CO.

"The grass was pretty high when we got there, and it was brass monkeys, remember the winter of '39-'40? Bugger me! The grass was stiffer than a bridegroom's prick, you could even feel it crunching like glass under your wheels when you took off or landed," he chuckled. "Talking of pricks, Dingo had the idea to prepare a runway of crushed grass using trucks, but when he tried taxiing on it his Hurricane slid right off, wrote it off. Remember that scar on the side of his jaw?" Granny grinned fondly, "Got it at Abbie-Drab, silly basket."

He pulled out his pipe and sniffed it, "'Course, it was a different story later, when it got a bit warmer. A lot of the local girls used to visit, *les aviateurs Anglais courageux*, and the long grass was warm and soft and fragrant in the early evening." Granny pursed his lips, and his voice was soft. "Somewhere to share a restful, or maybe not so restful, few hours together. Lovely."

Rose was silent. Was his friend wondering where the girls were now? What they were doing? And God help us all, what they were having to endure.

Thank goodness Jerry never made it across the Channel. He shivered inwardly at what might have been.

A distant crack, and the Sabre of one of the Tiffies on the boundary grumbled into clamorous life in an engine-test, the cloud of blue smoke immediately swept away by the spinning blades, Granny cocking his head professionally to listen. He was fond of saying, "Once a Brat, always a Brat."

"Mm. Unsteady, front plugs? Turn the ignition switch to the rear plugs, man, let the revs drop a little." To Rose's ignorant ears it sounded just fine but Granny smiled with satisfaction. "Ah, yes. There, that's better. Better sort out that fault, lads."

The throttle was expertly reduced by the erk in the cockpit, the Sabre idling for a moment, and then a final burst to clear the plugs before it was switched off and fell silent.

Granny sighed. "There was a Lysander reconnaissance unit based at Abbie-Drab, proper fire-eaters they were, bombing the crap out of Jerry and even shooting down some Stukas, Henschels and all sorts in those crappy kites, the brave sods."

His teeth flashed, "I had a good mate in that mob, Tony Doidge, didn't care that I was an NCO and he was an officer, not like a lot of the other snotty bastards, got himself a DFC and a Mention in just a few weeks." He nodded to himself, "And then one day he never came back, just like that, gone. A decent lad. Not a saint, not at all, none of us were, but a good, decent, brave lad who never came back."

Was that a hitch in his voice…?

Rose's voice was quiet, painful memories of bravery and youngsters lost in the interminable years of war. "Too many like that."

Granny nodded again, "Too many."

Suddenly there was a hiss and Rose jumped as two red Verey lights arced bright into the sky over the airfield, "Cripes!" and the butterflies in his stomach began to flutter.

The airman sitting at the trestle table snatched up the receiver as his telephone clamoured, and called out urgently to Rose, "Bandits approaching Harwich, Angels one. Duty patrol is attacking. Immediate readiness scramble! Scramble!"

Rose's Toffee Red Section were on immediate readiness, and young Byron was jumping into his Typhoon as Rose leapt to his feet, wondering how Jacko and Baggy were doing against the bandits.

Behind him, Granny called out, "I've lots more to tell you about Abbie-Drab, Flash, so mind your silly arse!"

*

Harwich and Lowestoft merged into the faint brown line of land to port in the dirty haze, the water beneath them a glittering dark green sheet fading ahead in the poor visibility.

Unbidden, a memory of Molly, a slim figure in misted cap and greatcoat waiting near Dispersals, eyes huge in her pale face, her smile the warmest thing on that damp, foggy morning after a night's flying at Dimple Heath.

Focus, don't let your thoughts wander to where and with who you'd like to be with, concentrate on where you are…

Rose craned his neck, up, back, and around, instinctive with the fighter pilot's mantra, seeking the tell-tale signs of enemy fighter-bombers which might be lurking in the eye-watering blue opacity above, sweat already running down his body, the silk scarf at his neck soaked, whilst the cloying grasp of anxiety had been rinsed away by the adrenaline zipping like electricity through him.

"Toffee Red Leader to Bunting, vector please." One gloved hand pressing against his pocket to check for the bear and the pebble, as he had done twenty times already.

"Toffee Red Leader, vector zero-eight-zero, bandits egressing west, Angels One."

Bloody hell! Jerry was heading out via The Stour, past the naval base and Lowestoft, straight for them!

"Red Two to leader, aircraft at eleven o'clock, Angels One."

Bless you, Jack! Rose squinted into the hazy light, but could see nothing, "Leader to Two, take the lead, I can't see 'em."

Byron's Typhoon, twenty yards to port and surging eagerly forwards, its exhaust smoke thickening and his nose pulling up gently, and Rose strained around to check that they were not about to be bounced, "Leader to Two, can you make out what they are?"

And then he saw them, ahead and above, three dark shapes, and just behind them, a fourth.

"They're 109's! Tally Ho!" Despite his best attempts to hide his excitement, Rose heard it in the boy's voice, felt a comparable thrill battling with the dread in his heart even as he grinned tightly beneath his mask, Tally-Ho, indeed!

"Toffee Red Leader, attacking," A last glance into the sky above and behind, safeties off, fingers brushing against Molly's picture.

Four to two!

Byron, curving to port, turning, "I'll take the front three, and you keep tail-end Charlie off me, Leader."

Dear God, see us safe through this trial…

He would have smiled again at the youngster's confidence and tone, but he replied, "Acknowledged, Two, you are leading."

And the enemy had seen them, beginning their own turn too late, for they would be unable to cut into the climbing Typhoons.

Rose's turn was slighter than Byron's, his enemy further, and now he saw that the fourth Bf109 was a FW190 Shrike, but there was no time to wonder at the enemy fighter mix.

The damned thing was turning into him, tilting inwards and coming down smoothly, tighter than a 109, and he was in range, mashing down on the gun button and feeling her slow, Sugar's cannon slashing out a staccato spray of deadly explosive metal towards the oncoming shape, squat and stubby and lethal, and Jerry was returning the favour, smoke trails from his guns and exhausts flowing behind, grey lines of smoke growing from the enemy's guns and thrusting close over him and to starboard.

In a flash the other aircraft was past, a blue-grey mottled streak, the snarl of its BMW powerplant audible over the thunder of Sugar's Sabre, and she rocked and slanted as she passed through the other's slipstream.

Don't let him get onto the boy's tail!

As if to reassure Rose that he didn't need any help with the 109s (but ta very much), there was a restrained exclamation of triumph over the R/T, "Got you!"

Oh, good boy!

He was pulling the stick back hard, harder, cut throttle, kicking the rudder and grimacing at the effort, the oxygen filling his gaping mouth, a loud gasp as he strained, and she was turning, *careful, don't stall her!*

The enemy pilot was turning too, but had broken to starboard, and Rose would be inside him, straightening and easing over, time enough to bring Sugar's nose onto the Shrike.

The 190 was unable to bring his guns to bear on Rose, but as he drew close Rose jammed his thumb down hard again and his cannon ripped out.

This time there was a flash at the base of his foe's starboard wing, and a second just behind the bright glint of the canopy's Perspex, a wickedly sharp splinter spinning out from the strike, and the enemy fighter-bomber flinched beneath, disappearing beneath his nose.

Again, he kicked Sugar around, continuing into another turn to port, heart crashing against his chest, sweat and cordite bitter in his throat. He grunted and gasped with the effort, each gulp pinching painfully at his creaking ribs and burning lungs.

Oh Jack, be careful, son… He fretted, even as his eyes flashed momentarily to the rear-view mirror, nothing, he's keeping his three (or should that be two?) busy, while his highly experienced CO has his hands full with just one…

His thighs and forearms were burning with the effort, but Sugar cut through the air smoothly, her Sabre singing a beautiful sound of baying power, quivering through him, and he wondered at the inexplicable pleasure that glowed warm in his heaving heart.

Turning, turning, and the other appeared once more, climbing and still turning to starboard but already its wings were tilting back into level flight, and he fired a snapshot before it disappeared again beneath Sugar's nose, but his deflection was well off and the shells fell away uselessly.

Rose cursed, pulling out of the turn and opening the distance at full throttle, one eye over his shoulder as the 190 sped away, *don't lose sight of it, one-two-three-four-five and turn,* and he was pulling back on the stick once more, kicking the rudder bar hard enough to throw her over to starboard, climb and chop the throttle, hauling up and around, wrenching Sugar into yet another tight turn, the harness holding him in place as the forces grappled with him, neck and muscles straining at the harshness, *Damn it! Where did it go?*

The haze was thickening, and he would have lost it, but the thin stream of white smoke which it was trailing (glycol?) helped him to catch sight of the Shrike again, more than a mile away already, and in a shallow dive and racing full tilt for home, the blue grey of its camouflage helping it to merge with the opacity.

Slam forward the lever, full throttle with boost, and he held on tight as she shivered and thrust herself through the gathering haze towards the faint shape of the 190, feeling the frenzy to catch the other taking control of him, a last glance in his rear-view mirror and his blood ran cold at the sight as a bright yellow torrent of blazing shells *zip-zip-zip-zip-zip!* scorched past, terrifyingly close to his port wingtip.

But as soon as his eyes registered the black spinner and radial engine huge in the mirror, he booted port rudder and wrenched the control stick back hard against his hip, limbs guided by instinct, the buckle of his harness digging into flesh, and Sugar half-rolled and dropped, skidding sideways and under, juddering in its propwash as the second 190 pulled up over him to avoid collision, thick black smoke pouring from its exhausts.

They were too low for the enemy to roll and escape by diving, but the German boy was already dropping his nose, pushing his mount for the protective shelter of the blanket of haze.

Another anxious glance into his mirror, caressing her controls to ease Sugar in behind the fleeing Shrike, her slipstream wrestling with Sugar, and he held her, even as she jerked and shuddered at full boost in pursuit.

And he was firing again, short second-long bursts with no deflection, the hard braking of recoil, tiny adjustments of the stick, pulling the fleeing dark shape of the 190 through his gunsight, *careful, not too much, hold it there*, cannon shells tearing swiftly across the space between them on smoke trails, firefly impacts rippling along the wings and tailplane of the pale grey-blue little machine, puffs of smoke and shreds of paint and metal blossoming and snatched at by the air through which it rushed.

The distance was closing fast, and he eased back the throttle, the 190 desperately jerking this way and that now, pieces of the aircraft ripped away by the deadly bursts from Sugar's 20mm cannon.

A flash of flame quickly extinguished and flaring again as more shells smashed into the 190's airframe, and then she reared up as her canopy exploded into a halo of short-lived sparkling fragments,

149

explosive metal tearing through the German boy to batter the powerful radial piston engine into useless scraps, and she burst apart abruptly as Sugar's fire pierced her fuel tanks.

As the 190 Shrike disappeared into an expanding ball of livid boiling fire, Rose was pulling back harshly, heart pumping and nerves shrieking as he willed Sugar to climb, and he blacked out for an instant, coming to in a climbing turn to starboard, Sugar's nose above the horizon.

He had not checked for other enemy fighters for some seconds now and he tightened his turn, licking the bitterness of cordite and enemy exhaust from dry lips, breath shuddering with effort, eyes sweeping the murk.

All that he could see of his enemy was a smear of burning fragments dipping on the oily grey waves below, a rapidly thinning bank of smoke whipped away by the restive wind, the euphoria and relief of survival tempered by a peculiar feeling of despondency that settled heavily over him.

Lord God, I let myself be bounced, but you saved me. Thank goodness Jerry had been a rotten shot, otherwise it would have been Sugar floating down there, burning pieces bright on the sullen waters.

It made him shiver despite the sweltering cockpit.

"Toffee Red Leader to Bunting, scratch one 190, any more custom?"

Bunting was warm with congratulation, "Well done, Toffee Red Leader, we confirm. No custom for you at present."

He had prevailed, through good fortune and skill, in what had finally turned into a two-against-one fight, but young Jack had faced three alone.

Please God, let the boy be alright…

His heart quailed as he called out over the R/T. "Toffee Red Leader to Two, respond."

150

A long moment, then, "Red Two to Leader, received. Angels ten, north of Harwich."

Good lad! Stay high, stay back, those gunners are a bit trigger-happy.

"Leader to Two, understood, re-joining. Any luck?" back on the stick and full throttle, Sugar soaring joyfully into the clearer air.

Hopefully he would be too fast to catch, but still his eyes roved keenly across the firmament.

The boy's voice betrayed his satisfaction. "Got one, damaged another, might even be a probable, but I lost him in the mist."

"Good man, well done! One and one damaged for me too." *But I lost the first 190 because I was daft enough to let myself get bounced.* "Damage?"

Less satisfaction now, "Got a creased wing, and she's dragging a bit to port, sir."

A flutter of anxiety in his stomach, eyes still roving the sky, clothes clammy with sweat and chaffing, "Can you get her back, Two?" He opened the vents at the rear of the cockpit and adjusted the cooling ventilation tube, but still the sweat rolled down him.

"I think so, sir."

"Right, don't hang about, old son, head for home, I'll catch you up."

"Two to Leader, received and understood."

The coast of Essex was no longer visible in the murk, the sun a pale disc of light to port, and he turned for Havelock Barr, head twisting and eyes flicking to the haze surrounding Sugar.

He'd allowed himself to be bounced once. It mustn't happen again. *Getting old…*

The mask was tight against the bridge of his nose and his sweaty cheeks, and he adjusted the straps, dropping Sugar down again to fifty feet above the surface of the water, and into the thin layer of sea mist, hoping that it might partially conceal him from unwelcome eyes.

He remembered Granny's story of Abbeville and wondered if the man he had just killed had someone waiting for him. A wife (or perhaps a French girlfriend like Granny's back in those warm days of early Summer), with whom he might have shared restful (or not so restful) moments in the long grass.

He risked a quick glance down at his own wife's photograph before resuming his sky, sea and cockpit sequence, hand quickly sliding over the bear and the stone still secure in his pocket, seeking reassurance.

Got another, Moll, and more importantly, I made it through.

One more time, Thank God.

Chapter Seventeen

Sid leaned comfortably against the side of the fireplace, and grinned cheerfully at Rose, ignoring the sour look he received in turn and raising his beer glass slightly in salute.

"We've been down the Crown and Trumpet, Flash, and I think we can sort you out."

Rose was sitting with Granny and Belle, and now she tilted her head, eyes turning with interest to Sid. "Oh? Sort Flash out? What with, Sid?"

Silently Rose groaned, *oh good Lord...*

Jacko looked uncomfortable but Sid was unfazed. "We're a bit worried about Flash. Him being a virgin and all."

Granny's eyebrows steepled, "What? *What?* I didn't know about this! You told me you weren't!" Belle smiled secretly, and Rose blushed under her knowing gaze.

Sid nodded, "I know. I was shocked an' all when I found out. I should've told the AOC but with Flash being a mate, I couldn't do it. We ain't grasses down the East end."

Rose rolled his eyes, "Yes, alright. Shut up, will you? You've had your little bit of fun, little bit of a laugh. Haven't you something better to do?"

Sid frowned, "Laugh? No, mon pauvre chien, this is very serious. I could be in hot water with the AOC if he knew I wasn't reporting a squadron commander who hadn't got his leg over!" he squinted through the tobacco smoke at Rose.

"Leg over," Jacko agreed anxiously.

"How are you going to sort him out, then?" Belle asked intently.

"We been talking to Gertie down the Crown and Trumpet, y'know, the barmaid? turns out she hasn't got a bloke. Just imagine, Flash, pints of beer every evening then a shag after," he looked at Belle, adding hurriedly, "'Oh, um, 'scuse me, ma'am."

Her face was serious, "No, that's alright, Sid. It's commendable that you're so concerned about your CO's welfare." She nodded with approval, "Quite right, too."

Jacko sighed wistfully, "Buckets of beer and a shag after…"

Belle looked amused, and Granny puffed out his cheeks, "Gertie? Wasn't she a barmaid there back in 1914? During the first little lot? She's a couple of years older than Flash, isn't she?"

More like thirty…

Trying to disguise his glee, his CO added, "But then, I believe he likes a mature woman, don't you my old pair of frilly drawers?"

Rose gave him a sour look. *Molly's five years older…*

Sid sighed insincerely, "Well, I'm sorry, I am really, but, Cripes! Stone me! Take a gander at his mug! Take a good look! Poor sod! He ain't much to look at, is he? Face only a mother could love. Sorry, Flash, old mate, but beggars can't be choosers, can they?"

Jacko shook his head sadly, "Can't be choosers."

Sid beamed reasonably, held up a finger, "I mean, you can't polish a turd, can you?"

His shadow whispered apologetically. "*Turd.*"

"And think of all the free beer he'd get!"

"Free beer!" sighed Jacko again.

Rose considered whether it was worth throwing his teacup at Sid and Jacko, but then, it wouldn't really do to throw one's cup (and its contents) at two of one's flight commanders, would it? At least, not in a crowded Mess in front of one's Wing Commander.

Probably not an appropriate form of admonishment for bare-faced cheek as set out in the King's Regulations. Any subsequent court martial would likely take a dim view.

Instead, he allowed himself to imagine for a moment what it would be like to knee Sid and then Jacko sharply in the groin.

In his mind's eye they lay groaning in agony, doubled up on the floor and clutching themselves, allowing himself to enjoy the vision for a moment. Bliss.

Granny inspected Rose as if he had never laid eyes on him before, "Mm. Can't argue with that. Fair point. So, what did Gertie say?"

"Well, to be honest, we didn't actually say anything to her. We thought Flash could ask her himself."

Cowardly bastards. They knew she'd give them each a slap for even suggesting it.

Granny smirked at him. "Well? What do you think, old sticky pants?"

"I've had Sid and Jacko as flight commanders ever since I took command of Excalibur, Granny. Isn't it someone else's turn to have them?" Rose queried earnestly, giving his lads a dour look, "I think I'll ask Will in the morning if he'd like to swop a couple of his flight commanders with mine."

Sid was unperturbed, "It's for your own good, Flash. We worry about you."

155

"But I'm married with a child, you pair of twits. How can I still be a virgin?" he asked plaintively.

"Yes, so you say, but I think you're telling us a little porkie, aren't you?" Sid held up a hand. "Them scientists say it's bad being a shagless man, coz you waste away, a little bit of how's your father's good for you, ain't it? It's the boffins you can't ignore, see, can you? I been chattin' to the doc, he's always reading *The Limpet*, regular like."

"*The Lancet*," his shadow growled quietly.

Rose threw up his hands in defeat, "For goodness' sake! Go on, then. I can see you're bursting to share your pearls of wisdom, so might as well get on with it! Let's hear whatever nonsense it is that you've dredged up this time."

"You'll thank me, Flash, you see if you don't." Sid slurped placidly from his beer and cleared his throat theatrically.

Rose sighed, *for what we are about to receive…*

"So, what they found, right, is that it's bad for a man not to have at least one shag every day, at least one, mind, and the longer he don't do it, the badder it gets."

Granny sucked at his teeth and jeered, "I could have told you that, you dented spanner!"

Sid held up both hands in a placatory gesture, "'Crickey, luvaduck, 'ang on a minute, Granny, will you? Give us a bleedin' chance." He looked apologetically at Belle, "Sorry, Ma'am."

She smiled kindly, "Oh, no. Not at all, don't mind me, Sid. Do go on, please. This is jolly interesting. I love sciency stuff."

Sid preened, his chest puffed out, and Jacko sidled into view from behind him to share in the limelight of appreciation.

"It *is* interesting, Belle, Ma'am, and I'm sure Flash will be glad to know." He focussed on Rose again, "So, the thing is, it's like a muscle, yeah? You don't use yer muscles, they dissolve away, right? Same for

156

little Timmy Todger. Don't use him and he'll soon make himself scarce." He grinned, "Don't use it and the sponge tends to shrink."

Jacko's head bobbed, "Shrink!"

Lord above, it was like some sort of conscientious objector's Punch and Judy show, utter nonsense sans the violence. He felt his hand curl into a fist, *although I could happily provide the violence…*

"Sponge? What do you mean, sponge? I thought you said it was a muscle?" Rose heckled, cocking an eyebrow disparagingly.

Sid paused uncertainly to take a sip, brow beetling, then, "Look, don't mess about, Flash, It's a spongy muscle thing, OK? Don't interrupt. I ain't a boffin, 'course I ain't, but I'm not silly."

Really? Rose *tutted* but his voice was contrition liberally laced with sarcasm, "Awfully sorry, old man, do pardon me."

"Made me forget now! Where was I?" Sid's brows knitted.

Jacko leaned forward and whispered, "Spongy muscle thingy shrinking."

Sid sniffed and made a face, "Gawd, Jacko, stop mumbling, will you?"

He ignored Jacko's incensed indignation, "We was talking about the spongy muscle, yeah? It's like a pole, is little Timmy Todger, but it's also like an iceberg, see? There's a lot of it hidden away inside the body, attached to the bone of the poultice."

"Pelvis," hissed Jacko.

Sid nodded at Rose, "So even yours probably ain't as small as it looks, cockle." He glanced apologetically at Belle again. "Anyway, when it starts to waste away, it does it on the inside an' all. If you don't use it, the old man shrinks, and it keeps shrinking, pulling in all the way back to the bone. It keeps shrinking until it shrinks away right back *into* the body, right?" He took another gulp from his pint mug and grinned, immensely pleased with himself.

Jacko's face was pale, reflecting his horror, "*Into* the body!" he whispered in dismay.

God give me strength. Rose found that his fingernails were digging into the frayed fabric of his armchair, and he made a conscious effort to relax, *Lord, protect me from Huns and chums.*

The whimsical thought of delivering several hard blows to them with his trusty old school cricket bat danced playfully through Rose's mind for a delicious moment.

Sid continued, "So, as it shrinks away, slowly, slowly, disappearing inside and pulling the skin back with it, OK? It shrinks back until you got the opposite of a winkle, see? You get left with an invigilation, see?"

Jacko sighed long-sufferingly, raising his eyes to the heavens, "An invagination."

Sid gave him an irritated look, "Yeah, that's right, one of them. And what does that mean for us if we don't know big words? It means that your willy turns into a fanny! And you turn into a popsie!" He turned to Belle, adding hurriedly, "Sorry, ma'am, 'course there's nothing wrong with being a popsie if you are one. I got friends what're popsies. They're nice."

Jacko tittered as she nodded graciously, but Granny looked thunderous, "Are you calling my senior WAAF a Popsie, you cheeky little basket?"

Belle's tone was thoughtful, her expression grave, "Oh, do behave, Danny. Thank you, Sid, that is fascinating. I'm terribly impressed by your knowledge. Quite breath-taking, in fact. I think you'd make an excellent scientist."

Sid preened, squaring his shoulders and standing a little straighter, while Jacko twittered behind his pint glass.

Granny turned to eye Rose sternly, "If this is true, Flash, you scruffy tart, I'm going to have to talk to the AOC. But we'll need an appointment with the MO first thing."

I wonder what the punishment is for punching a flight commander on the jaw, Rose wondered despairingly.

Belle shook a finger in remonstration, "Oh, I don't know. Don't be hasty, Danny. I think he'd look quite lovely as a WAAF, don't you? We could always make use of a good WAAF." She smiled prettily and Rose glared back at her, "and so many pretty ribbons and little rosettes on his chest! I think Flash might be ideal."

Belle leaned back in her armchair and considered him appraisingly, much as a farmer might gauge a prize dairy cow, struggling to control the smirk that was tugging at the corners of her mouth, "Hm, well, a touch of lipstick would help, of course, but at least his hair's well within WAAF regulation length…"

Rose heaved out a deep sigh and shook his head sorrowfully, "*Et tu,* Belle?"

Granny was laughing openly now, "Not a chance, Belle, I'm not having this randy little stoat running rampant amongst my WAAFS, bawling 'Tally Ho' and whipping up his skirts to waggle his crinkle at 'em! Be a breach of the Geneva Convention, wouldn't it? Wouldn't even expose Aunty Adolf to our Flash flashing the flesh in a frock. I mean, even in wartime, there're limits to what one can do to the enemy, aren't there? It just wouldn't be right!"

Belle looked down, trying unsuccessfully to hide her smile, "Shame. We've got women taking over men's jobs because of the war, it would be inspiring to see a chap taking over a woman's job. The papers would love it. Good for the war effort."

"Ex-chap, Belle." Granny corrected her gravely.

Rose felt his fingernails digging into the fabric of the armchair again, and he imagined wistfully for one perfect moment, that they were digging into Sid's eyeballs.

Thank the merciful Lord the junior pilots of Excalibur were too in awe of their seniors to be close enough to hear the inane drivel pouring from his A-Flight commander.

Sid beamed at him, "Yeah! From Tough Typhoon Rose to Tasty Totty Rose! Don't you worry, Flash, me old china. You ain't no work of art, it's plain for all to see, but I daresay if you look hard enough, you'll find someone to love you." He simpered, "I'll get you a nice long blonde syrup, do wonders for you! And anyway, some blokes just ain't as choosy as me! I'm a bit of a commissar when it comes to bints, see?" he added proudly.

"Connoisseur," Jacko mumbled crossly.

Sid ignored him, grinning benignly.

Rose got to his feet, and, resisting the urge to take a couple of steps to boot Sid in the privates, he pointed a finger to the other end of the room, "Oh, I say, look! I can see the MO! Shall I go and get him, Sid? See if you forgot anything?"

Sid peered apprehensively through the smoky room, and saw that the Medical Officer, Squadron Leader 'Snotty' Ragg, was indeed in the room, pounding the unfortunate piano into discordant submission amidst a group of the younger pilots with plenty of enthusiasm and a shocking lack of talent. He hurriedly picked up his pint, beer slopping onto his hand and already moving towards the door. "Uh, can't stay, folks, Jacko and I are off into town for a show, come on, Jacko..."

Jacko winked at Belle and gave Rose a cheerful little wave as he shambled off after his friend, "Ta-ta lovelies, cheerio! Off into town..."

Chapter Eighteen

The weather in the first week of June 1944 was unsettled, and 44 Wing's occasional North Sea patrols were often cut short or scrubbed altogether, whilst the Luftwaffe seemed unaware of the forces massing and gathering at the ports and harbours of southern England.

Byron and Rose were on the dusk patrol, even though 85 Group were now primarily responsible for the air defence of southern England, but Ops advised an early return, because of the worsening conditions, so there was still plenty of light when they came into land.

He noticed that all the Wing's aircraft were arranged on the far side of the field, and he led his wingman away from the others, back to dispersals, in case of a raid.

Helping him from the cockpit, Jimmy pointed back to the hangers, "We've got visitors, sir."

Rose noticed that there were two canvas-covered trucks parked beside the hanger. "Any idea of what's happening?"

Jimmy tapped the side of his nose and winked, "Something a bit hush hush, sir." he edged a little closer and his voice dropped, "Big Dave went over for a shufti, and he said they were unloading tins of paint, scores of them!"

"Paint?" Rose asked, apparently mystified.

Big Dave, already checking the ammunition bays, looked up and nodded shyly, "Pots of black and white," he rumbled.

"Big Dave reckons there's a special secret long-range mission, and the Tiffies are going to have black crosses painted on 'em to pull the wool over Jerry's eyes."

His voice dropped further, "I reckon he's wrong, the silly sod."

He ignored the dirty look he received from Big Dave, "Ever since he was dropped on his head, he's never been the same, poor lamb. I reckon the squadron's going to be assigned as night intruders for the invasion. All-black, with the tins of white to fox anybody who might have seen the paint and was wondering what it was for."

"Hm, you may well be right Jimmy." Rose kept his voice non-committal and his face neutral, calmly taking out his handkerchief to blow his nose, but inside his stomach clenched with a heady mix of excitement and fear. Like all squadron commanders, he knew of the invasion colour scheme, and he realised what this meant.

It was on!

*

Molly's eyes were red, the trails of tears silvering her cheeks, "Oh Harry, I can't bear it, why?"

Rose stared at his wife aghast, but found he was unable to speak, his lips moving soundlessly, helpless in the terrible actuality of her pain.

My love, how can I explain that Charlie and I only comforted each other in the absence of those we love most in the world, when the strain was unbearable? How can I explain that despite it, you alone are the most precious thing in my life? I love you. You are the centre of all that there is, all that there ever can be, the only shining constant of my being.

Her eyes were overflowing pools of pain, deep and dark, her expression one of fathomless despair, betrayal and hurt, the raw bleeding emotion as her face crumpled tearing like a blade deep into his heart.

He wanted to reach out and bring her in close to him, embrace her and comfort her, but he couldn't move, couldn't even raise his arms.

She hugged herself tightly, and her voice was thin with pain, "How could you? I've always been true to you. Don't you love me anymore?"

Oh Moll, I could never love anyone else the way I love you…

But he couldn't utter a word, couldn't breathe, and his chest tightened further as she turned and began to slowly walk away into the darkness beyond.

He wanted to call out, reassure her of his love, plead that she return, promise to be true forever, but he could only stand there dumbly.

With a jolt and a despairing gasp, he awoke, grabbing at the sides of the battered armchair, the black pot-bellied stove glowing before him, sullen but wonderful in the warm twilight of the Dispersals hut, the quiet murmur of conversation lulled, the far side of the room obscured in the fug of tobacco and cigarette smoke.

Rose tried to lick his chapped lips but his tongue was like bark, and the dried saliva on his chin like the trail of long-ago tears.

Nobody took any notice. It was quite normal for pilots to awaken with a start from the bad dreams that routinely plagued their sleep.

Oh, Thank God! It had only been a nightmare! He felt like weeping with relief. The look in the nightmare - Molly's eyes was still fresh in him, and he shuddered. *She must never find out about Charlie. I couldn't bear to lose her.*

He tried to slow his breathing, still sick with self-loathing for causing the pain in those lovely eyes.

Dear God! It had seemed so real!

He noticed then that Jacko was kneeling on the floor in front of him, eyes wide with shock in the darkness, like a comical living representation of the 'Kilroy was here' doodle.

I'm not surprised he's gawking mindlessly at me like that, he must think his CO's going right off his rocker... wait... what's the daft sod doing kneeling there?

Jacko smiled anxiously at him, adopting an air of tentative innocence, hands disappearing behind his back.

"Jacko," his voice was a croak, and he swallowed fitfully, dragging his sticky tongue from his palate, and tried again, "Jacko? What are you doing down there, you silly bugger?" He shifted himself forward and saw that his shoelaces had been tied loosely to the feet of his chair.

For fuck's sake! Commanding Excalibur was like running a bloody school...

"Jacko!" he roared it out this time, and with a squeak of fear, '*eeek!*' Jacko sprang to his feet and shot off like a whippet. There was no way Rose could get up and chase him with shoes tied to his chair, so he let him go and settled back, rubbing his stiff cheeks, still seeing the pain driven onto the face of the girl in his nightmare.

Thank God it was only a nightmare. If I lose her, I lose everything. Without Molly, my soul will never be content. His hand felt for the comfort of her photograph in his pocket.

Please, dearest Lord, let her never, ever find out. Never, ever. Never allow me to hurt her. Never let me break her heart. Let me only ever bring happiness to that incredible girl.

I love you, Moll. I might use this heart, but you alone own it.

*

At that very moment Group Captain James Stagg and his team of meteorological experts were analysing and assessing the weather conditions minutely.

Those on the other side of the water had a similar expert team of meteorologists also evaluating when an invasion might come, but Stagg had a secret advantage.

A shining star at the Met Office, James Stagg was tall, a lean Scot with sharply penetrating eyes, and the Chief Meteorologist of SHAEF. With the Enigma code cracked, observations and reports from the German side were available to his team in addition to their own reports and atmospheric charts.

With this rich bounty of data, Stagg's team were able to forecast the opening of a marginal window for the invasion on the Sixth of June.

With lesser resources from which to make an assessment, the enemy meteorologists in Paris predicted stormy weather for the next two weeks, and, believing that an invasion could not come in this time, commanders left to attend war games in Rennes, and leave made available to many of their men.

Stagg had returned from a meeting with Eisenhower earlier, managing to convince the Supreme Allied Commander that the fifth was a definite no-go. Strong winds, rough seas and low cloud conditions did not lend themselves to a successful outcome for what was to be an extremely hazardous venture.

Knowing that the next possible window after the Sixth would be a couple of weeks later, and knowing also that his forces were gathered, champing at the bit and ready to go, Eisenhower murmured a heartfelt prayer, crossed his fingers, and gave the orders for the launch of the invasion.

And four years after Blitzkrieg, for better or for worse, the wheels were set in motion for the greatest endeavour to be conducted yet.

Chapter Nineteen

Rose was awoken just after midnight by the cheery trill of his orderly, Edna, once belonging to an amateur theatrics group in civilian life and an implicit believer that the jaunty rendering of a song currently popular was the perfect way to rouse her charge to begin his day.

This morning's tune was Judy Garland's 'Trolley Song,' one which she felt had just the right tone to awaken her poor young Squadron Leader at this ungodly hour, well before dawn.

Rose did not have the heart to tell her he didn't agree, so endured the *'Clang, clang! Ding, ding!'* with a fixed smile as she warbled and chirped her way through her tasks, setting down a hot mug of tea on the desk and a jug of hot water for shaving beside the basin, before lighting the table lamp and tidying up his things.

To be fair, Edna's rendition was a particularly good one, but he would have been quite content with a gentle shake of the shoulder.

As he sat up, rumpled, and bleakly watched her bustle around his room (leaving the curtains drawn, for it was still night outside), he reproached himself for his surliness. He should be grateful for her cheery warble, even if it did not drown out the dull boom of engines endlessly rumbling overhead.

Edna wasn't *that* bad. Not really. Others had been a great deal worse.

Who could ever forget the sewer breath of Aircraftsman Birchley, considerately hunching forwards with hands on knees to quietly urge him awake with a mouth that was so malodorous that Rose truly believed the two ends of the man's intestinal tract had switched places, or fierce little Leading Aircraftswoman Horner who bashed around his room like a bull in the proverbial china shop, shocking him awake, bad-temper and impatience disguised by din and bash.

Yes, all things considered, Edna would do.

*

Rose yawned blearily as he parked his Hillman beside Dispersals, making sure to lock the doors in case some of his men (i.e., Sid and Jacko) decided to drive off in it for a laugh.

He stood for a moment, tired eyes turned up to the night sky as the engines of countless aircraft hidden in the darkness above rolled and boomed sullenly across the airfield.

He wondered at what awaited the men in those aircraft and shivered.

The invasion would be preceded by parachutist and glider troop landings, creating confusion and chaos along with the French Resistance to disrupt enemy reinforcements and to capture and hold key sites.

In addition to the troops would be drops of 'Ruperts', child-sized dummy paratroopers with pyrotechnics to create further concern and confusion.

He did not envy them. The weather conditions were less than ideal over the continent, some of the US aircrews not as proficient as would be desired, and the waiting defences brutal.

Many of the brave young men above on their bumpy way to occupied Europe would not see the dawn. Already, many thousands of others were heading for the beaches, jammed in the enclosed spaces of landing craft, soaring and falling repeatedly on the unsettled waters.

Around him there was the clank of metal on metal, and the thunder of Sabre engines being run up, and he breathed it in, savouring the freshness of the night air tempered by the scents of tarmac, dope, fuel and hot metal, the mixture of scents and odours strangely settling his stomach.

A figure appeared from out of the shadows, "Ah, Mr Rose, sir! I'm glad I caught you! I was on my way to see you. Q-Queenie keeps losing revs. The lads have been working on her all night, but I think we'll need to change the Sabre. I wanted to ask your permission to do so."

Rose cursed under his breath, "Is Queenie up for the first sortie, Chiefy?"

"No, sir. She's a spare."

"OK, then go ahead and do it. But I'll need her soonest. Big day today." As soon as he had said it he regretted it.

Chiefy knew the significance of the coming day.

The men and women of the groundcrews were true heroes, working tirelessly with little reward if any in all conditions to keep their aircraft in tip-top condition. He didn't need to tell them to give 100%, they gave it as a matter of course.

"Sorry, Chiefy, I know they'll work miracles. As always. Please carry on."

His senior groundcrew NCO smiled appreciatively, "Thanks, sir." He turned to go, then stopped. "Sir? Take care over there, will you?"

Touched by the words and the simple concern in the older man's eyes, Rose nodded. "I will, thank you."

He watched the NCO walk away, *I will, please God*, butterflies flittering inside his chest.

The men of Whip's C-Flight were already inside, sitting or standing quietly in small groups (but no sign of that blasted hound, thank the Good Lord).

He saw the two youngest staring at him. *Probably wondering why the old man looks so miserable...*

The Old Man. Dear God. It still astonished him that somehow, incredibly, after so many years of war, he had made it to being the 'Old Man' for Excalibur Squadron.

In their eyes he saw awe, and perhaps just a little envy. Did they wonder if he had already seen too much, and if he was going, as Granny would say, ruddy bloody bananas?

Inside he felt little different from the callow youngster of 1940, but now he was the one they looked to, the font of experience and wisdom.

God help us.

Whip grinned at him from in front of the black pot-bellied stove, a dark shape outlined by the glowing yellow flicker of light, "Morning, sir!"

Middle of the bloody night, more like...

Rose fixed what he hoped looked like a genuine smile onto his face, cheeks aching with the effort, "Morning, Whip, lads." He looked nervously at the door to the office, "Daffie not here, then?" his hand was close to the door handle, eyes sweeping the dimmed room, just in case he needed to escape death by slobber...

The Corporal staffing the telephone tried not to grin, but Whip shook his head, "Left her in my quarters. Shame, really. She likes you, sir."

He felt the relief surge through him. *Well, I don't bloody like her.*

"Yes. I see. Well then."

169

Outside there was the explosive 'crack!' of a Coffman cartridge as another of his Typhoons roared into life, the engines being warmed up and checked in readiness for the coming sortie. He rubbed the back of his neck to ease the tension there and sat down beside young Sergeant Gillespie.

The youngster was sprawled comfortably across the stained and torn settee, sound asleep with his mouth wide open, revealing a shadowed wall of stained enamel and grey metal, empty gaps where his upper first molars should have been, and the slivered remains of a barley sugar stuck to the occlusal surface of an upper premolar, testament to the boy's love for all things sweet and sugary.

Rose had been in his first year studying dental surgery in Whitechapel before joining up, so he stared for a moment with interest, but the light was too poor.

He felt a burst of affection for the sleeping boy. Young Gillespie would fly on Rose's wing today, much to Byron's jealous displeasure. With the very real possibility of losses in the coming campaign, it was essential that the CO had at least one replacement wingman trained and ready to fly should anything untoward happen to the first.

His back was stiff against the unforgiving frame of the settee, and he tried to ease his muscles against it, pressing his palm against his pocket, feeling the reassuring bumps of bear and pebble.

Rose's roving eyes found the curling aircraft recognition posters and Sid's pinups as he wondered if Molly was asleep, and wished he were with her, the ever-present disquiet edging into the emptiness.

Whip's stomach gurgled, and he rubbed it apologetically. "Oops, pardon me. I hope breakfast's on the way, my stomach thinks my throat's been cut."

The thought of breakfast made Rose's tummy turn over, and he felt the first burn of acid in his chest, trying not to think of the galvanised steel buckets, one filled with boiling hot milky, sweet tea, and the other slopping with its half-congealed contents.

Oh, dear Lord, please let it not be sausages again...

*

Excalibur's first sortie of the day was as the new-born glow of morning light blushed across the irregular smear of the northern coastline of France, Rose leading eight Typhoons at a thousand feet in the low-level outer fighter screen (which would hopefully protect them from the unwelcome attentions of excessively keen USAAF fighters), well north of Sword beach and (thankfully) out of range of coastal flak. They carried no bombs but would be free to attack enemy targets inland when they were relieved.

The burgeoning dawn revealed extraordinary sights, and they marvelled in awed silence at the seemingly endless lines of ships of all sizes and types, from launches of light coastal forces to the towering, armoured behemoths further offshore, the ships seeming to stretch from the English coastline all the way across the Channel to Normandy. *So many ships...*

There were even mysterious blocky things, towed by powerful tugs, and although he did not know it, these were the building blocks of the two portable Allied Mulberry Harbours to be set up at Omaha and Gold beaches.

Dieppe had proven expensively to the Allies that capturing a harbour was a massively difficult affair, likely resulting in the facilities needed being badly damaged, and the loss of so many of the attacking force demonstrating the cost required to achieve success.

The 2nd Canadian Infantry Division and associated Allied elements had paid for this knowledge with their blood, and now rather than try and capture the harbours essential to smoothly maintain resupply and reinforcements, they would bring their own.

The Mulberries would be put together at Omaha and Gold, should the bridgeheads be established, *please God*, and would be used by the US 1st army and the British 2nd Army to land their men and materials.

Smoke had been laid by 2 Group Bostons earlier that night to hide the approaching fleet, with hundreds of minesweepers forging busily ahead to clear minefields, and to this was now added the smoke from guns firing and ships burning, so that a thin miasma of smoke draped over the French coastline, hanging low and heavy above the water in drifting patches and extending further inland, sluggishly concealing the cliffs and beaches of Normandy.

The grey water, already whipped into surging agitation by the strong winds, was further furrowed by the wakes of myriad vessels manoeuvring close to the shore, some of which were also blazing furiously, pumping out dirty oily smoke into the gathering pall.

Sparkling pinpricks of intense light flashed in their hundreds, short-lived shifting constellations sparkling within the drifting murk, concealing the desperate struggle playing out on the shore, the intensity of the fighting shown by the thick of smoke rising from burning landing ships, tanks and gun emplacements and goodness only knew what else.

A safer distance further back, cloaked in the deepening haze, serried flashes rippled powerfully out from the faint, high outlines of mighty battleships, expanding hemispheres of pressure blasting aside the smoke momentarily, bombarding the enemy defences with unimaginable tonnes of explosive destruction.

Over to the east, a pall of smoke hung over Le Havre where the coastal guns which might have endangered the invasion fleet had received the first of many poundings by Allied heavy bombers.

As they patrolled, they were passed overhead by massive formations of Allied Bombers and their escorts going back and forth to add their thunder to the naval bombardment. Despite his apprehension, they were not attacked by Allied fighters, although once a flight of P47s flew closer to have a sniff before flying off to wherever they were meant to be.

Rose continued to eye the layered clouds with suspicion, the taste of this morning's sausages escaping from his throat to torment his taste buds with their memory, but the only aircraft visible wore either roundels or the stars and stripes. It seemed that the Luftwaffe were not going to make an appearance.

Rose had never seen so many ships and aircraft at once, it was unbelievable, and he allowed himself the thought, *how can we possibly lose now?*

And then almost immediately after that thought came the next: *Don't even know if they've established a bridgehead yet, so don't count your chickens, we have a way to go, a long way to go to Berlin, we'll have to fight our way across an entire continent yet, and there's many a slip, 'twixt cup and lip…*

*

An hour later, relieved by Scarlett's B-Flight, they climbed to a safer altitude, eyes stinging and bathed in sweat from the effort of keeping a good lookout in crowded skies and wrestling their Tiffies along the patrol line against the vicious wind.

His men were tired, but the boys on the beaches must be exhausted as they drove themselves against the merciless German defences, and every little bit of assistance mattered.

He took them inland, weaving to avoid the speculative heavy flak that rose to meet them before pushing down Sugar's nose when he felt they must have cleared the worst of the radar directed lighter flak, the ominous rattle and screech in his headphones subdued and erratic.

The eight Typhoons ranged down as two sections, in line abreast and half a kilometre apart, a few miles west of beautiful Lisieux, skimming the main road to beyond Thieberville.

Just before La Forge Des Ormes, they found a small convoy of trucks, four Opel Blitz three-tonners racing towards them, faded and drab against the road, but the dust cloud they raised behind themselves a dead giveaway as they rushed for the battle zone, giving Rose plenty of warning.

The enemy caught sight of the Typhoons too late, and Rose's first burst stitched a line of explosive bursts across the truck third in line, from the headlight, across the running board and tearing into the canvas covered rear, pieces of men, metal and canvas forming a growing cloud of debris through which the truck spun off the road and into a ditch, spilling figures in a mismatched assortment of standard field grey and the khaki of Fallschirmjager smocks as it rolled onto its side, wheels spinning uselessly.

Rose pulled the section into a loose turn to starboard, the sight of the wooden mat used for freeing the truck from mud flying from above its cab still in his mind's eye, "Whip, strafe the trucks and the troops, we'll provide cover."

He saw now that at least one of the other trucks had been hit by his men even as the second section ripped into the little convoy, and a third exploded in a boiling blot of blinding light.

Poor bastards must have been carrying ammunition, and then, *won't be killing any of ours with that little lot…*

The soldiers who had survived the first attack were scattered or hiding now, and a rifle in the hands of a half-decent soldier was as dangerous to the Typhoons as a flak shell, so he pulled his section up to eight hundred feet, praying that there were no flak guns situated anywhere near enough to catch them, watching the sky and horizon as Whipple's men obliterated the convoy.

A couple of minutes later, the Typhoons departed the scene, leaving behind them a handful of shell-shocked survivors, the dead and the dying amid the shredded, burning vehicles in the shadows beneath a rapidly spreading cloud of smoke.

Excalibur squadron had delivered its first blow in support of the landings.

*

Rose's next sortie was after a hurried lunch, and this time he was at the head of two flights of Excalibur's Tiffies.

Jacko had drawn the short straw and was on fighter patrol duties with his flight off the coast near Merville.

The fighting was continuing unabated, but the Allies had now pushed just beyond the coastal defences and established separate shallow pockets just inland of each of the beaches.

A huge pall of smoke hung like a dull shroud over the coast to starboard, climbing high into the sky and drifting, the stench of burning faint despite their oxygen masks. Once past the flak belt he led them down at full throttle.

Flying at high speed and low level gave flak positions little time to track before they were gone, and the same was true for small arms fire.

Using railway tracks as their guide meant there was no need to keep popping up to confirm their position, and the topography helped concealment, with little chance that enemy radar could track them at less than two hundred feet.

Mati and Rose had scrutinised the maps carefully, and together agreed that the squadron should hunt along the Amiens-Rouen railway line, hunting for trains bringing reinforcements into Normandy.

At the Rouen-Rive-Droite station, they turned eastwards towards Amiens, and it was the streaming banner of white smoke just ahead which told them of their good luck.

The Nazis armed their trains with deadly 2cm Flakvierling 38 quadruple mount guns, and it was prudent for any attackers to target these first in any attack, for to do otherwise would be to face the brunt of the focussed and combined fire of all the Flak one at a time. Flying in line astern or line abreast along the tracks themselves was just as perilous.

So instead, they flew a quarter of a mile parallel to one side of the tracks, a loose formation of two flights, eight Typhoons leading six. But as soon as they saw the smoke, they split, Rose's leading eight Typhoons leaping upwards to provide cover whilst Sid's A-flight opened the distance between themselves and the track to a mile, closing up in line astern.

For those on the train it would have looked like the British Jabos would continue flying eastwards, but as they disappeared behind a line of trees Sid banked his Typhoon hard over into a turn that placed his nose firmly onto the train, his pilots turning simultaneously so that B-Flight's line-astern formation swiftly transformed into one of line-abreast.

Today it seemed that the Luftwaffe would not make an appearance at all, and Rose allowed himself momentary glances to watch the attack even as he scoured the clouds, and he nodded with satisfaction at the skill of his pilots but fearing the storm they must shortly face.

The train was a chain of twenty flatbed links, flak wagons located just behind the locomotive, and another on the end.

176

The wagons bore a selection of light Sd.Kfz.221 armoured cars and a handful of the heavier Sd.Kfz.231s, and twenty four 20mm cannon stitched lines of torn soi; into the bank before smashing into the train at both ends, shells tearing into the locomotive itself and both flak wagons.

Sid and his wingman targeted the front of the train, shredding the tender, firebox and trailer, and as the locomotive disappeared inside an expanding cloud of smoke, soot, escaping steam and a blur of bright fire, the cloud was joined by a vertical jet of pure white steam shooting up out of the steam stack as if it were requesting clemency.

More cannon shells blew off thick chunks of the driving wheels, and the locomotive twisted and suddenly derailed, thrust off as the lurching tender behind drove into it.

The crew of the forward flak wagon were blown from their feet, disappearing into the jumble of flying metal, and then it was only the rear flak wagon which spat defiance, but the slash of fiery blobs were few in number and stopped almost as soon as they began as 20mm shells crept up and brushed over them.

As the locomotive and its tender crumpled and derailed, disintegrating as it did so, the flatbed wagons smashed into the back of them and the whole train seemed to shorten and fold as the wagons telescoped together, armoured cars and men torn from their positions to be smashed against the ground by the rolling ferocity of the wreck, and the attacking Typhoons had streaked past and were turning back in to strafe the wreckage.

The train was demolished, and the tracks broken and warped, but they had to be sure none of the armoured cars it had been carrying could ever be used again.

Far to the west, far above the clouds, a massed formation of USAAF bombers thinly etched hundreds of chalky trails into the sky, but of the Luftwaffe, there was still no sign.

"Good job, Red Leader, great shooting. One more pass then we'll have a bash!"

Despite a moment's regret for the fate of the SNCF crew in the steam engine's destroyed cab, Rose felt relief and a wild thrill of exhilaration grip his heart with Sid's success.

The lads fighting at the bridgeheads would not have to face any of the broken armoured vehicles below! And with the line blocked and the tracks damaged, at least for some precious hours, there would be no more reinforcements for Normandy using this route!

On the way home in crowded skies, they had the unusual experience of being joined by a mixture of other Allied aircraft, from four engine RAF bombers to single-engine USAAF fighters, in groups or alone, some distant, some closer.

At the debrief, Mati told them of USAAF practice, wherein a formation would circle a train before attacking to ascertain the presence and position of the flak wagons. If these were identified, they were dive-bombed first, as even a close miss was enough to disable the crews and their deadly mounts.

We were lucky that time, bloody lucky, Rose reflected thoughtfully, *Sid's lads gave a damned good showing knocking out the flak wagons in that first pass.*

Next time, we'll take at least one section armed with bombs, even if it's just with 250 pounders...

Chapter Twenty

Just after dusk on D-Day, the bridgeheads were attacked by a small formation of enemy bombers, several of which were shot down by patrolling Spitfires.

Earlier that day there were also a handful of fighter skirmishes inland, one of which led to three Typhoons being bounced and shot down when harrying enemy ground transport.

Although the landings were almost completely unopposed by the Luftwaffe, it was decided that fighter-bombers would be sent to raid airfields near the beachheads just before nightfall the following day to intercept any bombers being prepared for a night attack.

Jacko and Sid both led inland attacks, and whilst the former was lucky enough to find and destroy artillery pieces in company-strength rushing to the fighting, he lost his youngest pilot shot down in flames, a nineteen-year-old Sergeant recently arrived on the squadron, Arthur Driscoll, a farmer's son from Somerset.

Rose felt despair gnaw into the scars on his heart, an eager young face with whom he had promised to share a drink that evening.

Who had he been, and who might he have become, given half a chance? The farm in Somerset would have become an emptier place, but one filled with painful memories for those he had shared it with.

Later, still thinking of the lost boy who had been a part of Excalibur for so very short a time, he led C-Flight into the late afternoon sky, his faithful shadow, Byron, flying once more as wingman.

They made landfall just east of St Valery-en-Caux, continuing on through the broken cloud at ten thousand feet until well inland, with the grey and brown smoggy stain of Rouen ahead, its suburbs spilling messily into the rich green blanket of the great Roumare forest stretching to starboard, the Seine a dark squiggle snaking to port.

Weaving, constantly changing height and spread out as the first heavy flak clumsily tried to track them, black puffs erupting in the air below and behind, maintaining a heading for the great Luftwaffe airfield at Evreux, watching keenly for enemy fighters, but still there were none to be seen.

As soon as the forest edge passed behind his starboard wing root, Rose pushed Sugar down into a dive at full throttle, watching the altimeter unwind rapidly, fusing his bombs as he did so, his men following suit behind him.

Were it not for the thin cloud, Evreux should have been visible ahead now, but as soon as they passed through a thousand feet he pulled back and levelled out at two hundred, and, checking the others were close behind, Rose swung Sugar around into a wide circle to starboard, onto a heading of three-three-two.

Let the observers on the ground think their target was Evreux. The real destination was just ten miles ahead and with luck he would have foxed the defenders.

With the sun low in the west, they would circle around and approach the airfield at zero feet from the part of the sky that was painfully bright, but their eyes were searching for the enemy bounce that might yet tear their plans asunder, though at full throttle and at low level it would be hard for enemy fighters to pull off.

Nevertheless, *beware the Hun in the sun…*

The forest slipped past below, soft and green and peaceful, yet he hunched lower in his seat, heart racing and eyes stinging despite the extra armour protecting his cockpit, for there was no knowing what might be concealed beneath the spreading branches.

Any moment now, last quick scan of the instrument panel…safeties off…slow your breathing, haul in a lungful of oxygen…

Beaumont-le-Roger was an Armée de l'air airfield in 1940, almost thirty miles south-south-east of Rouen and half that west-northwest of Evreux, close to the villages of Beaumont-le-Roger and Beaumontel.

The victorious Luftwaffe had made it a major fighter base, used primarily by units of the legendary JG2 'Richthofen'.

The airfield was a grassy rectangle, dispersal areas located in each corner. Wary of the established flak positions, there would be only a single pass from out of the sun, and now he felt last-minute doubts, *should I have brought them from the shadows to the east and into the sun to upset the aim of the gunners?*

But he knew he had done the right thing, striking into the easterly wind with the sun in their eyes throughout the attack? Madness.

His nerves were crawling with tension, eyes stealing up to the mirror, but there were only empty clouds, the sun so low that Sugar's own rudder cast a shadow across the reflective surface as they closed on the airfield from out of the sun.

The shadows were long on the ground, but the stretch of green contained between the bordering roads showed them they were spot on.

I hope I haven't made a balls-up of it and brought us to the dummy airfield at Feugerolles…

And then there was no more time to worry.

Eight Typhoons, their Sabres snarling like unleashed beasts, the lethal silhouettes swept in over the trees and blasting as if from out of the dazzling sun.

Those on the left of the formation were perfectly lined up with the dispersals at the southwestern corner of the enemy airfield, and their cannon barked out at the camouflage-net shrouded shapes on the ground, and what looked like a Stuka dive bomber abruptly disappeared within an expanding grey cloud of twinkling flickers of fire, smoke dust and fragments.

In the corner of his vision, he sensed the flashes rippling erratically against some of the other shapes too, and he knew that the other Typhoon section would be dropping their bombs, momentarily vulnerable as the sudden loss of loads pushing them up, but his eyes were elsewhere, the Watch Tower and its accompanying buildings looming out of the settling gloom ahead.

A line of glowing tracer whipped outwards ahead, and he slewed Sugar's nose slightly to starboard and jammed down on the gun button.

Cannon shells sprayed out from his wings at the light flak position on the airfield boundary, his fire ripping out chunks of tarmac and concrete before smashing into the gun, and the glowing line of enemy tracer faltered and stopped.

The workshops at the western end of the field passed beneath them, the airfield wide and open, at first glance a seemingly empty expanse, occasionally broken at the edges by small huts and empty shelters, aware of the scattered flash of muzzles, but Rose's attention was on a row of aircraft ahead, marked out for him by their drawn-out shadows and the glint of dying sunlight on Perspex.

Sucking in oxygen to sustain his thrashing heart, Rose pointed Sugar's nose down, thwarting the relentless efforts of ground effect to bounce him upwards into an easier target for the flak bursting above them.

182

With the attackers at zero feet, the Luftwaffe gunners were fearful that they might hit their comrades on the ground if they lowered their guns further.

The bomb craters which appeared in the recce photos were mere facades, filled in, so that whilst the damage looked real from afar, operations would be unaffected.

I must tell Mati…

At the eastern end of the airfield flak unexpectedly stained the air, and Rose wondered what was drawing the attention of the guns just as an explosion flared silently in the approaching gloaming, and a dazzling blob of fire spiralled downwards, falling oh so slowly, almost floating into the trees beyond the boundary.

It wasn't one of his boys, so who was it? Might the enemy gunners have made some awful mistake and accidentally shot down one of their own? Or might there be allied fighters attacking from the east racing in towards them at any second? With a sky scarred with flak bursts and drifting smoke, it was impossible to know for sure.

And then he was firing again, the stick dancing in his hands as he sprayed the Heinkel 111 bomber on the far end of the line, tiny explosions flashing erratically as it seemed to twitch beneath the onslaught, dust and smoke billowing out as chunks were ripped from her, the spinning discs of her propellers disintegrating into jagged stumps, and he must have shot through her main undercarriage because she collapsed tiredly as he drew close and released the bomb lever.

Answering fire from the Perspex nose of one of the other bombers licked out, a burst of defiance that was well off the mark and came nowhere near him, the ground so close beneath a tiny part of him wondering how the tips of Sugar's propeller did not catch the ground.

Something bloomed out expanding light, a gout of ravening light and a sudden thrust of pressure as a bomber further along exploded and his stomach lurched as she was buffeted by the blast, his eyes focussed on the ground so perilously close beneath, one wingtip dropping.

With a slight touch of the rudder, Rose slid Sugar to one side, bumping through the boiling air and pushing her nose into the yaw before it had even begun, then pulling her back automatically as he looked for fresh targets with eyes stung by sweat and strain, desperate to ease the cloying embrace of the mask from his face.

At first, he thought there was nothing more for them here, bent forwards over a clenched stomach as shrapnel *plinked* against his canopy, rudder bar convulsing a little beneath his feet as something punched through it, yet still she flew beautifully, as if nothing had happened.

Rose was yearning for the sanctuary beyond the trees to the east where the sky dulled towards dusk, the taste of cordite harsh against his parched throat, but then he saw the irregular shapes hidden beneath the bordering trees.

Keeping her low, expecting the crash of enemy fire punching into Sugar and himself at any moment as he gasped in a breath, he kept Sugar low, sideslipping and aileroning as he punched the gun button, feeling her slow once more beneath the recoil and mindful of the stall, glittering strikes splashing against the propeller and cowling of a single engine fighter (FW190?) and its adjacent vehicles.

One of them must have been an ammunition truck or perhaps a fuel bowser, a sudden angry red-yellow mushroom marking the vivid impact of Sugar's fan of cannon shells, searing an after-image onto his retina as he looked away.

More eruptions beneath the foliage to port demonstrated that at least one of his men had also seen the hidden shapes.

And then suddenly he was hauling her over the trees, holding her steady, his wonderful Sugar, still at full throttle just above the treetops, chasing after his racing shadow, tendrils of tracer arcing uselessly behind.

Only then did he allow himself to see who else was with him, even as his eyes began that endless search once more for enemy machines above, heart gladdened by the sight of Byron's stained B-Bertie (*oh thank God!*), and then plummeting sickly as he picked out only four other shapes beyond that of his wingman.

He swallowed drily, not wanting to, but asking anyway, "Excalibur Leader to all, did we lose anyone?"

And Whip's terse response to his dry rasp, the pain unmistakable below the R/T's sibilant crackle, "Flak got Willy, chopped off his tail. Went straight in."

Oh, Willy.

Quiet Willy, Wise Willy, always sitting at the edges, grinning shyly at their jokes. Weariness drained through him, "OK, we're not out of the woods yet. Form up for home, route B." They would fly back well east of the strong defences around Caen, prior to climbing hard to evade coastal flak.

At least the journey across the Channel was not quite as hazardous as it had once been, with so many ships crowding the water, there was a good chance of being picked up rapidly before getting one's feet wet (almost).

Whip's was the missing Tiffie, so he must have egressed the airfield to the north. With a bit of luck, he'd join them on the way out.

The other Typhoons drew closer, smoke-stained sharks in the sea of darkness, and he swept the approaching gloom with careful eyes before drawing them down again to his controls.

Height, fuel, revs, pressure, sensitive for the smallest of vibrations in her engine or airframe, but Sugar's Sabre snarled as sweetly as before, and the controls felt smooth as always, *good girl.*

A last glance back towards the enemy airfield, blotches of flame burning, the columns of smoke like accusatory fingers merging into the encroaching night, slender arcs of multi-coloured tracer still crawling out for attackers now too distant to harm.

A silent prayer of thanks to God for his own survival, *thank you, Lord God, thank you*, and the profound stab of aching regret for yet another of his youngsters, the remains of a stout heart now lying in a foreign field amongst the chaos and debris of their enemy.

Another gone before he had really begun, lost to the ones for whom he had been someone, lost by mourning friends who would pretend to forget, but never would.

The sky blurred for a moment and he cuffed it away before settling his goggles into position again. *I'm so sorry, Willy. Those who survive this will remember you, I promise.*

Will I be one of those, or will I, too, become a fading memory in a broken heart?

Chapter Twenty-One

In mid-June, the Nazi robot bomb offensive began.

The Walter catapults began to unleash the first of many waves of unmanned evil at 200 miles per hour, with the speed building to over 300 mph by the time they passed over the English coast.

With the gradual expenditure of fuel the bomb would lighten, and its velocity would snap along to a phenomenal 400mph. At speeds such as these it was imperative for any interceptor to be in a good position for interception, as most RAF aircraft would struggle and swiftly fall back in a stern-chase.

Flying at an altitude that was between the ideal zone of fire of light and heavy flak, at speeds faster than the guns could easily track and fighters could follow, the defences scrambled frantically to establish methods to deal with this menace.

What they came up with were separate zones of action in which the guns and fighters would operate under ground control, whilst barrage balloons and misinformation would act in support.

And amongst the fighters hurriedly redeployed were the Typhoons of Excalibur squadron from their role in low level fighter cover and free ranging Rhubarbs into France.

Rose, with young Gillespie wide on his port wing was at three thousand feet, thirty miles to the east of Southend in the early morning of June the 17th, low cloud and rain hampering visibility, the rain blurring the grey, and making their eyes strain the harder for the sight of streaked blobs that might be enemy fighters lurking in the murk (or even more dangerous, God forbid, overly inquisitive trigger-happy Allied fighters).

With a warning from Mati, they had been sure to steer well clear of the trigger-happy gunners on the concrete barges which formed both an Anti-aircraft defensive line and a sea-barrier at Canvey Island.

Pleased to be flying with his CO again, Gillespie, a keen lepidopterist, burbled enthusiastically over breakfast in Dispersals to Rose about a 'particularly beautiful Purple Hairstreak' he had caught one evening earlier in the week. Pushing his breakfast of sausages (again!) and the accompanying fried blob of dried egg around the plate, Rose grunted a suitable response.

Personally, he couldn't understand why anyone would wish to capture something so fragile and beautiful and pin it to a board, but then, each to their own. Luckily, the youngster had ignored his CO's morning surliness.

"Hallo, Excalibur Leader, please turn onto a heading of zero-nine-five."

He cleared his throat and grimaced as his breakfast rose, "Excalibur leader to Ops, received. Heading zero-nine-five."

The visibility was truly terrible, and stare as he might until his eyes burned with the strain, Rose could not see the approaching bomb amongst the clouds.

"Excalibur Leader to Ops, how far is it?"

"Excalibur Leader, two miles and closing fast, will pass along to starboard of you, five hundred feet below."

Bloody hell! Rose cursed under his breath, feeling the flutter of anxiety through his heart, where on earth was the damned thing? "Can you see it, Two?"

"No, sir, can't see a thing."

Bugger! How are we supposed to see anything in all this clag? The sweat in his eyes and the smears of oil and rain on his bubble canopy made it nigh on impossible to see the tiny shape in this diffuse light. Thank God they were low down otherwise he would be contending with condensation as well…

Where are you?

Ops again, slightly anxious: "Excalibur Leader, bandit is passing a quarter of a mile to starboard of you!"

Too late! Damn it! He still could not see a thing but kicked hard rudder, stick over and back to turn hard to starboard, knowing that Gillespie would be following, eyes wide open, vision greying at the edges, as if it might help him catch sight of the elusive beast they were hunting in this bleak jungle of cloud.

He muttered a prayer of desperation, *Dear God, please show it to me…*

And his prayer was answered, for as he turned he saw the glow of light streaking past below, and glimpsed the bomb, a small, dull black cruciform, yellow light glaring brightly from its tail, and Rose fought to hold it in his vision as he pulled Sugar after it at full throttle, gasping against the pressure, the pinpoint of light seeming to weave wildly and leaving an after image of jagged lines in his eyes.

At least it's so bright we oughtn't lose sight of it that easily…

The distance closed quickly as they dived after the robot bomb, and as soon as he thought he was close enough he fired a one second burst, squinting and nerves cringing should the damned thing explode, but the bomb was smaller than he had first estimated, and the stream of cannon shells flew over and beyond it.

And then it was in a thin layer of cloud, the glow of the engine a faint beacon in the dreary, rain-soaked sky.

"Keep an eye on it, Two, you're to take over if I lose it in all this." The cloud was thin, but Gillespie's nearness was rattling him, "And for Christ's sake keep an eye on me, too!"

"Received, Leader."

The bloody thing must be far narrower than a fighter, let alone a bomber, how can I calculate range and deflection if I don't know how big it is?

And then reproach, *for goodness' sake! Stop being childish! You've got the best part of four years of operational experience, don't look like a damned amateur in front of one of your newest pilots! Stop being a silly tit and sort yourself out!*

Gillespie's Typhoon was sitting faithfully to one side, and Rose throttled back slightly as the cloud thinned away and the bomb puttered back into view, easing Sugar into position around three hundred yards behind the dark shape, and, sighting carefully as Sugar rocked in the bomb's pulsing slipstream, firing another one-second burst, adjusted slightly, and then a third.

The cannon shells seared harmlessly over the top of the enemy bomb, but his final burst tore catastrophically into its rocket motor, shattering it in an expanding storm of whirling metal splinters, a stream of fire licking back from it.

Sugar was buffeted by the explosion's turbulence but managed to avoid debris even as the flying bomb twisted into a flat spin, slowly rotating downwards to starboard, the spin quickening with each turn until it hit the waters below and broke up.

They turned above the expanding circle of water, but there was no more to see.

Dutifully, "Good shooting, Leader."

"Thanks, Two. Let's see if there're any more…"

He found he was still holding his breath, and hastily swallowed in a lungful of oxygen, eyes stealing a glance at her picture and fingers reaching down for the comfort of the shape of the little bear against his palm. *No time to rest…*

"Excalibur Leader to Ops, scratch one bomb. Any more trade?"

"Well done, Excalibur Leader! Stand by…"

Chapter Twenty-Two

The weeks of June 1944 were ones of intense stress and fatigue, the Allies fighting hard to keep the foothold they had gained, the beach-head pockets meeting, merging and slowly spreading outwards as soldiers from the Allied nations pushed hard inland.

Men, equipment and supplies began to flow smoothly through the Mulberry Harbours, with little interference from the Luftwaffe.

A similar flow of men, equipment and supplies was rushing to the enemy side, but the reinforcement of the German armed forces was fraught with peril as Allied fighter-bombers pounded the reinforcements and reserves from above.

Allied resupply was not all smooth however, for a great storm swept across the English Channel in the third week of June, an unusual event occurring only once every forty years, destroying the US's Mulberry 'A' harbour, and badly damaging the British 'B' one. The latter only saved because the waves which battered it were slightly smaller than those which had pulverised 'A'.

Although the harbours had been designed to be used for three months, 'A' lasted a fortnight, whilst the British 'B' at Arromanches lasted far longer than originally intended. By now, however, the supply lines had been secured.

Night temporarily became the friend of German logistic movement officers, though not for long, the heavy bombers kept up the pressure, aided and abetted by the moonlight Rhubarb experts of 2TAF's Typhoons, proving that they needed to fear the night as well as the day.

The long summer days filled with multiple sorties reminded the older veterans of 1940, never-ending days when they flew again and again against endless raids, the groundcrews striving to keep their hard flown charges in action, the men who flew them falling into exhausted but broken sleep whenever possible, the flying a constant effort under the grinding worry that they might yet be beaten.

As it was then, so it was now.

In 1940 and later, Rose had flown under the orders of others, Regulars and veterans of France, doing as he was told.

But now he was the veteran, the CO, *the Old Man*, responsible for both his young pilots and groundcrews, and the machines they flew and cared for.

The uncertainty and the doubt that flowed in the deepest eddies at the edges of his wakeful thoughts snatched at him and made him doubt himself. The acid that burned in his chest and throat were soothed by the MO's powders, but still he ate little in the evening, and slept with his head raised to still the blaze and irritation of reflux.

The V1s were coming over the Channel thick and fast, but Excalibur had found a decent measure of good fortune.

Every successful interception resulted in a shoot-down, although on occasion his Typhoons were having to pull back as more than one Allied fighter chased after a single flying bomb. After a few days, they had accounted for twelve, although the bombs had almost managed to pull one back when one of his little band of Belgian pilots, suave Montalmond, flew too close to an exploding bomb and was forced to return to base in a battered and rather scorched Typhoon.

The great storm which mishandled the Mulberry harbours also allowed a short respite from aerial operations, and this permitted the Allied aircrews a reprieve, albeit a short one. The silver lining of the treacherous storm which might have caused the invasion to fail meant that Rose and his pilots rested for a two-day period, a rest they were sorely in need of.

Mostly they slept and relaxed, but more than a few of them chose to drink, in some cases to remember the lost, in others to forget.

*

The dust of Normandy choked not only the men but the machines as well. Fine and light, it permeated everything and the Sabres of the first Typhoons to arrive at the beachhead airfields were almost immediately clogged and damaged by the scouring effect of the Calvados dust.

Unprepared despite months of planning, the Ministry rushed to get 2TAF's aircraft adapted for a dry, particulate-rich environment, and once the effects had been assessed, the RAF's Technical experts went into action to counter the effects.

Rose was told to report to the OC's office as soon as he had landed after another fruitful 'Buzz-bomb' chase.

Finding the OC's front office empty, Rose was about to stride into Granny's office when he heard the murmur of voices within and recognizing it was Belle and Granny, he hesitated, unwilling to disturb them.

"Damn it, Belle, I'm your husband, and you'll do as I say, d'you hear?" Granny's voice was raised, and Rose froze.

"I won't and you can't make me, Danny." Belle sounded tearful. What?

"Belle, please." His tone was softer now. "You must, please, love."

"Danny Smith, I have never stopped loving you in all these years, despite everything." Her voice shook with emotion. "Don't ask me to stop now."

"I never meant to hurt you, Belle." Granny sounded cowed.

"I know. I introduced Charlie to Flash, after all. I knew what would happen, I'm not blameless."

"Belle, my darling," his voice was reasonable. "Do it, for me."

"How can I? For better or for worse, remember?"

Granny sighed. "You've been true to me, my love, and you deserve so much better. I can't bear the thought of you being alone. If I don't make it, find someone who will make you happy."

"Don't talk like that! You're not going to die!" Belle began to cry, and Rose crept out. *I'll come back later...*

*

Fifteen minutes later, he found them quietly embracing, and he coughed at the doorway.

Smith *tsked*, grudgingly releasing his wife, "Flash, my old knobby dumpling! Any luck?"

"Got another just before it got to the Thames Estuary gun-zone. Bit of a close-run thing but turned out alright in the end." He shifted awkwardly from one foot to the other.

Rose stepped aside to allow Belle out, and his eyes flinched away from the redness in hers as she touched his arm, "Well done, Flash. Good to see you back safe and sound."

Smith slapped his desk with a one hand. "Good show, old pants!

That's three of the bloody things, now, isn't it?"

Rose nodded in response and took the seat Smith indicated, "Young Byron got his fifth, he has a good eye, and he's sensible. I'd like to put him in for a DFC."

"I agree, the lad's good, he deserves it. Four kills already, ground targets, and now five buzzbombs! I'll get Belle to put the papers together." He picked up his telephone, "Sissy? Could you organise a cuppa for Mr Rose and me?" He smiled, "Lovely, thank you."

He settled back comfortably, "You've heard about all the engine serviceability problems they've been having across the water? All that abrasive dust on the Landing Grounds has been scraping buggery out of the sleeves and leaving deposits on the spark plugs. Some of the engines are knackered and need to be replaced, but others can be restored and serviced."

At the best of times, any type of technical talk was enough to numb Rose's mind, for he just wasn't technically minded. It was twice as bad after a sortie hunting V1s, and he could feel his eyes begin to glaze, and wiped his face as if it somehow it might help.

"You're to take Excalibur up to Holmsley South, Flash, flight by flight, have an engine once-over and they'll fit specially designed dust deflectors over the air intake. Keeps the dust out and lets the air in. A mate told me that the Vokes ones are better than the Napier ones, so try and get them, OK? Which ones, old pants, old bean?

Rose rolled his eyes, "'Strewth! The Vokes ones. I'm not deaf, Granny."

"I know you're not deaf, old son, bit thick, though." Smith scratched his crotch thoughtfully, "It's daft, really. D'you know there was a special air intake made for the tropical version of the Tiffie? Designed for just this sort of situation? Could have used that now, but oh no! the Air Ministry knows best."

He sniffed disdainfully, "Tossers. The engineers found that Tiffies taxiing out would get dust into their ejection chutes, too, buggering about with the ammo belts and clogging up the chute, but Chiefy Schaefer from 181, remember him? The clever sod solved the problem by sticking loo paper over the chutes before take-off. When the pilot fires his guns, the shell casings and links tear through the paper and leave the chute clear. Clever, eh? Deserves a medal."

Impressed by the ingenuity, Rose nodded. "I'd never have thought of it, Granny, never in a month of Sundays."

The WAAF arrived with the tea, and they saw with horror that it was 'Handy' Hilda. Granny jumped to his feet to take the tray as she asked him, "Shall I pour it then, sir?"

Rose tried not look at her fingernails. Hilda worked in the kitchens, and it looked as if all the dirt from the potatoes she peeled had lodged beneath her nails. No end of threats and cajoling or orders would get those nightmarish nails cut short.

"Did you, erm, pour out the tea and milk, Hilda?" Granny tried to sound casual.

"Oh no, sir, cook done that. But I can be Mum, if you like?" She smiled hopefully and wiped her nose, smudging it.

Rose stood eagerly, "That's quite alright, Hilda, thank you so much."

Hilda's brow beetled, but Granny soothed her, "Yes, I'm training Mr Rose for the coming peace, thought he'd make a wonderful man servant, so although I'd normally let you make the tea, be a sport, leave it for the poor chap to do, eh?"

Looking him up and down, Hilda gave Rose an unreadable look, then shrugged, "Please yourselves. I'm off back to the cookhouse. Those potatoes won't peel themselves." Then she remembered, "Sir."

As the door closed behind her, Rose clucked his tongue, "Oh dear, I think you might have hurt her feelings, Granny."

Smith opened the teapot and stirred the tea. "I could care less. Better that than she hurt my poor suffering guts. Cripes, did you see her hands?"

Rose shuddered and nodded but thought of another scruffy cookhouse WAAF at RAF Dimple Heath, Elsie Dyer, aka 'Jankarella' the Jankers princess, a disciplinary nightmare and the nemesis of RAF Dimple Heath's long-suffering SPs.

Elsie had been instrumental in foiling a Nazi plot to steal top-secret technology, earning herself a very well-deserved Military Medal in the process. Elsie was now a Section Officer catering to the Brass at Bentley Priory.

If only Hilda would cut those awful filthy nails…

Smith handed him a steaming mug before holding out the little bowl of sugar, "You know that the Rafwaffe have been testing Jerry fighters, Flash?"

Rose nodded. "Know your enemy."

The 'Rafwaffe', more correctly known as 1426 Flight RAF, were a top-secret unit formed to assess captured enemy aircraft and evaluate their parameters of flight and performance.

Granny sat back. "I've heard tell that they can actually turn inside our fighters."

Rose stopped, the cup close to his lips as he blew on it, "What? No! Pull the other one!"

"Still your beating heart, old man. The fuel Jerry is using must be poorer quality or maybe contaminated. If I was filling Jerry's fuel tank, I'd piss in it. Obviously the Rafwaffe uses the same stuff as us."

Rose took a sip, and burnt his tongue, "Thank goodness for small mercies! If that's true, long may Jerry continue with shoddy fuel!"

"Amen." Smith produced a cigarette, and his lips twitched around it, "So, old dozy fart, remind me, which filter was it again?"

Chapter Twenty-Three

In the early hours of the 7th of June, combat engineers from the RAF's Servicing Commandos and the Royal Engineers Airfield Construction Groups landed on the newly captured sands near Vers-sur-Mer, around 3 miles southwest of Gold Beach. They were tasked with building one of the first Advanced Landing Grounds in France, and ALG B2 would become RAF Bazenville airfield.

All British Advance Landing Grounds (ALGs) were numbered and given the prefix 'B', whilst all the American ones were given 'A'.

The runways at these ALGs would be constructed from a wide variety of materials including Hessian surfacing, Asphalt and even Concrete, but the engineers at ALG B2 used Square Mesh Track (SMT) to build a runway almost a mile long, together with the other amenities necessary for an operational military airfield.

Occasional interruptions were due to sniper fire and artillery strikes, adding to the difficulties in building an airbase in record time.

On the third day of construction, when just about done, a Liberator bomber successfully crash-landed on it. Shaking their heads in exasperation while shedding a tear or two in frustration at the extensive damage done, the exhausted engineers sighed and grimly flexed their aching muscles before spending another two days to repair it.

Within a week of the landings, the Allies had prepared several new airstrips behind the lines in Normandy, thereby allowing the advantage of providing aircraft extended time over enemy territory, being able to refuel in France before returning to their bases in the UK and providing damaged aircraft an emergency strip to land on, saving them a stressful trip in a failing machine over the English Channel.

Close to the frontline, these airfields were hives of relentless activity.

By the second week of June these Advanced Landing Grounds were operational, albeit still under occasional hostile fire, and would be ready to host squadrons and wings longer term, with 2TAF's ground control being based locally in a Normandy church.

And so it was that Rose led Excalibur Squadron in to land at B2 on the evening of the 29th of June after almost two weeks of hunting V1 flying bombs across the approaches to south-east England, just as they had become adept in doing so.

Excalibur squadron entered the circuit from the south, emerging from the cloud with Normandy beneath them, the sun a pale golden circle low on the horizon, the muted sunlight catching the tops of the serried ships on the glittering waters and the glistening carpet of their swaying barrage balloons, the beautiful green of the countryside beneath similar and yet so very different from the one they had just left.

A flight of Spitfires from 443 Squadron was patrolling high above as cover, yet he found his eyes drawn to the east, as the enemy would be unlikely to attack from over the massed anti-aircraft guns of the fleet. Rose himself felt unease in the fleet's closeness, fearing trigger-happy gunners rather than the fading light to starboard. But there were still no signs of the Luftwaffe, just the distant and very welcome sight of more friendly aircraft.

Since take-off, Rose felt the apprehension, his innards contracting into what felt like an iron ball. It was the first time he would be landing on the continent in his career, and the occasional flash of an explosion, and the many drifting columns of smoke inland near the sombre glowing smudge of Caen itself showed how close they were to the enemy. The edges of the revolver he had strapped to himself dug into his thigh, and he wondered if he might actually have to use it as Villers-le-Sec passed beneath Sugar's nose.

In the early days, B2 had been under almost constant barrage from enemy 88mm guns, and the first week or two of operations had been fraught ones, with squadrons often having to abandon it when things got a little too hot.

Luckily, the airfield was now out of range of the enemy as the ground troops pushed forwards, and Mati cheerfully promised them it was safe now, even as he handed each of them a firearm and ammunition.

They had flown across to France too many times to remember but knowing they would now be operating from French soil seemed to make home, only a few minutes flight away, seem so very remote.

Rose glanced down at Molly's picture, a little part of him wondering idly what she was doing as Sugar passed over the end of the runway and he reproached himself for his inattention at what was possibly the most dangerous time of the flight.

The air seemed hazy, and he groaned inwardly, was that dust? If it was, the routine of taking off, taxiing and landing every day would be nightmarish.

They wheeled easily to port over Maromme to set up the approach, the squat grey stone parish church of Eglise Saint-Martin between La Croix and Les Noyaux jutting proudly upwards as they slid into line astern above it.

Rose had heard rumours that the church was the site of the Ground

Control centre from which all the aircraft of 2TAF were controlled, but he doubted it. GCI Control so close to the front line?

Pull the other one, chum…

On the final approach his eyes were drawn to the village of Crepon beyond, the brighter colours of day dimmed in the declining light, the ebbing rays gleaming from the few unbroken windows and casting long shadows across the buildings of the village outside the airfield's northeast border,

Most of the houses were either damaged or completely demolished by the fighting which had swept past, and he wondered how much the people had suffered, first under the heel of the invader, and now from the efforts of those who sought to free them.

Sugar was a little heavier than usual, her balance not quite what it usually was with every possible area of spare stowage being used to store both his belongings, tins of coffee, cigarettes and fresh loaves of white bread (whilst an additional six extra loaves, two blankets and a canvas bag of condiments shared the cockpit with him), and now he felt a stir of relief that they had arrived at B2 without incident.

The thought of getting into a hard-fought scrap with a Staffel of keen FW190s or trigger-happy friendly fighters, whilst slices of bread and tins of marmalade or jam spun majestically around the cockpit had been haunting him on the way over, although it did smelt awfully nice.

Had he been able to remove his oxygen mask, Rose would have munched his way through a loaf during the journey.

As soon as he dropped down the last few feet onto the SMT runway, more dust billowed into the air. Despite the rising cloud, Excalibur's Typhoons landed safely, no mean feat considering the limited experience of some of his youngsters, and he breathed a sigh of relief.

Rose and his men were guided to the western dispersals point by the simple expedient of a member of groundcrew hopping up onto a wing (easier said than done with the ferocious back draft from the Sabres threatening to pluck them off) and perching on the edge astride one cannon and holding onto the barrel for dear life as the taxiing aircraft juddered, bounced and swerved over the uneven ground of the airfield, directing the pilots with hand signals from their precarious roost.

A thick cloud of pale brown dust had been thrown up into the air by their landing and taxiing to dispersals, and Rose's hand released the bear and pebble in his pocket as the last of his boys edged into their positions on the ground.

A large formation take-off or landing could be horrendous and would require good coordination and skilled external control. Disaster was just a heartbeat away, and should a tyre burst on take-off or landing with forward visibility almost non-existent in the swirling dust, any aircraft following on behind would pile catastrophically into the wreckage.

The thought made him cold, despite the heat of Sugar's cockpit. *Dear Lord, protect us from danger…*

But military flying is a dangerous occupation at the best of times and very much more so during wartime when operational constraints expediently supplant peacetime practices.

*

Excalibur's ground element would arrive the following day, courtesy of the USAAF's Transport Command, but in the meantime, Excalibur would be looked after by the groundcrews of 121 Wing.

As the hardworking erks swarmed over Sugar refuelling and unloading her, Rose was handed a chipped and oily enamel mug filled with steaming tea by a grinning Corporal. "Welcome to Bazenville, sir! Corporal Martin. You must be parched! 'Ere, sir, 'ave a pialla o' chai."

203

Already he could feel the dust lodging into his eyes and nose and mouth, and he nodded gratefully to Martin.

The compo tea, brewed in boiling water from dried composite blocks comprising dehydrated tea, powdered milk and shovelfuls of sugar, was actually quite tasty and sweet when sipped hot, but would cool to a slightly less delightful brew which left behind it a gauzy scum on one's lips and tongue.

Knowing this, Rose washed down the slice of bread he had filched from one of his fresh loaves with frequent but cautious sips from his mug, before gratefully reaching for one of the roughly cut corned beef sandwiches from the dented tray the Corporal held out, "Git yer laughing gear 'rand that, sir. Nice bit of bully and pickle."

Like the tea, the sandwich had a light coating of dust, but he ate it anyway, and smiled his thanks to Martin as his pilots joined them.

Sid looked around with interest, eyes blinking in the dusty air, "Cor! No totty! What a dump!"

Jacko's lower lip quivered, "Dump!"

Rose saw Martin's face fall, "Belt up, you two," he turned apologetically to Martin, "Please excuse our rudeness, Corporal. We're grateful for the tea and the grub."

Sid was contrite, "Sorry, Corp, didn't mean to be rude, I was hoping to cherchez la femme francaise."

Jacko's eyes were downcast, and he bowed slightly to the Corporal, whispering conspiratorially, "Cherchez la femme, mon poulet grande de terre."

"Er… OK, sir." Martin grinned uncertainly as they were joined by a grubby figure dressed in a wrinkled set of overalls.

Rose was about to ask him where to report when the new

204

arrival smiled and drawled in a plummy home counties accent, "Hello, laddie! Welcome to B2, how d'you do? Name's Trent, Wing Commander, flying."

He noticed Rose's surprise, "Oh, do pardon the togs, old chap, but we were under occasional sniper fire until quite recently, so I thought it might be prudent to blend in a touch, got rather attached to these togs, but they do drive the brass potty." He pulled out a grubby hanky and blew his nose into it.

"Bloody dust!" He beamed at Rose, but his eyes were staring into the swaying stalks of the cornfield beside the dispersals, perhaps searching for a sniper, "Ah well, never mind, can't be helped." He hawked and spat, "There is a war on, after all."

Rose smiled, fondly remembering a rather scruffy and outspoken pilot officer who had flown Hurricanes with him in the dark days of 1940 but had magically transformed over the years into a rather debonair Typhoon Wing Commander.

By Trent's clothing, it appeared the process could go the other way as well.

Rose stuffed the remnants of his sandwich into his mouth and held out his hand, mumbling, "How d'you do, sir. Squadron Leader Harry Rose, Excalibur squadron, 44 Wing."

Trent grabbed his hand, shaking it vigorously, "expecting you, Rose. Good to have you with us, old man." Trent looked around at the circle of eager faces and sniffed, "Best disperse your pilots. Fritz still tends to lob across the occasional artillery shell, the cheeky scamp. Wouldn't do for one to land on us whilst your lads are bunched up like this, eh, what? Tiffie squadron in one basket and all that nonsense, hm?"

He watched the pilots hastily disperse, munching, coughing and spluttering, disappointed to see that the old lags and the youngsters coalesced into separate groups. The more experienced tried not to get too close to those less experienced, for the latter were more likely to be the ones to go 'for a burton.'

He could understand, of course, having lost so many dear friends over the last four years. Getting too close would be a torment of sorrow if your best friend ended up in a heap of burning metal on a foreign field. The imminence of death made them protect themselves the best they could, and one of the ways of doing so was to keep the new boys at arm's length.

It was unfair and unkind, but with time and with every sortie endured, the new boys, or at least the survivors, would gradually be accepted and included in the ranks of the 'old lags.'

"Tell your lads not to wander off too far, Rose, will you? There might still be a few Boche holed up nearby, the wily bastards, and not all of the locals are all that pleased to see us, either."

Trent sneezed explosively, a detonation no less thunderous than the Coffman starter cartridge on S-Sugar, and Rose, to his embarrassment, flinched.

"Bless me. The Farmer whose fields we've, er, commandeered is pretty vocal, said he had no problems for four years under les Bosches, and then we fall on his lap and wreck his farm. Doesn't stop him selling us his produce at shocking prices, mind, so he's not doing too badly out of it. If you need anything, ask him. He'll barter all sorts for cigarettes."

Trent thought for a moment, and his eyes met momentarily with Rose's before sliding off into the distance again, "Oh yes! For Christ's sake tell your lads to be careful eating in the orchard, the bees nesting there are voracious. I had to send one of my instrument basher's back to Blighty because the poor chap had been stung on the tongue! Damned nuisance, I can tell you!"

Looks as if it won't just be Jerry we'll be fighting this side of the water!

"I wouldn't wander beyond the perimeter if I were you. Better in than out, as the old lady said as she widdled in the sea." He stopped, confused, "Er, well, she actually said the opposite, didn't she? Anyway, don't go wandering off. There're lots of mines and anti-personnel devices still all over the blessed place, and for goodness's sake don't nip off sight-seeing into Bayeux, the tapestry's not even there at the moment."

The Wing Commander wiped the tip of his nose, "I went for a gander last week, but Boche have whipped the bloody thing off to Paris."

Rose tipped the last drops of his tea into his mouth, and handed back his empty mug, "Thanks, Corporal, much obliged, I needed that." The dust was irritating his eyes and, feeling wetness spill onto his cheeks, he fumbled for his own hanky to wipe his eyes.

Trent nodded, still squinting with suspicion at the shrubbery on the airfield boundary, "Heaven's man! Use your silk scarf to cover your nose and mouth! And do tell your chaps to keep an eye open for anyone skulking in the bushes, I reckon there's an enemy artillery spotter hiding out there."

He wiped his nose once more, eyes watering, "Right then, Rose, old man, let's get your lads settled in, shall we?"

Chapter Twenty-Four

In the initial weeks since D-Day, the Allies pushed outwards from the beaches to surge deeper inland to the south and west, but the hoped-for advances to the east did not materialise.

Their groundcrews were flown in on the 30th of June, and amongst them was Daffie, much to Whip's delight, and Rose's horror.

The latter ordered his C-Flight commander to keep the slobbering brute tied up in his tent during the day, ostensibly to prevent it from wandering off into the dangerous countryside or disrupt B2's flying programme, and to only walk it at night (once Rose had safely retired to his own tent, the ties safely secured against entry by demonic hounds).

The city of Caen, occupied by crack elements of Panzergruppe West in addition to other veteran units, was slated for capture in the first twenty-four hours of the Invasion, but turned out to be a tougher nut to crack than expected.

By the beginning of July, the city was still in German hands, the battered defenders very bloodied indeed, but still unbowed. An important focal point for transport and communications, Caen blocked the way to the easier open country to the south.

Unlike the obstacles of bocage country, this dry, flat landscape offered an ideal route for break-out and spread, as well as opportunities for creating the infrastructure required for support, including new airfields.

The space to the east and south would permit increased immediate air support, as well as easing the endless hustle and bustle of the existing ALGs and allow establishment of zones for marshalling forces and staging areas.

With comparative control of their sector largely established, the Wing settled into a daily routine of chipping away at the frontline to which Caen was an anchor, their main role now one of armed reconnaissance, interdiction and the interception of enemy road transport rushing to replenish and strengthen the occupiers of Caen.

And whereas Caen was a thorn in the side of the landings, the rush of enemy units to strengthen it helped reduce the pressure on the Allies west and south of the landings.

Occasionally 44 Wing would be called to destroy special targets, usually artillery positions set up in the ruins. The aim was to prevent damage to monuments, and a barrage was reasonably indiscriminate.

The emphasis now passed from larger, squadron-sized attacks to those of smaller formations of six or eight aircraft.

A formation of eight aircraft was termed 'fluid finger-fours' by the pilots, a stepped formation above the range of light flak with four aircraft above and preferably up sun of the lower four as cover, whilst a formation of six was stepped in pairs.

The battleground was mapped, organised into an atlas of checkerboard squares to help the pilots easily find the targets they needed to hit, while minimising risk to their own.

A good lookout and top cover were essential, as one squadron found to their cost, losing five Typhoons in a single disastrous ground attack mission.

By the first week of July, though, Caen was still in enemy hands, and in addition to being a thorn in the side and an obstacle which needed clearing, posed a considerable threat of counterattack into the Allied flank, thereby miring the advance.

A fussing Montgomery called for the support of Bomber Command, and in response hundreds of RAF 'heavies' dropped thousands of tonnes of bombs on the northern approaches to the city, churning the area into a vast concrete obstacle course.

Having further pounded the defenders (and those trapped civilians who had been unable to leave), the bombing also added obstructions and created defences for the British and Canadians to surmount, and further hampering the movement of Allied vehicles.

On the 8th of July, Excalibur squadron emerged from the boiling dust cloud of their take-off in support of the Operation Charnwood offensive, their target a unit of Panzers which had slipped back into position after the creeping barrage which had hammered into the villages leading towards the western peripheries of the city.

Even from a distance, Rose could see the billowing clouds of thick black smoke from the tenements on the jumbled outskirts of Caen, numerous thick columns surging up high to stain the sky and add to the drifting banks of smoke partially obscuring the view, testament to the earlier attacks in support of the British and Canadian troops fighting on the ground, myriad flashes of gunfire sparkling beneath the dirty shroud as the business of death continued tirelessly below.

A voice crackling in his earphones, brusque with tension and exhaustion, "Toffee Leader, red smoke coming down now, square ten, section four." Rose heard the accent and wondered where in Canada the officer was from, knowing he must surely miss the crisp, fresh scents of home in this firelit hell.

Using the bend in the Orne as his reference on the map, he pushed

Sugar forward into a dive, her nose pointing roughly midway between the river and the dimly visible x at the crossroads junction of La France. The panzers were lurking in the industrial estate there, the map showing the chimneys of the Cherelle complex as their target.

They spoke little over the R/T, most of their communications done by waggling one's wings or with hand signals, the plan of attack discussed already back at B2, so he just uttered a terse, "Going down now, fuse bombs."

The turbulent heated air clutched at Sugar as she thrust down through it, slipping unevenly across her fuselage and he grabbed at her with his heart in his mouth as she skidded, aware of the thin white blanket masquerading as innocent cloud but formed by the venomous prickling of light flak as he rushed towards it.

She lurched and despite the cool flow of the oxygen his mouth and nose were filled with the odour of smoke and ash, nerves screaming at him to pull away from the dirty explosions as shrapnel plucked at her, the wavering pressure pummelling at her flanks.

His eyes were searching for the streaming colour markers, trying to see past the smoke and the oil and dirt of her windscreen as he peered at the battered landscape below.

There!

Three chimneys, two together and one some distance apart, the twinkling of light arms as the panzer troops sheltering beneath them fired at him, eyes aching and shaken in the mad vibration of Sugar's dive as he kept them wide and focussed on the drab vehicles half hidden beneath the red smoke marking them.

At a thousand feet he released his bombs, even as he felt something punch into her behind his seat, his breathing harsh in his ears as he heard one of his men call out that on the RT to scream that he was hit, then nothing, pulling her back with muscles which felt like lead and kicking the rudder bar to drag her mushy reluctance into a climbing, vision-fading turn, out at full boost as several somethings clattered horribly against her canopy, and he flinched away from it as Sugar thrashed, *oh God, so slowly*, into the climb.

She slithered wildly as he aileroned her away at full boost, the concussion and the tap-tap of the shrapnel making his heart race from the light flak bursts pushing against Sugar, his tongue like a dry potato in his parched mouth, half expecting something to tear through the Perspex and into him, feeling the warm slopping wetness at his crotch.

For an awful moment Rose thought that he might have wet himself with fear, but it was only the sticky pooling of the sweat which rolled down off him to soak his buttocks and groin and thighs, the power of his climb forcing it upwards below his shirt against his back.

At last, he was clear, knowing with bitter anger that his bombs had fallen to one side, missing the angular grey shape entirely, instead ripping into the roof of a nearby warehouse, half-hidden in the noxious mire.

The intense lash of rough air and fragments dropped away to nothing, and Rose hurriedly scanned his instruments, but nothing warned of impending doom. Reassured, he allowed himself to fleetingly touch her photograph, but his eyes were on the dirty sky outside, seeking the tell-tale shapes of enemy fighters but seeing only the swirl of Typhoons milling around, others pulling off the target, the solid wall of smoke lit by explosions from within but hiding the real damage from their eyes and making the airspace one in which the risk of collision was a very real one.

Against the smeared backdrop above the target, he caught sight of the rapidly growing silhouette of Byron's B-Bertie as his wingman closed with him, blemished but whole.

His relief in his own and Byron's survival was tempered as he

212

recalled the panicky voice of one of their own over the target. Who had he lost? And, God help us, had he lost more than one?

Far above, the escorting fighters from Scarlett's C-Flight, catching the light as his scattered Typhoons merged back into formation over the flat patchwork of fields, diverse shades of yellow, green and brown, scattered patches of bright red poppies, so very different from the scarred landscape they had just bombed.

Counting his Typhoons collect and reform, each of them bearing varying levels of damage, Rose saw with leaden heart, that Flight Sergeant Sym's Typhoon was not amongst them.

Flight Sergeant Sym, a pre-war regular, beginning the war as a junior rigger and going on to retrain two years later as aircrew, first on Hurri-bombers and then on Typhoons, earning himself a DFM at the end of his first tour.

Surly with authority, Sym had refused all offers of a commission, content to remain with his friends. He had been one of Excalibur squadron's 'old lags'.

Remembering the braying of Sym's laughter at the morning briefing and enthusiastic reception of their dreadful breakfast, Rose felt that familiar hollow ache inside, and wondered at the absurdity that made men despoil the land over which they fought and died.

There was a chance that his Flight Sergeant might have escaped the maelstrom, please God, and he would save his tears for later.

If he survived.

*

Rose flew once more that day, flying 'clean' as cover escort for other Tiffie bombers.

Sym did not return, having received a direct hit from flak at the very moment he was pulling out, his Tiffie vulnerable as he curved off target. As he greyed or blacked out, he might not even have been aware of the moment of oblivion.

The Allied advance in what was the first part of Operation Charnwood had by that time fought their way as far as the western periphery of the city, but despite the almost continuous air attacks, the German defiance remained dogged.

The advance was slowing and stalling again.

It would not be long before Montgomery would call for the services of RAF Bomber Command again.

Chapter Twenty-Five

B2 Bazenville left memories that would stay with Rose always. It did not enjoy the peaceful quiet of an airfield in Britain, when just the occasional squeak of a tannoy or the running up of an engine would disturb night or day, dependent on its flying schedule and operations.

At B2, no matter the hour, there was no calm.

With aircraft landing and taking off throughout the day, the whine of the Luftwaffe calling only very infrequently in the hours of darkness, and the unbroken rippling thunder of distant artillery, Rose and his people quickly grew accustomed to sleeping whenever opportunity arose, the clatter of repairing, rearming, refuelling and maintaining of aircraft a background sound ignored.

The dour grumble of road transport and the grinding clank and squeal of armour on its way to and from the front along the nearby roads became a constant companion every hour of the day and night, much as the dust coating them and everything else at B2. The banging of their AA with its accompanying showers of hot shell fragments was not to be braved unless absolutely necessary, although the canvas tents provided little protection from the larger pieces.

Even poor Daffie cowered beneath Whip's canvas cot in the slit trench dug inside within his tent when the Bofors guns began to crack out their defence.

With their aircraft in the sandbag revetments of the wheat field north of the runway, they could doze amongst the swaying stalks, and dream of their loved ones. More often than not, their sleep was a brittle one, disturbed by nightmares and memories of the fallen, or the roar of engines.

With swarms of bees nesting in the trees of the peaceful and fragrant orchards, mealtimes could be as hazardous as operations. Being dive-bombed by ravenous insects whilst in the act of eating the latest offerings of the cookhouse was far from restful.

Rose hit upon the idea of attracting the little monsters by opening tins of Lend-Lease English Marmalade scattered around (all the bloody things are good for, he thought smugly), but with little success, for there were just too many of the wee horrors.

Rose's men preferred, whenever possible, to take their meals in their tents or the adjoining fields, and life became one of rest, sleep wherever and whenever possible, meals or flying.

As faces changed with injury or death, the young replacements found themselves kept at arm's length by the survivors who had lost close friends, the latter willing to mentor the youngsters, but unwilling to befriend today and become close to tomorrow's casualty.

Concerned by the rawness of the young replacements being funnelled into these hazardous specialist attacks, and with the heavy losses being experienced by their Typhoon pilots in the ceaseless operations of bridgehead support and ground-attack further afield, the call went out from Group for volunteers from other RAF fighter units.

Unimpressed at the offer, there were very few takers, and so replacements (much to their disgust) had to be drafted in from Spitfire units instead.

Whilst there were few enemy raids on B2 now, the airfield was a dangerous place to be. Twice a Vokes dome was hurled from a misfiring Sabre.

The first time it caught a propeller blade and buried itself into the ground not far from its Tiffie, but the second time, the scorching ejected hemisphere set fire to the canvas of a supply truck and destroyed it completely, much to the quartermaster officer's glee, allowing him to balance his books and write-off some of the items already missing from his shelves. Rose just closed his eyes and thanked God that it had not been an ammunition truck.

A far safer filter, also designed by Vokes, would soon replace these domes.

Benzedrine tablets kept them going, day after day, but the grinding unbroken stress and fatigue of high frequency combat operations was exhausting, whilst the intermittent access to mobile washing facilities meant that within a few days they were a hairy, faded, and unwashed group of men, their clothing a hodgepodge of scruffy uniform and personal items, stained scarves or handkerchiefs caked with dust protecting their mouths and noses.

Whilst the Spitfire's central role was of cover and escort, and the Mustangs ranged further afield seeking to sever the German logistic chain, it was the Typhoons which bore the brunt of frontline ground-attack operations in support of the troops on the ground as the Allies fought to expand the bridgehead.

Slowed reflexes claimed more than one of them, whilst others just disappeared amid the confusion of battle, but Excalibur's losses were relatively low, and despite it all, despite the slow drift from optimism to fatalism, Rose himself continued to survive.

Granny saw everything and, remembering the same grinding conditions of that long-ago Summer of 1940, arranged a rota for his pilots to fly back once a fortnight to RAF Havelock Barr for twenty-four hours, to allow essential servicing of their machines, whilst incidentally providing the men who flew them the pleasure of fresh meals and uninterrupted sleep between clean, crisp sheets.

An afternoon resting with a pint in the flecked shade of a pub garden amidst the peace of the village of Havelock Barr was a precious reminder of home and served to push back the exhaustion of those who survived the flak. Yet the interlude made the return to their dust-blasted corner of France no less difficult.

Thus, refreshed and knowing that they could repeat the trip on a twice monthly basis, they rallied and continued, daily flying three, four or even five short sorties to strafe and bomb the enemy.

On their flights back from Blighty, they would carry fresh bread and supplies to supplement the rations of Bezenville, full beer barrels specially adapted with ingenious modifications to improve aerodynamics slung beneath their wings.

*

Eglise-Saint-Clair was a perfect example of a Norman church built in the twelfth century, incorporating Romanesque, Gothic Primitive and Gothic Flamboyant styles reflecting many modifications over the centuries of its existence.

Located on the north-eastern fringes of Caen, the commanding officer of the Luftwaffe's 16 Field Division chose it as the perfect spot to site an 88mm battery. From this position it would be able to provide Heavy AA cover for the city, anti-tank defence and bombard the Allied forces encircling the northwest and south of the city.

"Flash, we're off to attack a church!" Granny grinned happily at him, fresh-shaven and eyes bright, monstrously cheerful at a time the teenage

Rose would have considered the middle-of-the-bloody-night, nursing a mug of compo tea in one hand and a soggy cigarette in the other.

What? Rose stared at his Wing Commander in surprise, heart fluttering, "Attack a church?" he echoed stupidly.

The odour of cigarettes, food (those blasted sausages!) and unwashed, sweaty bodies was greatly diminished at this early hour with the flap drawn back, and he sucked in the cold blend of tobacco smoke and muddy air into his lungs to help clear away the pervasive fug of sleep from his mind.

He still couldn't decide if a surly airman shaking him awake was an improvement over Edna's maddening warble.

Mati peered at Rose and Granny over the tattered map of Caen in 44 Wing's operations tent, absently sweeping dust and cigarette ash off it with one hand.

"The Canadian 7th Infantry have captured Abbey d'Ardenne at Carpiquet. They found the body of a Sherwood Forester Lieutenant, and Jerry might be holding our boys they've captured in Caen itself."

He looked up at Rose emptily. "The Wing are to strike a unit of heavy artillery dug in around a parish church in the suburbs to the northeast of Caen, in Herouville-en-Vexin. But you'll have to be careful not to strike the building. The Jerries have sited the guns on land between the church and the adjacent ancient cemetery."

The lantern cast a subdued glow across his face, "The Canadians have men unaccounted for. There may be POWs being held inside the church, and to cap it all, the place is a registered historical monument, too. So you must try not to damage it!" He shrugged apologetically and gave Granny an old-fashioned look, wagging a censorious finger, "And really, sir, you mustn't joke about it!"

Granny gave Rose a wink. "Don't get your bloomers bunched, Mati. I was only pulling your leg!"

Mati sniffed in cold disapproval. "You really mustn't, Granny! Command expect the boys to knock out those 88's without damaging the church or either of the two cemeteries. It's a tall order."

His thin face, thinner still with worry for the men he briefed before each sortie, and the anxiety of knowing that if the Germans were able, the Allies might still lose this desperate fight and be thrown off this small sliver of liberated France. "And what are they thinking? The artillery shells going up might blow you boys and the church apart."

"Don't worry your pretty little head over it, my old son." Granny spoke kindly as he scratched an armpit, his battered cap with its tarnished scrambled egg of rank set at a joyfully tipsy angle. He understood the strain Mati felt every time he briefed the pilots, his pinched expression when some did not return, wondering that he might have missed something important that might have saved them. "It'll be just six of us, no rockets or bombs, just in case, only cannon."

In the distance the muted rumble of yet another barrage settling on the stubborn enemy cowering in Caen, prolonged distant thunder foretelling of pain, blood and death.

"We'll barrel in low over the new cemetery from the northwest at low level in pairs, OK?" he picked at the torn corner, and Mati pulled the map away from him, "Will's lad's will be rocketing Panzers at the bend of the Orne, so it'll be Flash, Whip, then me, in that order. Quick in and out. There won't be any smoke shell markers, so give us a set of approach reference points for alignment, would you, Mati?"

He looked at Rose. "Flash, old pants, have a squint at the pics and sort me out a wingman, will you?"

Rose nodded, "OK, Granny," conscious of the sourness of his breath.

'Brat' Morton, Granny's long-time wingman had at long last been made a flight commander in a Spitfire Wing tasked with intercepting flying bombs on the east coast of England. Despite years of experience, and now with two DFCs and a DFM proud on his chest, the cheeky bugger still only looked like a schoolboy.

"Take-off in an hour, soon as it starts to get light." Granny retrieved a shred of tobacco from between his teeth and flicked it irreverently at Rose before hauling himself off the canvas chair, "Right then, you pair of stinkers, I'm orft to rustle us up some sausages for breakfast!"

He looked delighted by the prospect, but Rose felt the bloom of acid in his chest and sighed.

*

After weeks of bombardment, Caen glowed from numerous fires beneath an ever-present hazy pall of smoke, ash and brick dust, and despite the efforts of the night's rain, the air was dirty and spoiled. The sky was stained all along the frontline, but Caen was the piece de resistance of devastation.

Seeing the now familiar sight of the embattled city, Rose thought of the civilians who had not had a chance to flee, and now faced daily the onslaught, cheek-to-jowl with their once-mighty conquerors.

Six hundred years earlier Edward III's army had taken Caen in the first attack and then subjected the populace to days of brutality, horror and death. This time the battle was more protracted, but no less awful.

Perched on his parachute, the sweet flow of oxygen had cleared away the last of the cobwebs as well as the lurking pungency of the sausages from his nasal passages. Unable to eat the hideous things, Rose had appeased the acid with a dry crust of rough bread, washed down with a mouthful of searing compo tea.

With just the merest hint of the day's promise lightening the sky, they had taken off in clean air, the SMT beneath their wheels slick and streaky, the mud mercifully holding within itself the usual cloud of dust.

As they skimmed off the runway, the reassuring *bump* of the undercarriage tucking tidily into her wings, he felt the pleasure of Sugar's raw potency and speed subdue the insidious uneasiness of impending combat.

With the enemy position on the far side of the city, they would dog-leg back, first heading east to Courselles-sur-Mer, then turning onto a heading of one-six-zero to align themselves nicely for the attack.

Less than five minutes since take-off, Rose led them in, Byron on his wing, almost abreast of him, the first of the three pairs in line astern.

The six Typhoons dropped down to zero feet, and Rose stared hard into the soft glow of light on the eastern horizon, trying to make out the square outline of the simple church building against it.

But it was the long line of shadow it cast which caught his eye first, and he waggled his wings once, twice, automatically scanning his instruments and checking the safeties were off, as he had done umpteen times already, looking up to see the thin needles of the guns pointing at the sky to one side of the church, perhaps being readied to fire an artillery barrage into the Allied lines.

They must have been moved in position during the night, and he keyed his microphone, "Guns east of church, attacking," already easing Sugar's nose down and onto the 88 at the far right of the group, closest to the church's eastern bedside façade.

Incredibly, there were no flak bursts around them, no flowing lick of tracer, no muzzle flash from infantry, and he pushed down on the gun-button, the view ahead shuddering with the thumping recoil of his Hispanos, a torrent of shells ripping across the intervening distance.

222

The first flashes and spurts of dust were a little to one side and he adjusted his aim as the gun he had chosen loomed large, the shells streaking in to spark against the mounting and smash the gun to one side, a long tubular shape from its frame spinning lazily through the air, just missing the church's façade, an eruption of dust as a ricochet dug into stone, shells racing past to chop into the cab of a Hanomag SS-100 heavy artillery tractor, and the dim shape rocked as if in a great wind, the cabin exploding in an expanding bubble of glittering fragments of glass and metal, sparkling like fireflies in the boiling air even as Sugar swept over the destruction, the church bell tower with its high, narrow windows a blur which seemed terrifyingly close, close enough to touch.

Thunk! Something heavy punched into Sugar's side, just behind the cockpit, and his insides contracted painfully, but Sugar flew on as if nothing had happened.

Good girl!

They thundered out southeast over the River Orne and on into the countryside, staying low and weaving, Byron falling back to cover him as Rose pulled Sugar around a couple of miles to the east, just in time to see Whip and his wingman sweeping through the thick smoke rising from the battery position, a small explosion flaring fitfully in their wake.

Suddenly Byron cried out, "Bandits! Bandits! Three o'clock high!"

He saw them then, thanking God for the boy's sharp eyes, six dark shadows, lurking almost invisible against the hazy background, four small and stubby FW190As, the others covering them a thousand feet higher and behind, a pair of the sleeker, waspish Bf109s, and his heart tightened as he croaked out, "Whip, break, break! Bandits at your eight o'clock! BREAK!"

Whip broke hard to starboard, wingtips cutting white ribbons into the air, his wingman breaking to port, and the FW190's split apart into two pairs, the first pair racing after Whip, the second turning after his wingman.

But if he went after the 190s, the Bf109s would fall on them like a pack of wolves and tear them to pieces before he got to within effective range of the Focke-Wulfs.

With a dragging heart he pulled back on the stick and eased off the throttle, a gentle nudge on the rudder to converge with the 109s, eyes skittering across the sky for more of them, and knowing that Byron was close behind in support.

Whip cried out, "I'm hit, I'm hit!"

He dared not look as the pale shape of the Bf109 in his sights drew nearer, but he did anyway, just for a second, and saw that a thick ribbon of flame was streaming back from his C-Flight commander's machine, streaming vivid and awful back past its tail, a FW190 close behind, still firing into it.

The first 190 was being trailed by its wingman, which was itself under fire from a Typhoon following *it*.

It was too far to tell, but somehow Rose knew it was Granny.

The leading Bf109 ahead, pale grey with blue stippling on its upper surfaces, suddenly tipped into a turn as he lined up on it, but its number two reacted slower, perhaps only by a second or two, but it was just enough to allow Rose to close and fire as it passed through his gunsight, and as his cannon thumped out 20mm shells the second 109 quivered and shook beneath the onslaught, a bright flash of fire swiftly extinguished and a puff of smoke while it continued after its leader, passing beneath him and he pulled Sugar up over it, correcting as she yawed sickeningly, the blood thumping madly through him.

"Maddie, get after them!" he could not follow for he had seen movement in the corner of his eye higher up, and now he focussed on it, seeing that a further two shapes, possibly more 109s, were coming down.

Blast it!

Breathlessly, "Two more bandits, 109s, angels one descending from the east, turning into them."

Dear God, how many are there? Fear flowered, but he crushed it, swallowing the acid that rose with it.

Granny: *"Got you, you fucker!"*

Rose yanked back on the stick, kicking Sugar into a climbing turn to starboard, pulling her nose into the diving pair of 109s, heart juddering just as his cannon had thumped an instant earlier.

The attack on Eglise Saint-Martin had turned into an ambush, but the enemy dawn patrol had been too late to prevent them from having hopefully destroyed the battery.

Panting like a man many decades older, pressure heavy on his chest and his throat burning. *Mustn't let them get on Maddie's tail...*

The oncoming enemy fighters opened fire as they fell upon him, and he cringed as the lash of pretty but deadly lights tore towards him, but they had fired too soon, and the glowing lines flared past, their trajectory below and to one side.

"Scratch one bandit!" Byron breathless but victorious. At least the boy was having a bit more luck. *But there's another and the 190s, be careful!*

Rose pushed down on the gun button and Sugar's cannons ripped out again, the sound of screaming in his ears and the stench of cordite in his throat as he steadied Sugar. At first, he feared it was Byron, but realised that it was coming from his mouth even as the enemy swelled in the windscreen, and then they were past, his eyes taking in the dirty, oil streaked undersurface of one as it lanced past just over him, the expended casings of its shells a glittering cloud *plinking* like hail against Sugar's fuselage and wings, sparking against her spinning blades.

Sugar lurched and jerked unsteadily through the combined slip-stream of the 109s, and he stall-turned, mouth straining but silent now, muscles aching as she pushed into a turn to starboard, and his eyes flicked to the mirror, but it was empty.

He drew in a mouthful of oxygen. Where are the other 190s? Where are the others? Am I the only one still here?

Mirror? Clear.

A single 109, turning hard, visible now through the top of his canopy, turning in the same direction, light and dark green stripes, yellow spinner. No sign of the other one, keep her turning, stick right back but nose just above the horizon, turning gamely despite the extra armour, hoping Jerry's fuel was of the usual poorer quality so that Sugar might win this circling scrap.

Where's the other one? Collar slick against his neck, acid reaching up into his throat.

Instruments looking good, nothing in the mirror, glance, once twice, over each shoulder, ease back the throttle further and tighten the turn (*don't let her stall!*), one eye on the airspeed, and the green 109 was still there, but he was closer behind now, and the enemy pilot was looking back at him.

Another glance, smoke rising and the bloom of an explosion near the church, and he worried that an ammunition limber might have exploded and damaged the monument, and then he thought how stupid it was to be fretting amidst this whirling dance of death.

A slash of tracer, too far away to worry about, a second enemy fighter, half glimpsed as a fleeting shape swooping down and away as he sucked more oxygen into his aching chest.

The sweat spilled from him and then he caught sight of another Typhoon, a distant cruciform circling his fight, Byron? Might the other enemy fighters have fled the battlefield?

Mirror? Clear. Panting and chest burning as if he had run miles.

They had lost height, the ground turning crazily beneath them, too close for comfort, but the poor bastard ahead filled his gunsight now, and Rose pressed the button once more.

She slowed and he raised her nose a little, *more throttle!*

He feared she might stall and flip into the ground. The recoil had lost him position, but he had hit the enemy in that burst, and a cannon shell had blown a hole in the 109s port stabilizer, and it quivered, shook, and suddenly broke off to flutter down like a fallen leaf.

Got you!

Mirror? Clear.

As the 109 began to pitch forward and pivot the enemy pilot fought to control his machine, trying to pull back and level, even though it would expose him, and lining up for another shot, Rose eased out of the turn after him.

Mirror? Clear.

Losing too much height, the ground's too close, *be careful…*

Pressure once more on the gun button, the 109 wobbling uncertainly and sliding about in his sights as the enemy pilot strove to hold her steady, and he was rewarded with a flurry of short-lived stars sparkling white and rippling briefly across the dark silhouette.

Explosions ripped through it, *flash, flash, flash*, and he must have punctured the fuel tanks as a globe of eye-searing fire engulfed it for an instant, a smoking and broken burning shape emerging an instant later to spiral uncontrollably downwards, shedding incandescent fragments behind it.

They were so low that the 109 augered almost immediately into the ground, disintegrating and scattering burning debris and sparks as it dug a long furrow into the field below.

Mirror? Clear. Full throttle, pull out and check: around, behind and above. Body soaked and aching.

Clear, Byron's B-Bertie closing the gap, two more Tiffies protectively high. Surprisingly far, the church's tiny outline just visible behind the rising columns of smoke which only minutes earlier had been a Nazi battery of 88mm guns.

Lick dry lips, cracked by fear and tension to croak with dread, "Whip?"

But it was Granny who answered him from above. "No."

A single word, but one which doused the growing warmth of success and survival, brutally quenching his relief. *Oh, Whip…*

"Fanny?"

Flying Officer James 'Fanny' Adams DFM, Whip's best friend and wingman, an even-tempered and self-effacing Australian from Perth, another stalwart of 44 Wing.

And again, that single, ghastly word, "No." An empty sigh, "I'm sorry, chum."

Fanny Adams, who had smiled and nodded at Molly's picture, then shown his own. A girl in a summer dress, squinting into the Australian sunlight, hair bleached almost white, a confident, toothy smile and the scrawl, *Darling Jim, I'm counting each second! Your forever girl, Marj x.*

Hopes like a moth in the flame, cheery vigour to flaked ash, and the future lost in a single moment, his memorial the broken heart and bitter tears of a girl bereft beneath an Australian sun.

He felt sick, his restless eyes flicking across the sky, fingers trembling and wanting to scream.

God, why doesn't it get easier? Oh, dear God, why?

They flew back in silence, and whilst they may have destroyed their target, and shot down at least three of the enemy, Rose only felt a crushing sense of failure. Two of his family lost in a few seconds. Not just his men, but his friends, brothers for whom he was responsible. They had both been experienced veterans, decorated and successful, yet impartial death had taken them without consideration.

Yet in the midst of despair, he realised it could so easily have been him, but wasn't. If he had been in the second pair, or if the enemy patrol had arrived scant seconds earlier, it could have been over for Byron and himself instead.

Merciful God, thank you.

He shivered despite the cloying warmth of the cockpit.

Lucky again?

Then why don't I feel it?

Rose felt weak and empty, *Oh Moll. I can't bear it. How much more must we do? If Whip and Fanny can go like that, what chance have I?*

But her image was silent, her lips smiling serenely back at his red and tired eyes, blurred now by sweat and the tears of loss.

A loss that cut no less deep than it had the time before, or the time before that, or the time before that…

*

He jerked awake, a cry on his lips "Whip?", limbs entangled in his twisted and sweat dampened blanket, the image of Whip's blazing Typhoon streaming fire as it fell still caught in his mind's eye.

Again, he felt an unseen presence, but when he sat up to look, he saw the tent was empty save for himself, and he shivered at the sight of his flying kit draped across the chair. It almost looked as if someone was sitting there in the disordered squalor…

He licked his gummed lips to dispel the sourness of fear on them.

Are they here, those I've lost? Angry and bitter to have gone too soon?

As always, Molly's picture was in his hand, and he bought it up to his face, fingertips lightly tracing the dark cascade of her hair, hating each moment of separation.

Oh Moll, so many of my boys are gone, and yet I'm still here. Will I be haunted by them, or will my sleep be forever broken by guilt?

Rose closed his stinging eyes, trying to relax his aching muscles and feeling the tendrils of anxious disquiet and foreboding creep outwards from the recesses of his mind again.

Or will I soon be amongst them? Must I be tormented by the pain of their loss before it's my turn?

Outside the grinding slog of traffic to and from the front continued, but to his question, there was no answer, just the nagging certainty that the end was inevitable, and would be soon.

Chapter Twenty-Six

The following day it rained heavily, and the day's sorties were scrubbed.

The morning brought more bad news. One of the groundcrews had died from a fractured skull during the night in hospital.

Airman Gunn had been a youngster from Bethnal Green and an ardent fan of West Ham United, the winners of the inaugural Football League's War Cup (*'Come on, you Hammers!'*).

A broad smiling face, eyes brimming with mischievousness and a thatch of hair that stubbornly resisted King's Regulations, Gunn had fallen from the wing of a Typhoon as he guided the pilot from dispersals to the runway the previous week.

With uneven ground beneath their wheels, injury was a depressingly common occurrence.

Gunn had wanted to make the RAF his life, asking his CO's advice about the possibility, and Rose promised to write a recommendation for him.

With a heavy heart, Rose sat down to breakfast in the Mess Tent, eyeing the tin plate which was placed in front of him. It did nothing to raise him from the unflinching despondency.

To make his breakfast look more appealing, 'Shiny' Dewar, the

Mess Orderly who was anything but, had decorously arranged the two sausages, placed artfully to hide the burnt bits, on either side of the equally oily and amorphous splodge masquerading as a powdered egg omelette. A bright orange streak of baked beans curved gracelessly beneath it, as if the bloody thing were grinning at him.

To top it all, Shiny had really pushed the boat out and added a pair of biscuits purloined from one of the hundreds of Canadian Infantry Emergency Ration packs delivered accidentally the previous day to Bezenville.

The hard biscuits/crackers had been spread thick with the waxy yellow margarine and root-vegetable derived jam also provided in the packs. If asked, Rose would have chosen marmalade, which really said something about the conserves meant for the Canadian PBI over the sour-sweet lumpy mess that was meant to be either strawberry or raspberry jam.

Rose poked the egg tentatively and it slid slickly across the plate, a sausage hurriedly rolling out of its way.

Putting down his fork and looking to see if there was any fresh bread, he noticed an airman standing hesitantly at the tent's entrance flap.

Raising a hand in acknowledgment, Rose beckoned him in. It was Matthews, a fitter on Excalibur.

"Mr Rose, sir?"

Rose sighed heavily, putting down his fork. "Yes, Matthews?" he tried to smile but decided not to bother. He was the 'Old Man', after all. If he wanted to be a miserable old so-and-so, well, that was his prerogative, wasn't it?

The lad smiled nervously, "Um, I'm to collect the effects for Mr Whipple, sir, but I daren't because his dog's still inside the tent. If I try to take away the stuff while it's there, it might do me a mischief."

Mention of Whip's name kindled his sorrow anew, and then, *Dear*

232

God! Daffie! The poor creature had been tied up all day and night in Whip's tent, and she must be frantic with worry about her owner, "Has no one taken care of it?"

Matthews looked unhappy, "No, sir."

"Well, damn it, Matthews, there is a war on, what the bloody hell d'you expect me to do?" he kept his voice gruff, steepling his eyebrows threateningly.

Please don't ask…just piss off, will you?

"Everyone knows she likes you, sir." Matthews lips twitched hopefully, "I was hoping…"

"I'm at breakfast, man!" he eyed the greasy arrangement on his plate and felt his stomach churn dizzyingly, though whether at the thought of his breakfast or of confronting The Slavering Beast, he couldn't quite tell.

The way he felt, eating what slumped unctuously in the plate before him would be a trial in itself.

On the other hand, however…

Rose took a sip from his mug of tea, grateful that he had already emptied his bladder. Come what may, at least he'd not disgrace himself by wetting himself with fear in front of one of his men.

He sighed again to demonstrate his displeasure and stood. "Alright, then. Come along, Matthews."

Matthews looked mightily relieved, "Yes, sir, thank you, sir."

Contemplating the horror that was his breakfast, Rose picked up his plate, careful to hold it so that the ensemble did not slide straight off its puddle of grease onto the floor, even though that might be the best place for it.

Probably be best to go bearing gifts, in case the damnable thing was hungry, and if it went for him at least he could chuck it at the vicious brute before scarpering sharpish.

He tried to control his breathing, heart fluttering dangerously, watching but not seeing the billowing steam of his breath dissipate in the cold air as Mathews gingerly undid the tent flap ties on Whipple's tent. There seemed to be no sound, the airfield suddenly stilled as if holding its breath for what might come next.

Glad for the comforting weight of his revolver on one hip, Rose cautiously stepped inside, feeling like an idiot, entering the lion's den whilst clutching a plate of greasy food.

Perhaps I could jam the plate in its jaws before it can rip me apart...

No terrifying creature with outstretched claws and teeth launched itself out of the darkness. Instead, the heavy silence was almost mocking, as his head shook from the throb of his racing heart. Matthews cowered behind the flap, face pale.

At first it was so dim that Rose could hardly see a thing. Nothing leapt out at him, so he pushed his way between the tent flaps, heart in his mouth and the plate held out like a sacrificial offering.

You're not responsible for her, whispered the little voice in his mind, *send someone else in to sort her out.*

No, he told himself sternly, Whip was one of my boys, and Daffie was all he had. It's the least I can do to make sure she's taken care of. *I owe him that much, at least.*

Whip had been raised by his grandmother, but she had been killed in a tip-and-run raid a year earlier on Bournemouth, prompting his request for a transfer onto Typhoons.

There was a low moan in the gloom, a forlorn sound, and an echoing groan of fear inadvertently slipped from his lips as he waited for teeth to rend though his flesh. But there was no monster in the darkness, and he licked his lips and squinted into the dim tent.

"Daffie?" he quavered, feeling the weakness in his knees and the cold prickling of sweat on his brow.

The revolver was a comforting weight against his hip but he knew she would tear him limb from limb before he could reach the holster's flap, let alone pull out the weapon, and he gulped a silent prayer.

Dear God, forgive me my wrongs, of which there are many, and protect me from danger with your mercy, which is unbounded...

There was another moan from beneath the cot, a thin whisper of sound, and a shadowed shape unwound itself from the blankets on the floor.

The sound of his gasping breath and the thump of his heart was deafening. Surely the brute must be able to hear his fear?

The sinuous shape padded silently towards him, like a tiger in the night darkness of jungle, but just as he was about to drop the plate and bolt, she lay down at his feet, and with a barely audible whine, laid her head against his foot.

She knows. God help us all, but she knows.

Slightly surprised, and hugely relieved that he was still attached to all the things he had entered the tent with, Rose slowly went down on one knee.

"There, Daffie, there's a good girl." He was still holding the plate, and now he laid it beside her, but she didn't move, and he gingerly placed his hand on her head, half expecting her jaws to clamp down on to it.

But she didn't stir, and he felt the tremor of her muscles as he cupped her warm head in his palm, his fingers taking on a life of their own as he gently grasped one ear and pulled on it.

"Oh, Daffie." He remembered Whip's earnest, honest face, his eyes when he looked at Daffie, and Rose's voice caught as something twisted painfully inside him, "I'm so sorry, I truly am."

She whined again and sat up onto her haunches, the dark pools of her eyes gazing into his, the intelligence and sorrow within them reaching into him.

Rose felt a strange sensation of overwhelming calm settling over him, and to his astonishment he found that his cheeks were wet, and somehow her head was suddenly against him, warm and strong, gently pressing into the yawning hollowness of his chest.

He held her then, fingers buried into her fur as she whimpered and trembled, leaning into and against the wrenching anguish in his heart, his tears soaking into her thick coat.

Outside the tent, Matthews sighed and shook his head, strangely moved by the sight of his sobbing CO clutching the dog as if his life depended on it.

He looked away, feeling his own eyes prickling. *Fuck me, I'm turning into a bint. Better make sure the lads don't see, else they'll never let me forget it...*

Without a word, he turned and left, leaving the two deeply hurt souls to overcome their bitter loss together.

Chapter Twenty-Seven

By the third week of July, with the ground to the north and west of Caen taken and Ardenne Abbey and the badly damaged airfield at Carpiquet useful staging posts now in Allied hands, the city north of the Orne had been captured.

The next step of taking the rest of the city and the ground beyond began.

Operation Goodwood was planned as a series of armour-led attacks to the east and south of Caen, in an attempt to draw out the German reserves and destroy them through costly attrition.

In addition, Operation Atlantic would see them advance beyond the Orne against the enemy positions south of Caen.

After a week of bitter fighting, in which the torrential rainstorm had grounded fighter bombers and turned the battlefield into a muddy hell limiting the movement of friendly armour and motor transport, the Allies finally succeeded in rolling back the Germans out of Caen altogether and up to the ridge extending five miles to the east and almost seven miles southeast of Caen, with the Orne and the Caen-Canal approaches to the city now in friendly hands.

Caen itself was finally taken on the 19th of July, but the city was in ruins, the surviving civilians who had remained despite German instructions to leave finally emerging shell-shocked from the basements and cellars beneath the rubble of their homes.

The Allies had paid for their success with thousands of British and Canadian casualties, and almost five hundred tanks, but they had cleared valuable ground and Caen was theirs at last.

The enemy, reeling from the relentless hammering of aerial and armoured assaults, fell back to regroup behind their defensive lines on the curve of high ground overlooking the plains to the east of Caen.

Thwarting the breakout, the line of fortifications on the ridge of Verrieres (as it was known to the Canadians) remained in the hands of 1st SS Panzer Corps and the Wehrmacht 272nd Infantry Division, despite the incredible bravery and heavy losses shown by the Allies, particularly amongst the men of the 2nd Canadian Infantry Division.

In the Battle of Verrieres Ridge, General Guy Simond's threw his plucky Canadians forward day after day, but the strength and depth of the German positions, strict obedience to tenets, and calculated withdrawals and counterattacks made the task almost impossible.

The Ridge became a nightmare for the troops attacking it, but in so doing, many of the panzer divisions and supplies were being redirected from the American western flank, reducing the pressure on them.

By the 25th of July seven panzer divisions were confronting the British and Canadian forces in the east, whereas to the west the Americans were facing two panzer and one panzer grenadier divisions.

*

Caen had become a landmark for the Allies, the ever-present low shroud of smoke and dust partially hiding the ruins, scattered sparks and cinders glowing dimly where fires still burnt, a grim legacy of the desperate fighting which had all but destroyed the ancient city in its ferocity.

Now it glowered behind them in the morning light as they once again fought to cover the advance of Canadians with achingly familiar unit names such as the Black Watch, part of the Royal Regiment of Canada.

Verrieres Ridge was vicious to the Canadians, but the attack on the 25th of July resulted in the virtual destruction of the Black Watch as a combat effective unit, more than 300 of the 320 soldiers deployed becoming casualties.

Having lost their colonel and one major on their way to their starting positions, it was left to the remaining senior officer, young Major Philip Griffin, to lead the assault in broad daylight in the face of the fearsome defences as if he were fighting on the Western Front.

Griffin would receive a very well-earned Mention in Despatches for his courage, but like many of his men he would not survive. Verrieres Ridge would be a Battle Honour paid for with much blood.

The Black Watch had suffered at Dieppe, too, and they had more anguish yet to endure at the Battle of the Scheidt a few months later in 1944. Despite the repeated feats of gallantry by its men, The Watch were to receive little recognition for their daring and sacrifice, something which their war diary would later lament.

But the Black watch were just one of the many British and Commonwealth units that would finally prise the Germans from their positions after great bloodshed, and it is a bitter truth that bravery goes frequently unrewarded, the legacy to sacrifice often only the memories of those who had cared for them.

*

They circled above the battlefield, ten Typhoons in battle spread at six thousand feet, drab brown puffs of flak doggedly trailing after them as they bobbed and weaved gently, a thicker blanket of lighter flak below, just out of range, but the enemy gunners remained hopeful and continued to fire. The rest of his lads flew above them as cover, Jacko and Sid each leading a section.

At the morning briefing, they had been directed to the 'P' section of their maps, and Mati revealed that their target would be tanks. Thirty or so older MkIV Panzers had been dug into hull-down position in an arc south of Verrieres village.

They were not the first to attack, and the ground beneath them was partially obscured by the miasma of smoke drifting from Caen to join in with the smoke from the burning tanks on the pockmarked ground below, the broken layer of thin cumulus both a friend and adversary.

The tiny figures of the Royal Hamilton Light Infantry were vaguely visible on the ground, and there was no need to wait for mortar rounds to mark their targets for three of the tanks were pumping out smoke and flame in testament to Scarlet's own attack minutes earlier.

Despite the dirty air Rose could see at least four more of the metal monsters as they fired on the approaching Canadians, dark grey rectangles stark and sharp against the patchy mud-brown and green incline.

With the Nazi defenders of the village facing the Canadian assault, there would be fewer barrels pointing up at them as they rolled into the attack.

But the ridge was well defended by a varied assortment of weaponry, he was reminded by that insidious little voice in his mind. With tanks, flak, mortars and even nebelwerfers, there was still enough for everyone.

Granny was leading the attack, and now he steered the first pair down, young Gillespie close in line abreast on his Wing Commander's wing, the drop from six to two thousand feet done in an instant, sweeping through the harvest of deadly white bursts to pull out as their bombs fell away.

The speed of the dive made the images of their bombs appear strangely elongated, and they impacted and erupted together, the ballooning wave of compression hiding the disintegration of a panzer, clearing to reveal the blackened metal box in a scorched hole, thrown askew onto its flank and surrounded by chunks of torn burning metal, a rivulet of blazing fuel flowing like its life-blood down the slope through the bushes towards the ragged line of RHLI, and they parted from its approach.

Suddenly the turret was blown off to one side by a fountain of fire as ammunitions exploded within it. Another tank brewed up, and its surviving crew fled, only to be cut down by a massed burst from the attacking infantry. There would be little quarter given after so much cruel fighting.

Already the second pair's bombs were falling, and with a last glance to the side to check young Byron, yes, fifty feet from his port wing and a thumb poking up to tell him it was time.

A deep lungful of oxygen as the panzer he had picked as his target slipped beneath the wing and he pushed forward hard on Sugar's control column, the thread of fear gone as the flak rose to meet them.

The oblong shape appeared, growing larger in his sights, the intense flak bursts jostling Sugar, a bright stream of tracer passing close beneath, so close that he could have slid down it. He watched the altimeter spin down, something to concentrate on, hunched down against the sudden impact of tracer or flak shell, willing the needle around the gauge as it crawled away the altitude.

Buttocks and stomach muscles clenching tight, scrotum pushing

241

hard up into his groin like a blunt poker, keep the damned sights centred, *bloody hell!* A whimper in the cockpit as a blast close but not close enough pushed Sugar to port, feeling the bite of fragments against her wings and flank, ears ringing at the vicious *crack!*

And – release the lever! Stick hard back, *back,* hard into a stomach rigid as leather, vision greying and world fading as Sugar suddenly leapt up, the lost weight of her bombs releasing her, the funnel of enemy fire slipping off as she soared away.

Dear old Sugar!

The wall of mud and fire which had filled his windscreen now fell away to be replaced by the grimy sky, and with teeth set in a grimace as his senses returned, Rose jinked up and slightly to starboard, her Sabre bellowing angrily at full throttle, thrusting her up into the sanctuary of height and cloud, the force of it pushing him down against the seat, pooled sweat rising against his back and neck, one gloved palm clutching the pocket with the bear and the pebble.

He looked back as they levelled out, Byron's B-Bertie closing again, stained and scarred from the gauntlet they had run, a line of silver flowers stitched across her fuselage, and another thumbs up to reassure his relieved leader all was well, whilst below the khaki figures of the RHLI carefully picked their way past the guttering ruin of the tank they had just bombed, keeping a respectful distance lest the thing's ammo exploded.

Another four columns of billowing smoke marked their success, but it wasn't over yet, and there were still more which needed to be dealt with.

Chapter Twenty-Eight

The second sortie in support of the Canadians was that afternoon, this time Granny flying with Scarlet's 'Rockphoons', and Excalibur provided cover in two stepped formations at seven and ten thousand feet.

The RHLI had finally taken the little village, and British armour was moving up to support their foothold on both flanks. Overall, the situation remained grim as the Ridge remained substantially in German hands, a concerted one-two pincer counterattack from Kurt Meyer's 9th SS Panzer and elements of 5/1 SS Panzer now threatening the RHLI.

From seven thousand feet Rose allowed himself a stolen glance, just once from his endless scan of the sullen clouds and the horizon, to watch the attack unfold.

Beneath them, the handful of tiny metal rhomboids dully catching the sun as they cut sharp tracks through the swaying stalks near the crest of the ridge, Tiger tanks and smaller MkIVs, muzzle blasts ripping out from their guns and flattening stalks, the enemy infantry following just perceptible as grey shadows wending through the undulating crops, almost too small to pick out.

Granny led four Typhoons down simultaneously, line abreast and roughly fifty yards apart in a steep dive screaming towards the enemy-held crest of the ridge, cannon thumping out shells and expertly firing his rockets in rippled pairs.

But he must not watch, for despite the saturation of the Normandy air with Allied fighter-bombers, still the Luftwaffe managed to slip fighters through to strike at them.

Rose was squinting suspiciously at the cloud cloaking the sun as the last rockets were slipping from the rails beneath the wings of the diving Typhoons, the air spotted and speckled by light flak, when suddenly the area behind the rocket-blasted crest of the ridge flared with bright white light.

From amongst the flashing explosions and rapidly expanding pressure waves, fiery trails snapping straight back at them as if in reciprocation, and Rose heard Granny's exclamation of surprise, suddenly cut off.

Knowing he ought not to, but looking anyway, he saw one of the four attacking Typhoons had disappeared, in its place a twisting meteoric ball of fire which smashed straight into the conflagration on the ground, setting off more explosions and flinging fragments far and wide.

Rose felt a cold stab of fear. *Dear God! Please let that not be Granny!*

Of the three remaining Typhoons, one was streaming a long banner of flame, its flight wavering drunkenly as its pilot strove to keep his damaged machine in the air, but he was losing his battle.

The other Typhoons were fleeing for home, and Rose ordered the rest of his escort cover to head back as he lunged down to cover the damaged Typhoon's flight.

The German counterattack had been repulsed, and the Canadians victorious on the northern slope, as numerous fires burned on the ridge crest and reverse slope.

The Typhoons of 44 Wing had assisted in their success, possibly had even been the ones to have won it, but at what cost?

As he drew closer, the destruction and tracer behind them now, he saw that the flames streaming from the wings had burnt off the paintwork, and the aircraft was going down.

Through the smoke he could see the pilot bashing at the canopy, but it wouldn't move. He looked closer, and it was difficult to tell, but with a sick sensation he was certain that it was Granny struggling in the cockpit.

Allied soldiers scattered as they drew closer to the ground, and then the damaged Typhoon hit the ground, skimming upwards into the air again before hitting the ground a second time. As it smashed down again it seemed to come apart, sparks and blobs of burning fuel and wicked fragments shed outwards, until only the front continued, skidding and rolling in the muddy ground before smashing into an outcrop of ground and exploding.

Disbelieving, feeling as if his chest were being crushed, Rose circled the deep furrow in the ground, the back half of the Typhoon forlorn at the point of impact at the edge of a ditch, the canopy still incredibly unbroken glinting close to it, wings and smaller unrecognisable shreds of burning metal scattered along the scarred earth.

A welling void of blackness threatened to engulf him, and he bit down on the scream of anguish that was swelling against his windpipe, biting his tongue at the same time.

The sudden pain swamped his senses, and he swallowed his unborn thin cry of despair, felt the tears pouring from his eyes. He had to get back, see to his men, see who they had lost.

He laid a shaking palm on her photograph, but there was no comfort.

Might it be one of the others?

Please God, let it be one of the others.

He felt deep shame for even thinking it, but nonetheless continued to pray for it to be so as he flew back to B2, muscles stiff with the shock, the gaping emptiness of his chest threatening its collapse.

Granny was not amongst the pair who had returned. The young sergeant pilot looked pale and strained, the trail of smoke from his cigarette wavering in reaction, whilst Red Douglas, his new C-Flight Commander after having stepped into Whip's shoes, could not meet Rose's eyes.

Flying Officer Guy Montalmond, a member of his 'chorus line' quartet was one of the missing pilots.

Montalmond had fought with the Belgian and French air forces as a bomber pilot during the Blitzkrieg, before being welcomed into the RAF as France was overrun, switching from bombers to fighters.

The suave young man from Mechelen with the slickest curled waxed moustache Rose had ever seen, deepset dark eyes which excited great interest at dances (although rumours were of a wife waiting for him in Brussels), and a chest resplendent with the ribbons of the French and Belgian Croix de Guerre, veritably studded with glittering stars and palms, his DFC, DFM and bar almost dowdy by comparison.

The other missing pilot was Granny.

Rose offered what he hoped looked like a reassuring smile to the shaking boy, but his face hurt as he pulled back his lips, his mind whirling with despair, sudden weakness in his knees threatening to give way.

Suddenly Mati was there, surprisingly strong hands dragging him into the deserted Intelligence Tent, pushing the unresisting Rose into a canvas deck chair.

Rose stared at him with brimming eyes, his mouth working as he tried but failed to speak. Mati breathed out and leaned back against the Maps Table, dry rubbing his hands together. "I know, Flash."

He felt he was falling, the sudden sense of vertigo making him close his eyes and lean back against the chair, his bitten tongue throbbing, the howls of despairing emptiness in his chest stopped by a throat constricted with pain.

I can't bear it! I can't! he could feel his sanity slipping as waves of utter misery washed over him, *Dear God, I think I'm going to go mad! I must get back to my tent. I need Daffie. I need her support.*

He tried to speak, but knew if he did he would begin to weep inconsolably, and he dare not cry in front of his friends. An airman sauntered in but fled at Mati's expression.

Mati patted his gloved hand kindly, eyes bleak, "Let me get you a cuppa, Flash. It'll help."

Help? *Help?* How the bloody hell could tea help?

Granny was *dead*, couldn't Mati understand what that meant?

Granny. Was. Dead.

Oh, merciful God, Granny was dead!

How could this be? Granny couldn't die, he was forever.

But he wasn't.

He wanted to shake Mati, make him understand that he needed to get back to the gentle creature with whom he could entrust his grief. She alone in Normandy could help. A mug of bloody Compo tea could not help in the slightest.

He felt his throat tightening wretchedly, felt the shudder of sobs building, and covered his mouth with a shaking hand, pushing against his lips as if that might stop the cries that bubbled and pushed to escape.

Suddenly the telephone jangled. They stared at it, before Mati shook himself and grabbed the receiver, worried eyes fixed on Rose's pinched, stricken face.

"Intelligence Officer? Call from the Canadian CP? Yes, alright, put it through." He listened for a moment, an expression of bewilderment on his thin face, and then incredibly a wide smile spread across it. "Oh, I say! It's you!"

Rose felt like wringing his neck or slapping him. What was wrong with the idiot? How could he smile at a time like this? He looked at Mati and felt the burn of hate.

"The CO of Excalibur squadron? Certainly, sir." Mati leaned forwards with twinkling eyes and held out the receiver. "Flash, it's for you."

Rose felt that should his lips part, the wailing would escape them. Who could it be? Might it be the Colonel of the RHLI, wanting to thank them for their support? Head spinning, he grasped it, wondering how on earth he would be able to speak to whoever was on the other end.

He swallowed, breathing into the receiver, and a voice crackled in his ear, one he had heard so many times before. "Flash? Is that you, silly drawers?"

And Rose fainted dead away.

*

"It was a perfect approach, ripple-firing rockets into the Hun, but as soon as I was close enough to the bastards on the crest, they fired the fucking things at us, and I thought we were goners, pissed myself good and proper, and I don't say that very often."

The 'fucking things' were Nebelwerfers, otherwise known as 'Moaning Minnies' because of the haunting sound of their flight, a cloud of them shooting out from ten tubes mounted on a Sd. Kfz. 4 half-track chassis in the face of Granny's attack.

Only one had hit, blasting poor Montalmond apart instantly, fragments spraying P-Popsie and mortally damaging her. Red and the youngster had been lucky to escape unscathed.

"It was like a fireworks display, flame bursting out all over the bloody place and this barrage of rockets were shooting up towards me like the hounds of hell! So I pissed off sharpish, toot-sweet!" Granny let out a shuddering breath theatrically, wiping his face as if it might erase the memory of the rockets leaping out at him, sitting on his left buttock to keep the pressure off his injuries, "Still can't believe that I wasn't hit by one!"

He let out a heartfelt sigh, "My bum cheeks clamped down together so flaming hard that I thought I was going to get sucked up my own arse!"

Rose laughed, relief still flooding through him, but the thought of being on the receiving end of a volley of rockets was terrifying.

Smith had been incredibly fortunate. (*Thank you, God!*)

When P-Popsie hit the ground a second time, she broke apart under the force of the impact, and still struggling with a stuck canopy and trying to bang on his harness release, Granny found himself still attached to the rear end of the fuselage, a shallow ditch having caught Granny's P-Popsie a blow on her radiator and breaking her apart.

The jarring force cracked Popsie's mainspar instantly, the rear of her fuselage (with Granny and seat still attached), caught against the raised edge of the ditch, her wings folding forward, detaching and fragmenting, whilst the still-burning front end of P-Popsie spun and rolled and bounced onwards to explode against the outcropping.

As Popsie broke apart the force ripped Granny's harness and he was thrown from her, flung face-first into the ditch, its glutinous mud cushioning his fall and the sides of the ditch saving him from the force of the Sabre's explosion. It did not save him however from the metal fragments that buried themselves into his right calf and buttock.

Rescued from drowning in the ditch by grateful soldiers from the RHLI, the fragments of P-Popsie were extricated from the muddied and bloodied hero by a weary young Canadian MO, and with his wounds dressed and the taste of mud washed away with Seagram's Whisky from the RHLI Colonel's own special hoard, Granny was collected by Trent.

But Granny's tenure as 44's Wing Leader was over.

By happenstance, AVM Harry 'Broady' Broadhurst, the commander of 83 Group was touring his Normandy squadrons, arriving unannounced at Bezenville in his personal Spitfire XIV an hour and a half after Granny's triumphant return.

Seeing Granny's injuries and Rose's pinched and tortured face, Broadhurst ordered Granny straight onto the next casualty evacuation flight back to the UK (at gunpoint if necessary) making Scarlet 44's acting Wing Commander until a new one could be appointed, whilst Red Douglas would be acting CO for Orna Squadron.

The bluff AVM momentarily considered sending Rose back on the same flight but dismissed the idea with regret.

There was a war on, and he needed as many of his brave boys in Normandy as possible, particularly his veterans.

The future was at stake.

Chapter Twenty-Nine

With the British and Canadians maintaining a relentless pressure on the Germans, and with the diversion of most of the supplies and reinforcements to the eastern flank, conditions were perfect for the US forces to break out from their front.

As the British and Canadians faced the ferocity of the formidable German defences on the Verrieres Ridge with incredible bravery, the US First Army finally broke through beyond St Lo in Operation Cobra, taking the Cotentin peninsula, with the US Third Army taking Brittany and spreading practically unchallenged south and west over the following week.

Bravery and sacrifice concentrated the enemy's attention and resources to the east, saving the lives of many thousands of Americans during Cobra.

But despite the bitter fighting and the heavy casualties of Operations Charnwood, Goodwood, Atlantic and Spring, the Allies prepared to strike yet again.

In the lull before the next attack, with the Germans desperately rerouting troops and supplies (too little, too late) towards the American breakout, Rose prepared his replacements as best he could, praying they might survive the drive onwards.

Flying a Typhoon requires immense energy and stamina, the relentless airframe vibration and deafening Sabre physically gruelling for young men and their slightly older leaders. In combat, even more is needed to include tactical thinking and a high level of constant awareness, maintaining a focus and clarity of thought which becomes more difficult as commitments and the tempo of sorties increase.

Alighting and departing amidst obscuring dust clouds, with the inherent accidents and crashes more likely through exhaustion, their nerves were further eroded knowing the probability of unpleasant death whilst mourning the loss of friends.

With building fatigue comes a blunting of ability, and Rose and his men found that with the attrition of the reflexive edge, flying and formation-keeping increasingly careless, landings rougher (adding further to the risk of a calamitous tyre puncture at an undesirable moment), and tired minds straining for the enemy, whether on the ground or lurking in cloud.

And on top of it all, the effects of so much time spent breathing pure oxygen burning their lungs, combined with erratic and broken sleep, a poor diet and excessive smoking amongst many creating nausea, bouts of faintness, and chest pains as their tortured bodies rebelled.

Yet still they continued to climb into their machines every day as often as needed to maintain support for the men on the ground, for whom the war was no less of a trial.

*

On the night of 7-8 August, Operation Totalize was heralded by the surging throb of over a thousand Lancaster and Halifax bombers

252

as aerial bombardment initiated the Allies latest attempts to punch their way out of Normandy.

This time around, it would be the 1st Canadian Army including British, Polish and others, which would be the ones to face the defiant German defences. With the US Armies spilling south and east, the initial plan for the southern thrust was to split apart, down to Paris and up to the Seine.

Hitler's frenzied directive to attack in the west at Mortain rather than allow a calculated fighting retreat committed the enemy to push west even as the Americans thrust southeast. Ultra would reveal the enemy aim to cut off American thrust into two, and the German push collapsed, in no small part because of 84 Group's Typhoons which had been tasked with dealing with the enemy armour.

Realizing that they might encircle and trap a major part of the German Army in France if they acted soon enough, Eisenhower and his commanders decided to link up east of Falaise instead.

The RAF heavy bombers dropped their loads on the flanks of the planned route of advance, pulverising the threats from the sides before the Allied ground forces rolled forward, a massive artillery barrage rolling ahead as eight columns of armour advanced behind it, the latter closely followed by infantry now mechanised and mounted in Kangaroo personnel carriers converted from self-propelled guns.

Additional artillery and smoke supported their flanks as they crunched into the punch-drunk German defenders, their paths of advance lit by flares guided by searchlights, Bofors guns and radio beams.

For the enemy it must have seemed like the Nine Circles of the Inferno had erupted over them.

With little danger from the flanking edges of the advance, and their infantry now mechanised, the pace was initially swift, but slowed and stalled as they met enemy units which had been kept further back in reserve.

Heavy flak and a tragic misunderstanding also resulted in USAAF bombers bombing the Canadians and the Poles, killing hundreds of Allied troops. Nonetheless, by the end of the operation the Allies had decisively breached the deeply emplaced defences of the German lines south of Caen and were halfway to Falaise.

Throughout the operation the fighter bombers of 83 Group bombed and rocketed the enemy positions beyond the once impenetrable Ridge, the Typhoon pilots pounding the dazed Waffen-SS survivors of the bombing unforgivingly, again and again, pushing them back.

The call came to 44 Wing to cover the withdrawal of the British Columbia Regiment and the Algonquin Regiment. Sent to take the high terrain near Quesnay woods, the Canadians found themselves in the wrong place and coming under heavy fire from retreating Tigers and Mk IVs of the 12th SS Panzer Division.

But the lost Regiments which comprised Worthington Force were mistakenly on Hill 111, and when 44 Wing came to their rescue, they arrived instead at the real Hill 195 and found no sign of the troops they were to support.

Mati had spoken of panzers and anti-tank emplacements hidden in the woods near the highest ground in the area, so Rose led two flights of Excalibur in to attack. With little indication where the enemy formations were beneath the thick foliage, Rose detailed his men to bomb the thicker clumps of trees in the hopes that the enemy was hiding beneath.

No signs of drifting marker smoke, no signs of friendly tank columns, and his stomach burned with acid as he anxiously prayed that the troops they had been sent to support were not being held as prisoners beneath that luscious green canopy.

In pairs the Typhoons dived to drop their bombs, pulling out and climbing to port from the cauldron of fire to avoid rising terrain, battered but whole, jinking and weaving away for sanctuary.

Incredibly, despite the intense layers of flak, they dropped their bombs without losing anyone, although Jacko lost part of one aileron and flew back to B2 with one wing lower than the other, the remainder of his flight bearing battle damage in varying degrees.

Excalibur's bombs had blasted leaves and branches and dirt into the air, the racing shockwaves causing the foliage to ripple out in ragged expanding circles, the bright flash of their explosions flaring within, blasting debris into the air as trees were uprooted, but the brown haze of dirt vented by the explosions made them difficult to identify.

An orange flash, and fuel-fed smoke began to gush thickly from beneath the canopy, black and stark against the verdant richness appearing to indicate that they must have hit at least one panzer, but everything else was still hidden beneath the awning of leaves, albeit frayed by their bombs.

With that much AA, there must have been something important, surely?

They had survived, but the apparent paucity of the results made his heart settle emptily in his chest.

Merciful God, thank you for your mercy in bringing us through that storm of fire safely. But despite their salvation, he could feel nothing but emptiness, and this time the magic of her image could not dispel his gloom.

His mouth tasted of metal and his swallow was painful as tired eyes blinked away the slick grease of sweat to search the clouds for danger.

Oh Lord my God, how I wish for the embrace of my darling Molly's arms, her warm fragrance filling me so that I might close my eyes and just sleep…

He felt guilty for his thoughts, grateful for the solace of Daffie's

255

company (*forgive my ingratitude for the gentle creature's understanding and empathy*), no longer awakened by the disturbing sense of a brooding and unseen presence in his tent, but nothing could replace the blessed haven that was Molly.

Jimmy cast a reproachful glance at Rose when they had landed once more, and this time it was his special '*Bloody Hell! What have you done to her now?*' look.

It was a look Rose was seeing more and more often. "'Strewth! Can't you take Sugar somewhere she's less likely to get a pasting, sir?" The fitter shook his head and stroked her patched fuselage possessively, but his relief in Rose's safe return was palpable, the dust-scoured face thin and pallid with the pressure of those who kept the battered Typhoons flying hour after tiring hour, the demands of Invasion no kinder to the groundcrews.

He had seen too many of his friends gathering forlornly at an empty dispersals bay after a sortie which had claimed one of their own, and he dreaded each sortie.

*

The only Typhoons to find the embattled Canadians on Hill 111 thought them German and strafed them instead of the 12th SS, before realising their mistake and fleeing into the anonymity of cloud without thinking to reveal the location of the battle.

Without support, the troops grimly continued their lonely fight, waiting for the light to fade.

Under cover of night, those still able finally escaped the killing field, leaving behind their dead and seriously wounded.

Chapter Thirty

With the failure of Operation Luttich, the German armoured push to the west against the American breakout, the enemy began to fall back, and Montgomery initiated Operation Tractable.

Unlike the massed columns of Totalise, Tractable was a thrust of only two armoured columns, 2nd Armoured Division and 4th Armoured Brigade, smashing a path east of Falaise towards Trun, with 3rd Infantry Brigade's mechanised infantry again following close behind the tanks to mop up the dazed defenders.

This time it was the RAF who erred catastrophically, the bombers sent to attack Quesnay Woods in support also mistakenly bombing Polish and Canadian troops, just as the USAAF had done during Totalise.

Totalise and Tractable were cruel to Excalibur. Day after day, one mission followed another as the Allies delivered a succession of blows against the German defences, knocking them back. The names of their targets just so many names, merging together, indistinct and half-forgotten in his exhausted mind.

Save, of course, for those in which Excalibur suffered its losses. The names of those places and the names of his precious dead would remain forever stamped into his mind, entwined together for eternity.

Rocquancourt: 'Pops' Graham, a pre-war Regular and at thirty-four the eldest of his pilots, decent and patient, the man to which Excalibur's youngsters had turned if in trouble.

Le Castelet: Peter Thomas, one of the two survivors of his quartet, the ex-Guardsman who marched everywhere as if he was still on Horse Guards Parade, always fragrant and smooth-shaven with that absurd monocle, despite the grubbiest of conditions.

Saint-Sylvain: Percy 'Cock' Foster the gloomy, raw-boned Tynesider who drank like a fish and managed to find the worst in every situation, never the same since quiet Willie's death.

La Ruette: Herrick, lost on his first sortie, his unopened bags returning the very same day on the evening flight back to Blighty.

Urville: Gerry Andrews, the last of his 'chorus line' quartet, the handsomest man on the squadron, reputed to have slept with a bevy of Hollywood starlets one night when a guest at one of their USO parties.

Saint Germain le-Vassy: Alexander Leslie of Trinidad, soft voiced and always wearing a smile, a talented pianist and poet.

Potigny: Alan Winters, he of the fearsome Ginger beard and the booming and baffling cry, *"Drop your bloomers, the Navy's here!"*, disappeared without a trace in cloud on the way to the target.

Ussy: Farley and Dobbs, replacements who collided over the target, bombarding it with torn and flaming pieces of man and machine.

I shan't ever forget you, I won't, Rose silently promised them as he shivered at the memories of his dead. At least the wounded were able to escape this torment, though their minds might not.

Will those yet unborn, he wondered, the recipients of the peace who will only know a time of reconciliation free of fear and pain, think of these men-boys who died before they had even learned what it was to live? Will the yet unborn remember, let alone be grateful for the supreme sacrifice made for them?

The thought they might not was too awful to contemplate.

Daffie raised her head from beside his flying boots and looked at him, sensing his despondency.

I'll never return to these places in peacetime, for their names will always be excruciatingly painful reminders of those I lost on the drive to Falaise.

If you survive to see peacetime, that is, the snide little voice in his mind reminded him.

Rose drew Daffie into his arms as she slobbered at his face, the grey misery draining into the warmth and vitality of her, clutching thick handfuls of her coat to still the trembling in his fingers.

Well then, he told himself briskly, *If I don't make it, then it won't matter a jot, will it?*

His eyes drifted to the picture frame on his cluttered desk, and he knew that of course it would.

*

The Civil War Union General Sherman, after whom many hundreds of tanks fighting in Normandy were named once said of war, "It is all hell."

The later quotation 'War is hell" was derived from these words, and all those who have served and known the closeness of death first-hand on the battlefield are witness to this truth.

It is one thing to destroy objects, inanimate beings, the mind focussing on an enemy aircraft, ship or fighting vehicle, perhaps a building like an aircraft hangar or a blocky radar installation, but it is quite another to see your shells and bombs tearing into a living breathing creature and shredding it apart.

Racing across a landscape at low level, the terrain streaming past at high speed, eyes flicking from ground to sky, searching for the enemy fighters lurking for the perfect bounce, or the tell-tale structures that warned of telephone or electricity cables ready to claw them down.

A mile to the west of La Boissiere, Rose's thumb pushed down even as his eyes were registering the men in field grey jumping to their feet and scattering from the onrushing fighter-bombers now descending on them.

The infantry column was settled beside the road that led from Caen to Lisieux when the Typhoons slid into line abreast and fell upon them, their transport parked on one side beneath trees.

As his shells bit into and across the tarmacked edge, exploding on the grass, Rose toed the rudder pedal, spraying a snaking swathe of flying metal at the mass of men, almost feeling the shock as they were torn apart beneath the onslaught, smoke and dirt and tufts of grass a greenish-brown haze rising before him, spawning groups of men running to either side of it, feeling that guilty exhilaration as others were thrown back and bowled over and torn apart beneath the explosive impacts.

Few of the fleeing men in grey even thought to return fire at the swooping, thundering gull-winged birds of prey, their senses overwhelmed and the desire to escape swamping all else as the terrifying bellow of Sabres and the thump of Hispanos deafened them, the pressure waves of cannon shells and aircraft beating at their bodies and wits.

As he fought the ground effect, pushing Sugar's nose down against it to keep her cannon pointing into the clumps of infantry, his shells smashed against a truck, and it detonated in a blurry orange flash framed by a ballooning cloud of white, making him yank back on the stick.

His chest was painfully tight as Sugar bumped against the wave of pressure, Sabre at full boost to fight her way through the tormented air, just conscious of a white flapping shape (a seagull?) hurtling past Sugar's wingtip to starboard, and he felt relief that he had not hit it, and regret that an innocent bird had been caught in his spray of shells.

Rose felt the first tendrils of blackness twitch against the peripheries of his vision, but then she was back into smoother air, and he soothed Sugar down from the climb, the road ahead of him empty and the enemy behind, the excited chatter of his men on his earphones.

He pulled her to port between the slopes on either side, eyes keen against the crests and clouds for the airborne enemy, but the sky was empty save for Red Douglas's flight above.

A string of dots appeared, closing up behind in his mirror as the other Typhoons swarmed after him, the destruction wrought by them now hidden by the high ground.

Later, as they noisily gathered around Mati with their mugs of dusty tea, 'Basher' Beaty from B-Flight called out, "Did you see the Hun Bun wagon go up? Blew the cook right up into the air in front of us, thought he was going to hit the CO!"

Rose thought back to the flapping white shape he had mistaken for a seagull soaring, surprised that, unlike the regret he had felt for what he thought was a dead bird, he felt nothing for the dead man.

Cook or infantryman, the wretched man had been a soldier first and foremost, a part of the thing that was guilty of destroying so many lives and spreading so much poison in the world.

Yet there were innocents amongst the enemy, too. And while he did not consider the men and women of the Reich's armed forces innocents, there were the decent as well as the evil, whilst amongst the German civilians there would be those who were truly blameless and helpless.

But there were also the innocents in servitude of the enemy who also suffered.

Rose and his men slaughtered some of the blameless in service on a day that would create within him the deepest feeling of self-loathing, memories of a handful of minutes never forgotten, never forgiven.

Yet he would repeat his actions when called upon to do so again.

They were directed to a point midway along the road from Rouvres to Sassy, hunting a reported column of artillery pieces. The Germans had always been heavily reliant on horse-drawn transport, and at this stage of the war, fighting on so many fronts, this was very much the case for many of the infantry and artillery supply trains.

Tilting Sugar over into a screaming dive, his nerves curling in horror at the sight of the beautiful animals running in terror, coats glistening in stampede as they towed clouds of dust behind the big guns to which they were harnessed.

But Rose knew that there was no choice and that he must lead by example, that refusing would allow others to hold back. If they did not destroy the enemy artillery now, it would be used to destroy their own later.

He had seen many awful things in this war, but still he felt the sick self-revulsion as his bombs ripped through the bodies of the innocents in servitude below, the cannon shells transforming the smooth harmony of teams of horses into a rolling mass of torn flesh, shattered bone and blood.

The big guns being pulled behind finished off the job, each catching up with and rolling over its team as they collapsed, a cruel slaughter that those who lived beyond the war and into the peace would never be able to forgive themselves for, one which would haunt the more sensitive throughout their lives.

And this would not be the last time they would destroy German horse-drawn vehicles.

Afterwards, he bawled out young Owen, the Welsh farmer's son, for refusing to drop his bombs or strafe the enemy and its blameless slaves.

The self-loathing and anger with his orchestrated massacre made him shout harder and his words sharper, wishing that he could have done the same as the boy, but knowing that there could be no mercy until this madness was done.

And God help him, he found to his shame that haranguing the boy eased his anger and shame.

How different the stained and dusty Harry of today was to the fresh-faced youngster he had been in 1940! Four years of war and a soul scorched ragged by fear, strain, and the losses of too many friends.

Rose cared not at all for the enemy dead, even though the true blame lay with their leaders. They had shown little kindness and compassion but much cruelty for the peoples of the nations they had stamped across, occupied and enslaved.

Sow the wind and reap the whirlwind.

After the victory there might come a time for mercy and forgiveness, when those who had not known almost constant fear nor personal loss might forget the years of suffering and look back in kindly benevolence, when a period of peace soothed away the hatred and the anger, dulling the memories of sacrifice.

But until the peace, there would only be war.

And the odds were that fate would not be merciful to him, for now Rose was certain that he would not know the final victory. All he could do was ensure that he gave all that he had to win that success.

For a peace and safety enduring. For the citizens of the time to come after this hateful war.

For his little boy, his darling child. For Daniel.

And for the love of his life and the only source of true happiness that there could be for him in this world. For the keeper and custodian of his heart.

For Molly.

Chapter Thirty-One

With the Allies hammering again and again against the Normandy lines of defence, battering the enemy southwards to Falaise and Trun, concentrating much of the German armour and supplies, the sweeping thrust of the Patton's Third Army curved up to meet their Commonwealth Allies.

The senior officers of the German 7th Army and the 5th Panzer Army, bound by a madman's orders, saw they would be enveloped, and hastily made plans for withdrawal, praying that it was not too late.

But of course, it was.

*

"Cab Rank control from Toffee Leader, eight at four." Eight Typhoons at 4000 feet.

"Thank you, Toffee, armour and transport in F6, edge of the wood at the crossroads, light flak half a mile south."

"Obliged, Cab Rank." Eyes slide from the bright sky to the gauges and then on to her picture. *Wish I was with you, my love...*

"Toffee Leader to Flight, orbit starboard, Blue fuse bombs, Red ready rockets." *Try saying that after a few pints...*

Check the map strapped to his leg and peer out through the oil-stained Perspex.

Um...oh, there they are, a clump of dirty grey-green vehicles, a dozen or so, keep turning Sugar to starboard and check the bombs are ready to drop, make sure we've got the sun shining behind us to bugger up their aim...

The flak is silent, wary of drawing our attention, but it'll open up as soon as we begin the attack. *OK, then, best let the rocket boys sort out the armour...*

"Toffee Blue, sort out the panzers. Toffee Red, we're for the flak."

Just enough time for a quick prayer and a last gulp of oxygen, a last glance at her picture because it might truly be the last time, "Going down."

As the Typhoons tipped after Rose, the enemy gun position opened fire, and whilst the streams of tracer were terrifying up close, the aim was off and the firing wild, and he knew that there was little danger of being hit as he pushed down the gun button in response.

The deadly flicker of the 20mm quadruple mount was in his gunsight, and he adjusted to allow the shells to dance across and into its platform vehicle.

Another flicker of light showed that there was a second gun, and like the first it was dug in and artfully concealed beneath a camouflage net heaped with branches and leaves.

Flashes rippled unevenly over the target and surrounding ground as he held her steady, and he could only imagine the damage his cannon shells were doing as he released his bombs into the expanding cloud of smoke obscuring the enemy position.

She seemed to lift and wallow with a whiplash of tracer slashing in a glittering arc horribly close to his port wingtip, and he pushed her back up into full boost, easing his thumb from the gun button, wondering if his aim was good, the sky fading at the peripheries and the line of flak suddenly gone.

Higher up he turned hard to starboard, young Byron faithfully on his wing, watching the other two Typhoons of his section pulling through thickening smoke, his eyes straining for the fleeting shadows of bandits in the haze, but the Luftwaffe was elsewhere, and the stained sky still clear.

There was no more flak and he allowed himself thanks, the words tired, *Thank you, merciful God...*

Something was burning on the ground, and he saw the bombs of his second pair explode, *flash-flash-flash-flash,* pressure rippling out to shatter half-seen vehicles through the smoke.

To the north the others were slaughtering the enemy, straight trails of grey smoke needling from their wings and intersecting with the ground in violent eruptions, and Rose caught sight of a dull metal shape, a Panzer V Panther, flung up and away from a blast like a child's toy, shedding fragmented tracks, pirouetting almost delicately, the turret spinning from it as it slammed into the ground again.

Molly adored ballet, Rose dozing his way through three of the Sadler's Well Ballet Company's acclaimed performances. The sight of the smashed panzer twirling gracefully through the air reminded him strangely of the delicate and elegant brilliance of Moira Shearer in *Coppelia.*

He sighed then shook his head. *Stop thinking of women, you dirty dog,* he admonished himself sternly, *you're on a bloody battlefield.* He felt her eyes on him reached out his fingertips to lightly stroke the picture, avoiding her gaze and studiously keeping his eyes on the sky around them, *I hadn't been leering at Moira, Moll, honest.*

He thought of how Charlie's body felt against his and sighed again.

Another dark shape, low down and further away, heaved a long streamer of vivid fire straight up into the sky an instant before being shattered by a devastating explosion from within.

The clump of vehicles had become a line of blackened and twisted shapes, burning brightly, lit by the pyrotechnic display of their own exploding munitions and spewing oily black smoke into the sky.

Of the flak position they had bombed, nothing remained but ash and charred fragments.

With an enemy in full retreat, 44 Wing and 2TAF continued to push them back, foot by hard-fought foot.

In the second week of August, the Wing destroyed scores of panzers, artillery and motor transport, columns of smoke winding upwards on the road to Falaise from Dozule, Livarot, Bernay and Aily.

The third week of August began in support of Red Douglas' boys as they rocketed SS Tigers hidden in woods to the west of Trun, Excalibur flying 'clean' as escort. For a tense thirty seconds they tracked a quartet of Focke-Wulfs, but the distant barbs of the enemy turned away as soon as Sid's A' Flight curved after them.

The Germans had transferred so many fighters to the defence of the Reich and the raging conflagration in the east that what was left to protect their ground forces was sorely lacking. But they were not a spent force by any means, and led by veterans, they picked their fights. The Allies might control the air, but they needed to fight to hold it.

It was the third week of August in which the German Army was almost encircled by the Allies with the frontal flank units sacrificing themselves east of the pocket, dying to keep the Allies from fully encircling them, dying to keep the route of escape open for the desperate retreat of the fleeing army, once proud formations now fragmented and riven from the air and from the ground.

For Rose and his men, it was a time of maximum effort, life a confusion of flying, eating, and sleeping, occasionally scribbling a few words on a piece of paper for loved ones, some memories standing out from the jumble.

Memories. Awakening before dawn to the usual sound of preparations and the grind of reinforcements on the roads, the warmth of Daffie's presence and the taste of the day's first mug of tea, a quick sponge wash with icy water, the pervasive dust on its surface scraping at his skin, before climbing into his grubby battledress, checking the daily orders and intelligence before briefing the boys on the dawn strike, watching Mati chalk up the names and wondering apprehensively which of them might not come back. Then breakfast (if he was not on the dawn strike) and the simple pleasure when Shiny would lay a plate of fresh bread or fried eggs before him, knowing guiltily that poor Daffie was waiting for his return with those bloody awful burnt bangers Shiny saved specially for her.

Memories. Jacko, sound asleep in his cockpit, head thrown back even as the great blades of his propeller were slowing to a stop after yet another sortie. Echoing memories of the endless sorties of the summer of 1940.

Memories. British troops capering around on the battlefield as Excalibur squadron pulverised a position held by a trio of Tiger tanks and a couple of Stug IIIs sheltering on the reverse slopes near Vaston, the crossfire of their big guns creating confusion in the Allied advance before Rose, flying one of the wing's Rocket Typhoons while Sugar was being patched up (again), planted a pair of rockets on the crest and flipping one of the Stugs onto its back like a beetle, the pathetic sight of the surviving Tiger trying to hide its lumbering bulk beneath a few trees, seconds before rockets slammed it into oblivion.

Memories. Sid leaning against stacked ammo crates, a tin plate balanced on one knee, mouth filled with bread and meat but stilled by fatigue, his eyes empty and face bearing the wan pallor of those who had faced too much stress and fear and continued to do so.

Memories. 'Maddie' Byron's delight amidst his friend's catcalls when Rose handed him the thin sheet of paper, confirmation of his DFC and promotion to Flying Officer. Rose was grateful for Byron and Gillespie. The youngsters were unflappable and excellent wingmen, brave as lions following Rose through the thickest of flak.

Memories. A handful of Panzer IVs fleeing for the cover of a dense wood, smoke and dust obscuring the air above them, Typhoons curving after them and sliding into echelon smoothly, one metal monster flipped over onto another, the bizarre stack of panzers wobbling and teetering before sliding sideways into a ditch.

As shocked crewmen in panzer black clambered unsteadily from the hatches of the wrecked tanks, a bomb pierced one and the fuel tanks went up, a bubble of expanding flame englobing the tanks and those who had just crawled from them, dense choking smoke spewing black from the ferocious petrol-fed fire, the armour a threat no longer.

Memories. Returning from a strike at Vimoutiers, Excalibur's A-Flight bounced by USAAF Mustangs, trigger-happy and hungry for a kill, but Sid was no slouch and he turned instantly into them.

Realising their mistake, the Mustangs dived away, helped on their way by a burst of cannon fire from Jacko at the head of B 'Flight. Rose had exclaimed, heart still beating at the thought he might have lost Sid and his men through rank stupidity, "Jacko! What if you'd hit one of them?".

Sid answered for his grinning and unrepentant friend, voice loud with released tension, "Wot? Nah, Jacko could've if he wanted to, but a USAAF star would've looked right out of place in that line of swastikas painted on his Tiffie, see?"

Memories. The wrecked convoy on the Falaise to St Pierre-sur-Dives

Road, a long line of destroyed motor and horse drawn transport in a shallow valley, twisted charred bodies, metal and melted rubber, a myriad of dead scattered amongst the vehicles.

But not all the dead were clad in field grey, and Rose caught sight of white uniforms and long hair blowing in the currents of hot air formed by the fires. A convoy which had included ambulances, doctors and nurses, the traditionally untouchable slain and lying amongst the corpses of their fighting brethren.

Memories of four years earlier, an English fighter airfield in summer, rent asunder by a Luftwaffe attack, blood, brick dust and ash, lines of dead girls in RAF blue hidden by dirty tarpaulins.

And now someone had done the same to these German girls. Despite the plenitude of death, he had wept for the dead German nurses.

Certainly, they were the enemy, but the sight of them thrashed despair in his heart. *I'll not tell Moll of this; it'll only awaken memories of her lost girls.*

Molly no longer spoke of them, but he knew she would never forget those killed that terrible day at RAF Foxton.

Rose had spoken quietly of what he had seen to Mati, but Scarlett had heard the conversation. "For Christ's sake, Rose, grow up, can't you? What d'you think we're doing here? This isn't a bloody tea dance. If killing the Hun is too much for your delicate constitution, I'll send you back. Stop being a baby. I'm sure some old fart on Monty's staff could do with someone to drive them around and make their cocoa. Getting windy?"

Ignoring Mati's strained smile and fluttering hands, the excited chatter of his lads as they loudly recounted their latest feats, Rose mentally flipped two fingers up at his acting Wing Commander. *Well sod you as well, you miserable old so-and-so…*

As if to confirm Scarlett's words, the next day found Excalibur in an attack on a hastily rigged pontoon bridge across the Seine. A convoy of vehicles on either side and across it halftracks, panzers and ambulances, black uniforms of the SS spilling from the Red Cross vehicles as the Typhoons of Excalibur thundered into the attack.

The flak was heavy, but he lost none of his men, and there was no quarter for the SS as they ripped away the thin pretence from those who were responsible for so many atrocities.

No dead girls here after they were done, just bobbing corpses floating downriver amongst the shattered remnants of the bridge.

Yet despite the grind, he felt their pride in themselves, the discipline and self-control in the desperately tired young men under his command, sometimes even flying an unbelievable ten attacks a day, pushed beyond normal limits, many of them civilians just a short time earlier.

More often they were lucky and found little or no flak, their attacks seemingly unopposed, the retreat gradually becoming more and more hopeless as units seeking an elusive safety they would never reach.

The Luftwaffe were notable in their apparent absence, reminding Rose of Granny's reminiscences of the BEF's retreat to the coast, the RAF squadrons sacrificing themselves against swarming enemy fighters, slaughtered as they covered the withdrawing British and French forces, desperately trying to keep the advancing panzers at bay with their own lives.

The shoe was on the other foot now.

It seemed that what was left of the Luftwaffe in France would not do as the RAF had done during Blitzkrieg, for the canny enemy pilots bided their time and sought opportunities that favoured them.

One such was the bounce of a flight of 183's Typhoons at Vimoutiers. Without cover, the eight RAF fighter-bombers were bounced by five times their number, the victorious Bf109s downing half the Typhoons and killing their pilots, the remaining four only escaping by the skin of their teeth because of the timely intervention of Spitfires. But in a sky thick with Allied aircraft, such occasions were thankfully few, and the Luftwaffe were suffering their own casualties. Rose and Gillespie caught a Heinkel 177 bomber before it could attack the convoys pushing along the road to Falaise and the youngster dispatched it with the minimum of fuss.

But flak continued to whittle away at their numbers.

The area around Falaise and to the east was one that they were now very familiar with as the southern American pincer closed with the northern British Canadian one.

Now they found themselves vying with the Tiffies and Thunderbolts of 2TAF's 84 Group as the number of targets shrank, the constant attrition of air and ground attack obliterating the mighty German 7th Army, once numbering more than a hundred thousand men.

In the last week of August, with the surrender of the German garrison in Paris, Rose and his men attacked targets along the river Seine, pushing beyond the outskirts of Paris, the tower against which Hitler had taken his picture in 1940 an outline on the horizon.

After an attack in which his guns tore apart a halftrack laden with troops, their stricken faces obscured by the sparkling flashes and billowing of metal, dust and shreds of paint, Rose idly wondered if he might just hope that one day, he might look out over a peacetime Paris from the Eiffel Tower's highest galleries with his family.

The supremacy of the Panzers over the Allied armour and any hope of a German victory was lost by the impact and close support of the fighter bombers. Rose and his men knew that they and those like them had played a decisive part in the destruction of the 7th Army.

The Hawker Typhoons of the RAF had been the grim harbingers of death for the enemy, yet also the heralds of deliverance for their own.

The war in Normandy was over, and the Allies triumphant.

*

By the end of August, Excalibur's scoreboard showed that they were responsible for the destruction of over two hundred panzers and six hundred trucks, plus numerous trains, river barges, and other war materiel.

Rose alone had accounted for 10 panzers, Sturmgeschützen and other armoured fighting vehicles, plus 43 trucks and other soft-skinned vehicles.

S-Sugar could not sport all his successes, even though the score painted beneath his squadron-leader's pennant was notable enough, for some of these victories had been gained when flying rocket-firing Typhoon 'D-Dolly' borrowed from Red Douglas's Orna squadron on the occasions when poor battered Sugar was being serviced or patched up after a particularly 'dicey do'.

But the numbers that mattered the most, the ones that mattered to him above all else, were of his fallen.

In Normandy, Rose lost twelve of his pilots, youngsters and veterans numbered amongst Excalibur's honoured dead. In addition to his pilots, three of his groundcrew had died in accidents and by enemy action. What was left were the survivors of the merciless fighting which culminated in the destruction of the 7th Army, and there were no longer any youngsters in Excalibur, only veterans.

These men, his men, the living and the dead, were the heroes of Normandy.

Sixteen Typhoons had been destroyed or damaged beyond repair (not counting the one destroyed or the two damaged in the early July dawn raids by FW190s), but somehow, Sugar and he had survived the breakout, the sporadic advances, and the final encirclement and destruction of the enemy.

He still found it hard to believe that he and his lucky few had survived the storm of shot and shell.

The Light Brigade only did it once, he mused. We rode our mounts though the Valley of Death so many times I've lost count. How did any of us survive? And even more improbably, leading them in, how did I?

Rose took Sugar and young Gillespie for a flight across the hard-won pocket which was the final resting place of so very many of the enemy.

The urgency of the push was eased, for the enemy had been driven across the River Dives, and the ground forces were making the preparations for the next stage, the drive east across France. Beneath them the movement of friendly forces was relaxed and unhurried, and the sky seeming a great deal emptier than it had throughout August.

As they drew closer to the narrow river, the total devastation wreaked on the enemy became progressively more apparent. The charred lumps of smashed equipment and the attendant dead became thicker and wider, until it seemed as if the ground beneath them was comprised only of blackened tanks and trucks, abandoned artillery pointing accusingly at the sky from whence the fighter-bombers had mercilessly blasted them.

And so many dead, *oh dearest Lord God, so very many!*

Bloated, twisted and black, the bodies of the enemy forming a wretched and uneven blanket over the ground, and he turned his eyes away from the scene of horror, turning gently back for their airfield, grateful for the oxygen which would mask the hideous stench that must blanket the area for miles around.

He had played his part in it, but now the dreadful sight brought tears to his eyes, and he wondered once more at the selfish conceit of those who sent their young to fight for them when they sought to steal what belonged to others.

Rose shivered despite the hothouse temperatures of his cockpit. The land below was haunted now and steeped in the blood of those who had occupied it. Once his time here was done, if he survived, he would never return to this place.

Normandy was a place of great beauty, but after the fighting of 1944, the landscapes had lost their charm for Rose, and would be haunted forevermore.

*

Bezenville B2 was a hive of activity when they returned.

83 Group's AOC, Harry Broadhurst, had ordered 44 Wing's recall for rest and re-equipping, a Canadian Typhoon Wing flying in in the morning to replace them.

The Wing's time in France, at least for the present, was over.

The first of the DC3 Dakotas had already arrived for the ground elements, and Scarlett was organising the Wing's return.

Naturally, the acting Wing Leader would lead Orna squadron back that evening, and Rose would be left to ensure that the remaining ground echelons were safely loaded up and flown back in the morning, with Excalibur providing the escort.

Scarlett and his lads would be dining in Britain this evening, whilst Rose and his boys would be enjoying whatever culinary delights Shiny Dewar and his circus would rustle up.

Thanks, I don't think.

"Enjoy your evening, Rose. Don't dally over breakfast," sneered Scarlett before climbing into his Typhoon.

Wanker.

276

As Orna squadron and the Dakotas disappeared into the dusky sky, Mati turned to Rose, "He'll be a Marshall of the RAF before he's done, Flash. *Don't dally over breakfast!* What an arrogant prick that bloody man is."

Chapter Thirty-Two

Rose wiped his sticky eyes and glared at the little Frenchman, trying not to look at his watch again. "I think I must be bloody dreaming! Could you just repeat what you said?"

For goodness' sake! it's just after four in the bloody morning!

The grumble of military traffic from the roads outside seemed to answer, *so what? Don't you know there's a war on?*

With a Sten gun hanging from one shoulder, the man stared back at him, unfazed. "My name is Guy Ricard, m'sieur, and I am the leader of the Resistance in this area. I have received word from my friends in Amiens that the Bosche will be flying important cargo from Glisy airfield at dawn. It must be destroyed." Two large, flat-faced men loomed silently on either side of him.

Rose's gummed mouth tasted like the inside of his flying boot, and he stroked his temples as if it might clear his mind. "*Must* be destroyed? Important cargo, you say?"

Dear Lord above, I sound like old Mr Micawber! Lawks, guv'nor!

He closed his eyes, felt the floor move and opened them again, "I'm sorry. What sort of cargo is it, Monsieur Ricard?"

The Frenchman leaned closer, and Rose's nostrils caught the scent of aftershave and *Gauloise* cigarettes. The Good Lord only knew what the other made of Rose's dreadful aroma of bad breath, sweat and unwashed dog.

The Frenchman's nostrils flared, though whether from Rose's scepticism or his fragrance was unclear, "M'sieur, it is the important pieces of the flying bombs."

Ricard shifted restively from one foot to another, eyeing Rose and wondering doubtfully if this unshaven and bleary-eyed young RAF officer really was the one he needed to talk to. The line of frayed ribbons on his grubby battledress seemed to indicate he was.

"Enough for two hundred bombs." He raised his eyebrows and spread his hands theatrically, "More!"

Rose felt like screaming. *I'm supposed to be taking my boys home in the morning!* He looked at the Frenchman suspiciously, "How can we be sure this is true?"

Anger flashed in Ricard's dark eyes, but he shrugged expansively, "My friend is reliable, capitaine, a patriot. If it is true, the parts will be used in two hundred bombs against your compatriots. Non?"

"Yes, I see." God! Two hundred bombs! What choice did he have?

Rose felt himself sag. Just when he had come to believe that he might actually be going home to Molly and Danny, this happened.

"Thank you, Monsieur Ricard, for your and your friends' efforts. I shall, er, visit Amiens airfield immediately." The thought of it made him cringe.

The Frenchman inclined his head gravely, "There are five aircrafts, M'Sieur Capitaine. The strange ones with three engines."

Five Ju52's. And of course, there'll be fighter escorts, too. Lots of them. With Allied control of the air as it was, the Luftwaffe had taken to moving around in larger formations.

Safety in numbers.

Blast!

Rose shook the man's hand and thanked him, before calling an airman to take Ricard and his hulking companions to the Mess tent to sample Shiny's inimitable cuisine, poor buggers, before turning back to Mati and the duty Warrant Officer.

"Mati, I'll need whatever you have for Amiens-Glisy. Could you have a word with the Wing Commander Flying and the Spitfire Wing's CO's, too, please? I'll need cover. Mr Soames, would you kindly prepare Sugar? Remove the bomb racks, if you've enough time, top up the fuel and cannon shells. I want to be in the air before dawn. Are the dawn readiness fighters ready? Full fuel and ammo?"

The WO nodded stolidly, "Yes sir."

I'll ask for a section to go with me. "Grand! Right then, see to it, please, Mr Soames."

"Sir."

"Thank you," Then a thought, "Mati, old chap, could you see that Molly gets my letter, and would you sort out something for Daffie if…?"

The Intelligence Officer nodded soberly, "Of course, Flash." He spoke timidly, "Shall I talk to your flight commanders? Sid and Jacko will be cross. They'll not want to miss the party."

This is one party I'd *love to miss…*

"No, the lads are beat. Dawn's, what? About an hour away? Let 'em rest. They'll still be dead to the world." He grimaced at the poor choice of words. "Besides, a single Tiffie might be able to nip in unnoticed where a squadron wouldn't."

"I'll take some of the dawn readiness Spits. We'll spread them out to the northeast and southeast to catch Jerry in case I'm too late."

And if Jerry's out in force they'll tear my boys to shreds. I couldn't bear to lose them after all we've survived. They aren't dispensable, no matter what the Brass think. He knew that Granny would have told him to take the whole of Excalibur (*'you gormless plank!'*).

But Granny wasn't here. Rose was.

Mati's voice was pleading, "Let me phone this through to Group. Flash?"

Best they know where I'm going, and he nodded, "OK chum, but there's too little time to wait for an answer. While the brass're humming and hawing Jerry's going to get away. Should be able to sort 'em out with the Spits. See if you can rustle up any more kites from Ops, though, would you? Send them after us just in case we don't get 'em all." *Or if they get me…*

Mati nodded firmly, "I'll call my friends at B10 Plumetot and B17 Carpiquet, too, see if they can't help."

"Thanks, Mati." *I must get dressed and give Daffie a last hug goodbye…*

*

He adjusted the scarf around his neck, and smiled down at her, lying on the floor, once a fearsome beast, now something immensely precious. He kneeled and took her head gently in both hands and kissed it, seeing her love in those dark, expressive eyes.

A single word of farewell. "Stay." She whined softly but did as he asked.

It was time.

I'll do it, but I'll do it without my lads. They've earned their rest, and with a bit of luck, they'll be back in Blighty for lunch. They survived Hell, and they've earned their reprieve.

Here am I.

Send me.

Both the Spitfire COs offered their Dawn Readiness sections as cover for the sortie, but of course cover was needed to protect B2 against an early morning strike, and they settled on providing a pair of Spitfires each.

Rose met with the four pilots before take-off, asking them to take up positions five miles northeast and southeast of the city, whilst he would make a high-speed pass across Glisy airfield.

If the Junkers were still there, he would strafe them on the ground. The Spit boys would be his eyes in the sky and his last gasp lest the trimotors leave before his arrival.

In the back of his mind, the little voice whispered, *what if they already left in the night…?*

Amiens-Glisy was a pre-war French Military airfield, but Mati had assured him that it was essentially abandoned with the frontline so close, and there might not be any manned flak positions. Rose would use the distinctive Amiens Cathedral as his reference point. Set on a ridge, the Gothic structure was visible for miles.

Rose took off first, thirty minutes before dawn. With his experience as a night fighter, flying in the darkness held few terrors for him.

Her photograph remained in his pocket, for whatever happened in the skies over Amiens, Molly would be close to the undeserving heart he had lost to her.

But he wasn't alone.

Arriving at dispersals, stomach empty and fluttering, he saw that a second Tiffie was waiting ready alongside his with bombs on its racks, and the slight figure standing sheepishly with the sleepy groundcrew.

Gillespie.

Rose had ranted and raved, but the boy was adamant. Quavering, but adamant. "You ain't flying alone, sir. I'm your wingman. I'm coming."

Touched by the boy's loyalty and willingness to risk it all once again when safety was so very close, he felt his voice begin to shake with emotion, and rather than bawl like a baby in front of his loyal wingman and the watchful 'erks', he shut his mouth, settling on giving the boy a frown which sternly held his wobbling lip in place.

They flew in silence at two thousand feet, well back from the coast and high enough to clear the ridges of the Seine valley.

There was no flak, not even the rattle in their earphones of the radar-controlled stuff, and he grunted in satisfaction as he saw the dulled snaking glint of the Seine once more, and he steered them a little to starboard to clear the rambling patch of blackness that was Rouen, at which Joan of Arc had found martyrdom.

Did the spirit of France's greatest heroine, burned once at the stake then twice more to make her ash, observe the distant shapes of their racing Typhoons, and wonder how fate decreed that the men from the country which had once been the enemy now fought and died half a millennia later for France's freedom?

A single glowing line of golden tracer licked out silently, curling away ineffectually.

As soon as they cleared the high ridges east of Rouen he pushed Sugar quickly down from two thousand to two hundred feet, no lower lest they be snared by electric pylons seen too late, feeling Sugar's desire to stay in the high clean air.

As he had hoped (and prayed), the skies above the ancient city were empty. With Allied radar so good, the Germans knew that any concentration of fighters would attract overwhelming attention from the RAF. With a bit of luck they would be scrambling into the air for a dawn rendezvous, keen to avoid attracting attention for the valuable cargo.

Then a cold feeling of doubt. What if the skies were empty because the cargo had been flown out during the night? Surely, they hadn't had enough time yet?

A quick glance to port, faithful Gillespie at fifty yards, a new prayer uttered under his breath, *If you take me, Lord, please keep the boy safe*, the glow on the horizon bright now as dawn lingered just beneath the horizon, Amiens a busy collection of dark buildings catching the faint golden-pink gleam of almost-light in its arrayed windows.

Pinpricks of light from Amiens, but the sparse flak was too far behind and too light to worry them.

His heart was thrashing as he searched for and found the lofty, proud edifice with the high windows that was Amiens cathedral, a single slim spire climbing higher above its imposing bulk, a structure capable of containing twice that of Paris's Notre Dame.

A last check at the controls, safeties off? Yes.

Turning automatically on to a heading east-south-east, the four or so miles between the cathedral and Glisy airfield speeding past them.

Please God, let there be no flak as Mati promised.

There, just ahead them, a pair of runways arranged in a rough T-shape, dull grey lines lighter with dew-shine in the pale light than the surrounding fields and hedgerows of Picardy, and he felt a rush of relief, *Thank God, there you are! Found you!*

Now, if only they had arrived in time!

He tried to recall the layout, the PRU photographs revealing two large hangers and two smaller ones, the wreckage of a pair of Messerschmitt 410's destroyed by 8th Air Force P47s bulldozed together...*what!*

Even as they cleared the boundary, the muzzles of Gillespie's G-George flashed shockingly bright, spitting fire-bright lines of shells dragging thin trails of smoke at something Rose couldn't see, G-George dropping back a little as it slowed. *Thank heavens for fresh young eyes!*

Against the shadowed border at the far end of the seemingly empty airfield, something sparkled from hits, partially obscured by a thin haze of smoke spreading into the still air.

And no flak! Mati was right, God bless him.

There! Shapes lit up by the strikes, and he caught sight of a group of boxy trucks, and just beyond, the angular lines of aircraft.

They haven't taken off yet! They're late!

Excitement raced through him, pushing aside the doubts and the whisper of anxiety. Slip her gunsight onto the jumble of shapes until they were quivering within it and toe the rudder gently, to one side of Gillespie's hits, right, left, right, spraying the target from side to side, fighting the ground effect swell beneath Sugar, counteracting it as he pushed down on the gun button. Something had begun to burn as his 20mm banged out cannon shells.

Still no flak.

Rose dropped her nose further, adjusting trim as the hammering cannon braked her, up a little to keep the red dot on the flickering shadows.

An explosion, another, then a blindingly bright ball of flame wavering and rising against the growing dawn, more explosions, and they were so close now that he could differentiate between each aircraft. Three of the trimotors were smashed and well alight, the flickering flames making the nearby trees appear to dance.

A Feisler Storch, men jumping sluggishly from it as if caught in amber, wings crumpling like a moth in flame before exploding into smithereens as the boy's cannon found it, the carcasses of trucks flaming bright, blown to pieces, his shells ripping the tailplane off another trimotor, the impression of movement as the last aircraft

285

moved away from the destruction, propellers spinning, frantically trying to escape.

Light blooming in a vivid yellow explosion (*Gillespie...?* No, his bombs), and he was pulling up, dragging his thumb from the gun-button and pulling back as the trees beyond the boundary loomed, gasping with effort and fear as the force of Gillespie's bombs reached out, jostling and clutching at Sugar.

He let her slide and fall, just enough before taking control and recovering her, and they were speeding out over the carpet of green. Ahead of him, the dawn had breached the night, the sky much lighter now, yellow, pink and mixed lilacs.

And still no flak.

He sucked in a dry mouthful of oxygen, feeling the glow of success lighten his muscles, eyes automatically searching in the fighter pilot's mantra, seeing that the boy had survived their run, a few hundred feet higher, bounding into the air after releasing his bombs.

I should have kept my racks and brought bombs along, too. Thank goodness for the boy, the stubborn wee bugger.

George slipped alongside Sugar, and Rose looked back. One of the Ju 52's had managed to get moving, but Gillespie's bombs had brought its desperate take-off run to a sudden, savage end, and now it lay broken beneath the torrents of smoke pouring from the ill-fated attempt to salvage the vital components of Hitler's terror weapon.

That's 200 bombs that won't fall on home. Thank goodness for the French Resistance, Rose thought gratefully. *Might even make ol' Ricard smile when he hears of it. Best let the Spit bods know what's happening.*

"Excalibur Leader to Crumpet Silver and Crumpet Gold, target destroyed, clear to return. Thank you!"

They were acknowledging him when Gillespie's wings rocked urgently, "Two to Leader, Bandits, ten o'clock, angels one!"

Before them four dots had emerged from out of the burgeoning light, growing wings as they drew closer.

Instinctively Rose eased Sugar up and into them, muzzle flash already sparkling from their wings and spinners.

A *Schwarm* of Bf109s.

Dear God.

But a *Schwarm* of four was better than a swarm of forty.

He held his fire, knowing that his ammo must be dangerously depleted after their long run-in to the trimotors, cringing as grey smoke trails reached out for him, and at last he pushed down on the firing button.

The enemy aircraft on the far right of the formation exploded suddenly, the flaming, expanding globe dimming the dawn behind it momentarily, and its wingman flinched away.

Rose's target seemed untouched, and in a flash and a shrieking surge of sound, they were past one another, Sugar bumping awkwardly through the slipstreams of the enemy fighters, and he pulled back urgently on the stick and kicked the rudder bar to turn her hard after the enemy.

Somehow, the boy's shells had clipped the Bf109 wingman with the same burst that had ripped into its leader (*the jammy beggar!*) and it was dragging a trail of glycol behind as it fled to the north.

Rose's shells, however, had not connected with the enemy, *but at least theirs didn't connect with us…*

Yet despite the temptation to pursue the damaged 109 for an easy kill, faithful Gillespie was steadfast beside him, *good boy!*

The remaining enemy pair, doubtless shaken, had turned as well, climbing higher into their turn, and like knights of old jousting, the two pairs of aircraft raced madly at one another again.

"Two, once we're past, head down and keep going, get out of it at full boost, we'll out-run them," gasped Rose. Behind them the rising sun was a brilliant ball of light.

"Sir?" breathlessness tempered with doubt.

"We're going the right way. We'll separate and scarper for home." He huffed out, the straps tight against his chest and cringing with fear at the prospect of another high-speed pass, "Don't hang about, laddie, I'll see you back there."

No time to argue, they were closing with the 109s again, but at least the sun was in the enemy's eyes.

A burst of tracer flowed terrifyingly close over the canopy, so close that he leaned forward as far as he could, as if it would make a difference, and he responded with a hopeful one second burst.

A 109 flashed past above him and again Sugar wallowed, "Go, two! Get out of it!" *God let him not have been shot down! Let him get away, please…*

Rose booted the rudder bar hard and wrenched Sugar around again, *the ground's too close, watch your altitude,* vision greying at the edges just as he looked up through his canopy to see one of the 109s pull up and twist, throwing the sleek little fighter into a stall-turn, but the other continued onwards towards the higher terrain west of Amiens *splitting after Gillespie…or coming after me?*

The oxygen mask was sucking at his face, damp rubber irritating the bristles on his sweaty cheeks, but there was no opportunity to adjust it because now he was banking strenuously after the 109, his turn tighter despite Sugar's additional armour, a quick glance for the other but there was no sign of it. Beneath them their shadows undulated wildly across the ground.

Where are you, you Nazi bastard? Eyes sliding quickly forwards, the sky around and above still clear, the ground circling his wingtip, dangerously close, nose above the horizon, no sign of the boy, *run lad, run!*

Sugar's nose pulling into the enemy fighter, reeling it in.

The 109 pilot threw his fighter into a dive as he must have been instructed to when being chased by a Tommi, thick black smoke streaming from his exhausts, and Rose fired a burst at him even as the German pilot realised he was too close to the ground, twitching up out of the dive as he caught sight of the terrain looming ahead, losing speed and slowing.

But he had allowed Rose to catch him and now Sugar's cannon furiously ripped out once more and impacts flickered bright on the starboard tailplane and the delicately slim grey-blue striped fuselage of the 109, just behind the hateful black cross.

He continued firing into the enemy, a piece of the cowling ripped away and an aileron detaching, a thin flame leaking a long line of gauzy smoke, the sleek shape shaking beneath the explosive impacts, and then suddenly there was only the hiss which told him he was out of ammunition, and he cursed in bitter frustration.

But that final burst had done enough, for even as he checked his mirror considering the moment he might make a risky break for home, the 109's tail section folded upwards as if in slow motion, the fighter beginning to yaw and fall, one wingtip dipping as it slid into a flat spin, and he lost sight of it as it dropped away below and behind him.

Rose did not see the 109 slam into the ground because his eyes were in search of other enemies in the ever-brightening sky, but as he peered back over his port tailplane, he saw the sudden flash and the dark billow of oily smoke of the vanquished 109's demise against the grassy slopes, matching the distant tangled columns of smoke rising from Amiens-Glisy, and further still a blotch of faint dots low on the horizon, a cloud of deadly midges in the glare of sun-haze.

Midges catching the sunlight, metal and Perspex glinting and lustrous.

Enemy fighters, looking to create mischief, or an inexcusably late fighter escort?

The Luftwaffe formation was too late, their charges already ash and glowing fragments. And there was no chance they might catch him for Sugar could out-run them effortlessly.

Yet as he turned Sugar westwards for home, more dots cleared the crest ahead, a loose group of fighters heading straight for him, and his heart lurched painfully at the sight.

Dear God, now what? Enemy fighters in front and behind, and empty ammo trays! Sugar and he were the filling in a Luftwaffe sandwich…

So this is where it ends…If only I could have held Molly and Danny one more time…

And one of the fighters ahead was firing already, too early for they were still out of range, and then a wave of relief when he saw that it was firing on its leader, which began to burn.

As they drew ever closer, he finally realised that the group ahead consisted of a single Bf109 closely pursued by a quartet of Tiffies!

The unfortunate 109 maybe the last of those they had been attacked by, was a blazing shape now, and the wreck curved downwards meteor-like for one last contact with the earth.

His earphones crackled, "And just where do you think you've been, young lady?"

"Been, young lady?" chirped the accompanying echo indignantly.

Throat tight with emotion and suddenly released tension, Rose opened his mouth to answer, but was unable to speak.

The Typhoons of Sid, Jacko, 'Maddie' Byron and loyal young Gillespie slid protectively around him.

Surrounded by his friends, Harry Rose flew back one last time to the ALG B2 at Bezenville, a grateful survivor of the vicious and unforgiving Battle for Normandy.

The New Zealanders of 485 Squadron from Carpiquet B17 had been alerted by Mati and found the five Typhoons west of the Seine, the twelve Spitfire IX's escorting Rose and his little band of brothers the rest of the way home to B2.

At last, he had the courage to pull her photograph from his pocket, still not quite believing that he might be going home after all, tears blurring the lines of her face.

Soon, my darling.

Merciful God, thank you.

Epilogue

The indescribably wonderful sound of his son's wild laughter, Noreen's semi-hysterical shrieks in Hindi and Daffie's excited yelping and barking made the glass rattle in its pane and Rose feared it might crack or implode despite the trellis of tape pasted across it.

Standing, he placed his palm lightly against it, to feel the sound as well as hear it.

He watched them for a moment, enjoying their easy camaraderie, eyes slipping from the garden to the gently rolling fields and woods beyond.

Rose felt the pleasure and tranquillity of its calm beauty, and suppressing a shudder, remembered a ruined landscape so very like this one across the Channel.

Behind him Molly puffed as she slowly got to her feet, and her arms curled delightfully around him, her breath warm on his shoulder and her cheek smooth against his neck.

Normally he would have enjoyed the soft swell of her breasts against him, but now her rounded belly pushed gently against the small of his back in their place, and his hand slipped from the cool glass to rest against the curve.

He felt the kick of their unborn child and laughed. In this world where death and injury had become commonplace, life was even more beautiful and precious, and he marvelled in the sheer wonder of it.

Her voice was a murmur against his ear, "You might be a sex-mad fiend, Harry Rose, but I love you with all my heart."

"And I love you with all of mine, Moll." He felt the gentle kiss behind one ear and revelled in the simple pleasure of her warmth against him.

"Zaleel khuta, harami! Chaurdho mhuj koh!" (Bloody dog, bastard! Let me go!) squawked Noreen like a demented banshee from the garden, eliciting another fusillade of excited barks from Daffie in response.

"Crikey!" Molly tittered at her old ayah's exaggerated yells, "Anyone would think she hated poor Daffie"

He smiled fondly, and closed his eyes, enjoying her closeness. "I know. I don't think she realises we notice her feeding and cuddling the beastly little thing all hours of the day."

Molly giggled, "Beastly little thing? Who do you mean? Daffie or Danny?"

Another high-pitched screech as Noreen tumbled beneath Daffie's weight into a rose bush, hair a wild grey corona around her head as her scarf caught on thorns and slipped from her shoulders, *"Aiyeee! Pughlee Khuteeya!"* (Aiyeee! Silly bitch!).

Daffie, her coat free from the dust of Normandy and now sleek and shining, slept beside Danny every night, and was his constant companion and guardian, sharing a friendly rivalry (most of the time at least) with an adoring Noreen.

It was ten days since the successful raid on the aerodrome at Amien-Glisy and Excalibur's subsequent return to Britain, the endless gratitude in their hearts for having somehow survived the Normandy maelstrom tempered by the desperate sorrow for those that would never return home.

Like all of those who had fought from the beachheads to Falaise and beyond, 44 Wing endured much in France, but their sacrifices had not been overlooked.

As soon as he could, Granny hobbled from the hospital with Belle's help to the AOC's Group HQ and submitted an extensive list of recommendation for decorations.

'Broady' Broadhurst had expedited the list's approval and added to it a second bar to Granny's Distinguished Service Order. Rumour claimed the great man even muttered something about 'another ring'.

Just imagine! A fourth ring! The scruffy but exceptional Pilot Officer from 1940 now a smartly turned-out Group Captain! If it turned out to be true, that would be a truly deserved advancement by merit. In wartime all the petty politics is generally put to one side, only to resurface when the fighting was done.

Rose's men had also done well, the survivors of Normandy either receiving a DFC, DFM or a Mention.

Young Byron received a Mention to put alongside his DFC, and Gillespie's DFM had been approved, with a recommendation for a bar and promotion to Pilot Officer in recognition of his exemplary conduct during their dawn raid on Amiens-Glisy.

Red Douglas, his promotion to Squadron-Leader confirmed, Jacko and Sid each received a bar to their DFCs, and it had been a similar story for the men of Orna squadron, with Scarlett (*miserable old so-and-so!*) receiving a DSO.

Chiefy had earned himself an MBE, and there was a generous smattering of BEMs (one of which Jimmy received) and LSGCs for the tireless labours of the hardworking groundcrews. Big Dave had been silenced completely to learn of his LSGC.

Had Rose been able, he would have ensured that each of his people received recognition for their exemplary service, for they had certainly earned it. Theirs were the efforts which kept the Typhoon force continuously operational throughout the worst of conditions.

But so many heroes responsible for the quite incredible defeat and rout of a powerful defensive force which had been prepared and waiting for them remained unrecognised.

Rose was also pleased to hear that both Belle and Charlie were to receive MBEs, the former for her service as senior WAAF at Little Sillo and her work in preparing the Wing for the move to France, whilst dear Charlie's Night Fighter Trial, though short on results, had provided a vital contribution to the advances needed to develop a true all-weather interceptor.

For Rose himself there was another Mention for the Amiens-Glisy mission, his third, and in addition for his efforts and those of his priceless people, there was a bar to his DSO.

And for Molly? Molly was but one of the legions of those who kept the home fires burning and the country working as they waited every moment with dread in their hearts for The Telegram that might dash their dreams and break their hearts forever.

Molly's reward was Rose's safe return to the heart of his family, with the knowledge that her husband had been fortunate enough to survive the enemy's best efforts over many months to kill him, just as the Luftwaffe had tried in that frenetic summer of 1940 when they had first met.

True, his eyes were haunted, the grey hairs at his temples more numerous, and his body thin but strong from hauling a heavy fighter-bomber around a hostile sky. His voice and trembling fingers revealed his utter exhaustion, and the neck she brushed with her lips was rough, skin coarsened against sweat-soaked silk by years of twisting his head this way and that beneath an indifferent sun.

But, most important, he had returned to her.

His first night at home, Rose slept in the parlour with loyal, loving Daffie watchful at his side. He had been afraid, he grudgingly admitted to Molly, that he might twist and thrash and catch her as he slept, fearful for their unborn child.

Molly was Rose's antidote from the poison of war, and he discovered that beside his wife, his sleep was deep and untroubled, her presence easing and diminishing the turmoil of his subconscious mind, and which would, given time, heal him as best it could.

With experience, expertise and more than his fair share of good fortune, Rose had endured and survived a pivotal campaign upon which the future would be founded, and having done so, could proudly count himself amongst the group of extraordinary men and women responsible for forging the return to Europe, and bringing fresh hope to the hearts of those existing beneath the crushing bondage of oppression that liberation would be soon.

The war is not yet over, but for the moment, Rose can rest.

Acknowledgements

With heartfelt gratitude I would like to thank:

The incredible James Faktor, Rebecca Souster and all the superlative folks at Lume Books who make dreams a reality.

My friends April Stone, John Humphreys, Raymond Fitzhugh, Christine Harris, and of course, Russell and Angela Gallon, for their endless support and encouragement.

And lastly but most important of all, the ones who fulfil and enrich me so very completely, my wonderful wife and children.